MY BONES WILL KEEP

Gladys Maude Winifred Mitchell – or 'The Great Gladys' as Philip Larkin called her – was born in 1901, in Cowley in Oxfordshire. She graduated in history from University College London and in 1921 began her long career as a teacher. She studied the works of Sigmund Freud and attributed her interest in witchcraft to the influence of her friend, the detective novelist Helen Simpson.

Her first novel, *Speedy Death*, was published in 1929 and introduced readers to Beatrice Adela Lestrange Bradley, the heroine of a further sixty six crime novels. She wrote at least one novel a year throughout her career and was an early member of the Detection Club, alongside Agatha Christie, G.K Chesterton and Dorothy Sayers. In 1961 she retired from teaching and, from her home in Dorset, continued to write, receiving the Crime Writers' Association Silver Dagger in 1976. Gladys Mitchell died in 1983.

T0315546

ALSO BY GLADYS MITCHELL

VINTAGE MURDER MYSTERIES

With the sign of a human skull upon its back and a melancholy shriek emitted when disturbed, the Death's Head Hawkmoth has for centuries been a bringer of doom and an omen of death - which is why we chose it as the emblem for our Vintage Murder Mysteries.

Some say that its appearance in King George III's bedchamber pushed him into madness. Others believe that should its wings extinguish a candle by night, those nearby will be cursed with blindness. Indeed its very name, *Acherontia atropos*, delves into the most sinister realms of Greek mythology: Acheron, the River of Pain in the underworld, and Atropos, the Fate charged with severing the thread of life.

The perfect companion, then, for our Vintage Murder Mysteries sleuths, for whom sinister occurrences are never far away and murder is always just around the corner …

GLADYS MITCHELL

My Bones Will Keep

VINTAGE BOOKS
London

Published by Vintage 2014

2 4 6 8 10 9 7 5 3 1

First published in Great Britain by
Michael Joseph Ltd in 1962

Vintage
Random House, 20 Vauxhall Bridge Road,
London SW1V 2SA

www.vintage-books.co.uk

Addresses for companies within The Random House Group Limited
can be found at: www.randomhouse.co.uk/offices.htm

The Random House Group Limited Reg. No. 954009

A CIP catalogue record for this book
is available from the British Library

ISBN 9780099584063

The Random House Group Limited supports The Forest Stewardship
Council® (FSC®), the leading international forest-certification organisation.
Our books carrying the FSC label are printed on FSC®-certified paper.
FSC is the only forest-certification scheme supported by the leading
environmental organisations, including Greenpeace. Our
paper procurement policy can be found at
www.randomhouse.co.uk/environment

MIX
Paper | Supporting
responsible forestry
FSC® C018179

Printed and bound in Great Britain by Clays Ltd, St Ives plc

CHAPTER ONE

Edinburgh

'. . . famous alike for its romantic history
and the surpassing beauty of its natural situation.'
Muirhead's Blue Guide to Scotland, 1949
'. . . a penniless lass wi' a lang pedigree.'
Old Saying (possibly Glaswegian)

THE hotel overlooked West Princes Gardens. Laura was admiring the view from her bedroom window. Away to the right stood the Episcopal Church of St John, where Princes Street and Lothian Road made a right-angle. Beyond it, and a part of the Gardens, or so it appeared, was St Cuthbert's; and here and there, although they were not readily identifiable from the hotel windows, were the statues erected to the memory of the faithful departed – the poet Allan Ramsay, the surgeon Sir James Simpson and the visionary who promoted the ragged schools, Doctor Thomas Guthrie.

On the other side of the railway, which appeared to cut the Gardens in two, there was the dominating feature of the view. This was the castle, built so high on its formidable eminence that from where Laura stood it was almost impossible to decide at what point the work of man and the work of nature met, so entirely did the castle buildings and defences seem to be part of the rock on which they stood.

She knew all about the Castle. She had been familiar with it, on and off, since the age of four, when she had stomped on sturdy legs, hand in hand with parent or uncle, across the bridge over the moat, past the effigies of Bruce the Scot and Wallace the Welshman, to the portcullis gate and up the narrow, sloping road towards the King's Bastion.

Memory and imagination carried Laura farther. Most of what she knew of Scottish history had been learned upon these occasions, for that rabid Scottish Nationalist, her Uncle Hamish, after whom she had named her young son, had been wont to embark enthusiastically upon stories of Scottish kings, Scottish plotters, Scottish institutions and Scottish heroes, until an intelligent and imaginative child could see the builders of the Wall of Antoninus, Saint Ninian's church at Whithorn, the landing of Saint Columba at Iona, the murder of Duncan by Macbeth.

She saw, and deeply felt, the humiliation of William the Lion, compelled, as a prisoner, to acknowledge the supremacy of the ill-tempered, energetic, wrong-headed Henry II and she rejoiced in the long-term revenge of William when he formed the first Scottish alliance with France. She sorrowed over the death of the four-year-old Maid of Norway and thrilled to the story of Bannock-burn.

The tales were endless, but Uncle Hamish was a born *raconteur* and carried the child's mind along with his as they stared in fascination at Mons Meg or visited the bomb-proof vault in which the Honours of Scotland repose serenely within their iron cage. Many a time they stood on the King's Bastion, after visiting the Scottish War Memorial and Queen Margaret's tiny Norman chapel, while the man pointed out the Forth and its bridge, the Lomonds in Fife, and the Ochil Hills famed in ballad. Out to the west were Ben Ledi and Ben Lomond, magic names in a child's Cloud-Cuckoo-Land.

> ' "Yea, in my mind these mountains rise,
>   Their perils dyed with evening's rose;
>   And still my ghost sits at my eyes
>   And thirsts for their untroubled snows." '

Since that time Laura had seen most of the mountains of her native land, but, grand, aloof and sombre as she had found them, she had never recaptured the ecstasy with which she had first seen the shadowy corries, the proud, defiant peaks, from the supreme vantage point of the King's Bastion.

She shrugged off these infantile sentimentalities and began to plan a pilgrimage round Edinburgh itself when she was released from her duties for an afternoon. In imagination she saw herself climbing the two-hundred-feet-high monument to Sir Walter Scott; visiting the Royal Scottish Academy and the Raeburns in the National Gallery; revisiting Lady Stair's house and the Thistle Chapel in St Giles; avoiding a visit to John Knox's house, for her detestation of the scourge who had ranted about the 'Monstrous Regiment of Women' was unrelenting; standing in the full force of the wind on the Waverley Steps; above all, traversing the narrow and ancient wynds, closes and courts of the Old City and hoping zestfully for the adventures which, in Edinburgh, had never come to her except mentally, inspired by her uncle's stories.

She had visited, in her thoughts, George Heriot's School, where a cousin of hers had been educated before going on to the University, and was on her imaginary way to the Greyfriars churchyard, when there came a tap at the door. Laura, coming to herself and recognising her employer's knock, went to the door and opened it.

'What ho, Mrs Croc., dear!' she said. Dame Beatrice Adela Lestrange Bradley, wearing tweeds which did not suit her, cackled harshly, waved a skinny, yellow claw and came into the room. She was consultant psychiatrist to the Home Office and was in Edinburgh to attend a Conference, not a government-sponsored affair, but, in the words of Laura, 'a get-together of the psychiatric squares for gang warfare and personal combat.' Dame Beatrice had been

11

asked to read a paper on *Some Aspects of the Politico-Criminal Mind* and, with a fearful and wonderful leer at Laura, who had brought her the telephone message, she had consented to express her views to a possibly hostile assemblage. Now here she and Laura were, with the Conference fixed for two days ahead.

Laura's part, so far, had not been assigned to her, so she mentioned her plans, and then, referring to the Conference, ventured to ask for instructions.

'Oh, that!' said Dame Beatrice. 'I meant to tell you.' She accompanied this obvious lie with another cackle of eldritch mirth. 'I thought, though, I'd better wait until you had rid yourself of your beloved encumbrances so that you will be free to do exactly as you please as soon as we have coped with my notes.'

'Do you mean it's all for nothing that I've ordered my husband to spend his leave fishing for barracuda, and parked my son on his long-suffering grandparents? What are you at, Mrs Croc.?' demanded her secretary. 'I was sure I should sit through the Conference and keep you supplied with over-ripe tomatoes to chuck at your chosen foes. I was looking forward to it.'

'No, no, I shan't need you, and I can supply my own tomatoes. In other words, just come and go as you please. I expect you can find ways of amusing yourself, can you not?'

Laura affected to be stunned.

'You don't *need* me? Not for a whole *fortnight?*'

Dame Beatrice waved a claw.

'Don't get into mischief,' she said. 'It is some time since I was in Edinburgh. Go along out and enjoy yourself. Tomorrow you can take me sight-seeing.'

Laura wasted no time. Basely abandoning the programme she had planned, she took a bus to Linlithgow and studied the inscription on a fountain: *St Michael is Kind to*

Strangers. Then she went to visit the Church of St Michael, but, returning to the High Street after an early tea, she tripped on an unexpected double kerbstone and took a heavy fall.

People rushed to her assistance. Laura tried to tell them that she had suffered no hurt, but kindly hands insisted upon helping her to a seat under a tree and kindly Scottish voices asked her where she wanted to go. As the only place which Laura wished to visit was Linlithgow Palace, she announced this, and therefore (so extraordinary is the common reaction against a show of courage), she was abandoned on the spot by her well-wishers and undertook a somewhat limping pilgrimage alone.

'St Michael is kind to strangers?' thought Laura, hopping painfully up to the chief apartments of the palace in the wake of more active visitors. 'Oh, well, we'll wait and see.'

By the time she had seen the Great Hall and the chapel, and, in addition, the room in which Mary, Queen of Scots, was born, she had forgotten St Michael and his kindly interest in strangers and was anxious only to catch the bus and get back to the hotel.

It was a distance of seventeen miles and Laura was sure that she would be back in good time for dinner, as she had promised. When she got off the bus her injured leg not only hurt but had stiffened, so she decided to take a taxi instead of walking the comparatively short distance to the hotel. There were no cruising taxis, but she knew where there was a rank close at hand. To reach it she had to cross the road and it was while she was standing with a fair number of people on an island in the middle of the street, waiting for a stream of traffic to go by, that (her hearing being abnormally acute) she heard a man's muttered words : *Ready? The blue car this side. He's going to cram past. Now's our chance.*

Suddenly there was an exclamation, followed by women's

screams, a screeching of brakes, and, next to Laura, a fainting girl. In the street the blue limousine, unable to pull up in time, discharged its chauffeur and a portly gentleman, the only other occupant, to gaze helplessly at a man's body which lay in the roadway. A policeman came up. Laura and another woman took charge of the fainting girl, both glad of any excuse not to have to look at the mess in the road.

'Terrible! Terrible!' said a man nearby. 'It was sheer suicide. What way would a body be doing a thing like that?'

'But, of course, it wasn't suicide,' said the shattered Laura to Dame Beatrice when, having walked after all, she had rejoined her employer at the hotel. 'It was murder. I'm certain of that.' She recounted the mutterings she had overheard. 'The only trouble is that I haven't the faintest idea who said it. There were quite a pack of us waiting to cross, and, as soon as the words were out, the deed was done. I waited and told the policeman. He made a note of my name and address but said that it was undoubtedly the man's own fault and that the words I'd heard "held nae significance," as the other people he had questioned after the ambulance had driven off had all been perfectly certain that the man had simply thrown up his arms and chucked himself under the wheels. So what do I do?'

'It seems to me that you have done what you could,' Dame Beatrice replied. 'Besides, the policeman may have been right, you know. The words you overheard may have had no bearing on the matter at all.'

Laura tried to take comfort from this thought. On the following morning they went to Holyrood.

'So that's that,' said Laura, when they had visited the Picture Gallery with its somewhat oddly conceived portraits of the Scottish kings from the brush of Jakob de Wet. From him, Laura suggested, may have stemmed the legend that the Scots are a mean, ungenerous, parsimonious, cheese-paring race. Dame Beatrice asked why and was informed that de Wet had been commissioned to produce one hundred and ten works of art (and pay for his own materials) in return for the average sum of two pounds four shillings per portrait.

'No wonder they're lousy,' said Laura. 'Let's go to the Zoo.'

'The Castle first. I like the view out to the Forth.'

'Have you ever been into the dungeons?'

'Yes, I was shown them once, but I believe that there is no general admission for visitors.'

'I'd like to see them. I specialise in the macabre. What's interesting about them?'

'Well, if your injuries of yesterday will stand up to it, we will go and see. I know the mother of one of the senior officers of the Black Watch and the great-aunt of a captain in the Argyll and Sutherland Highlanders. We should be able to bluff our way through.'

There proved to be no need for this. As they got out of the car on the Esplanade at the top of Ramsay Lane, a middle-aged man in the uniform of the Scots Guards saluted Dame Beatrice and exclaimed :

'Well, well! It's been a long, long time!'

'Alastair McClennan!'

'The same. And when are you going to Gàradh again to see my cousin Margaret Stewart? She talks often of you in her letters.'

Dame Beatrice introduced him to Laura and mentioned the latter's desire to inspect the dungeons. She had seen the dark hole which had formed the sixteenth-century prison of the Countess of Glamis, Laura explained, but not the dungeons under the Old Parliament Hall nor (for it seemed a time to strike while the iron was hot) the West Sally Port.

'Before I take you to see that, Mrs Gavin,' said he, 'you must promise me two things : first, to sing "Bonny Dundee" – for, as doubtless you are aware, it was from there that

Viscount Claverhouse left Edinburgh in order to raise the Highlands to fight for the Stuart cause——'

'Although why anybody should want to keep James II of England on either throne is more than I can fathom,' said Laura. 'What else must I do?'

'You must persuade Dame Beatrice not to leave Scotland until she has visited my cousin at Gàradh – unless you'll go and visit her yourself? I know you'd be more than welcome.'

They visited the West Sally Port and then were taken to the dungeon prison of the ninth Earl of Argyll before his execution. Lastly they were taken to inspect the quarters of the French prisoners of Stevenson's *St Ives*. When they were taking leave of their conductor, he said, looking keenly at Laura :

'Mrs Gavin, what did you see in Argyll's prison?'

'Nothing really, I suppose,' said Laura. 'I have a grandmother who's supposed to have the Gift, but I don't think I've inherited it.'

'Well, I won't press you. I'll merely say this : many people firmly believe that parts of the Castle are haunted, so, if you did see anything, you're in good and honest company.'

'It wasn't a ghost,' said Laura. Neither of her hearers urged her to say any more, neither was she herself at all certain that the impression she had received was anything but the result of too lively an imagination; for, in the dungeon from which the noble Argyll had gone to a felon's death, she had thought for a horrified moment that she saw the face of the man who had been run down and killed at the road-crossing. She might have dismissed this as a nervous fancy, although nervous fancies were entirely foreign to her nature, but she thought she also heard a groan.

She soon threw off the effects of what she felt was a piece

of childish nonsense, the result of a certain amount of delayed shock, and she and Dame Beatrice went to the hotel for lunch and then visited the Edinburgh Zoo. When they were on their way back again, Laura said :

'Do you really think I could visit his cousin at Gàradh? I've heard about those gardens.'

'I do so wish you would go, child. I am sure you would enjoy your visit, and I should very much like you to meet Mrs Stewart, who is an old friend of mine. Look here, suppose I give you a letter of introduction? Then you can please yourself whether or not you go. The gardens certainly are worth seeing and I think you would find the coast scenery and the drive to Gàradh very fine. There is only one eye-sore, to my mind, along the road you would probably take, and that is the newish hydro-electrical plant near a small place called Tigh-Òsda. Apart from that – and you may not object to it, since, of course, it provides not only electricity but employment – it is an interesting and mostly a very beautiful road.'

'I'd love to go,' said Laura, 'and, although I'm not shy, I'd like a letter of introduction to prove my *bona fides*, don't you know.'

'Your face is your fortune,' said Dame Beatrice absently, recollecting her own last visit to Gàradh, 'but I'll write the letter tonight.'

Two Houses in Wester Ross

'By perilous paths in coomb and dell,
The heather, the rocks and the river bed.'
John Davidson

DAME BEATRICE not only wrote the letter but rang up Mrs Stewart of Gàradh and it was arranged that Laura was to call on her, the date of the visit to be arranged by telephone later so that Laura did not need to be tied in advance to any one particular day.

'Won't she think that a bit thick?' Laura suggested, for she was at hand while the call was being made. Dame Beatrice put the point, and then replied :

'She says good gracious no. She has no plans for the next fortnight and will be delighted to see you at any time. You are not to dream of spoiling your holiday. So there you are.'

The following days, therefore, found Laura (in her own expression) 'stooging round the Highlands in a hired Tin Liz' and thoroughly enjoying her freedom. She devotedly loved her husband and her small son, but it was a welcome change to be a grass widow and mother for a bit.

She left Edinburgh for Inverness, but stayed a night on the way at Pitlochry and another at Kingussie. In Inverness she put up at an hotel where they knew her, and on her first evening she saw a shabby man take a good-sized salmon out of the River Ness right under the hotel windows. This she regarded as a splendid omen for the success of her trip. Every diner left the table to see the fish taken, and, the ice thus being broken, Laura, who was a sociable soul, found plenty of people to talk with over coffee in the lounge.

Before dawn on the following day she crept quietly out of her room, left the hotel by a side door she had used for early-morning excursions on previous visits, retrieved the hired car from its lock-up garage and drove along the shores of the loch in the hope of seeing the Monster.

This attempt to add herself to the small but convinced band of Nessie Spotters was doomed, like all her former ones, to disappointment, although she drove all the way to the western end of the loch and parked there until hunger drove her back to the hotel for a very late breakfast.

It was all very well, she thought, bearing the learned gentleman a certain amount of resentment, for Dr Maurice Burton to scrutinise all the evidence for Nessie's existence and then attribute her energies merely to expanding gases in a waste of vegetable matter, but what of the stories of swimmers tossed out of boats who had found their art of no avail and whose bodies had never been recovered? What of the stories of divers who refused to speak of what they had seen in the depths of the loch, when they had been sent down to salvage those bodies? What of the unimpeachable evidence of many accredited eye-witnesses? As for the discrepancies in their accounts of the actual appearance of the Monster, well, Laura had heard her husband's opinion of the way in which witnesses in police court cases could fail to identify – or could wrongly identify – people whom they had seen far more clearly and at much closer quarters than anyone had ever seen the elusive Nessie.

Yet Dr Burton, reflected Laura, comforting herself with the thought, seemed to have ended his researches with a divided mind. He was even prepared to accept the hypothesis that there might exist some sort of *amphibious* creature, nocturnal, on the whole, in its habits and looking rather like a long-necked otter, a creature so far unknown to zoologists. On the whole, perhaps such an animal was

19

rather more delightfully terrifying than the completely aquatic and apparently purposeless Nessie herself.

Laura enjoyed her late breakfast, decided to spend the morning shopping, loitering and writing letters, have lunch at the hotel and then make her way to Freagair and hope to put up there for the night. If the one hotel at Freagair could not take her, there was always Strathpeffer.

The hotel at Freagair had a room for her. She ate Scotch broth, trout and good Scotch beef for her dinner, refused the sweet and asked for roes on toast, drank a half bottle of undistinguished Burgundy and went to bed in good time, having decided upon an early start for Gàradh so that she would be able to call upon Mrs Stewart before lunch.

She arranged to return to the hotel for the following night, breakfasted at eight and was on the road by a quarter to nine. She had been warned that after the first ten miles the road was single-track all the way to Crioch and, a mile out of that resort of wide and shining sands, single-track again to her destination. There were passing places, but it could take a long time to make the full journey.

Laura, however, was lucky. There was very little traffic, the hired car behaved well and the road was extremely beautiful. The morning was sunny, although not particularly warm, and although the narrow road needed concentrated attention, she was aware of green hills to her right, a sluggish, broad river bordered by rough pasture to her left, and beyond the shallow valley there were the mountains. A single-track railway line ran alongside the river.

Later, on the right, she passed a smallish loch with islands, one of which was wooded, another of which had been built on (she had a glimpse of a white house) and the rest were no more than rocks.

Later, she passed another house, but it was beyond the river and the railway and, although she noticed the trackway which opened off the road, she did not see the house.

Some miles further on she came into Tigh-Òsda, at which the single-track railway terminated, and, except for a disfiguring new hydro-electric plant, the views for the rest of the way were superb. The long windings of the narrow road descended to a loch twelve miles long, guarded by grim mountains on the far side, partly wooded on the near side, islanded and tantalisingly beautiful. Laura drove slowly past it and although she still kept a wary eye on the road for approaching cars and passing-places, she managed to see enough of its loveliness to make her decide to come that way again at some time and enjoy it to the full.

At Crioch, on the coast, she passed a post-office and wondered whether to stop and send her employer a card, but a glance at the clock on the dashboard suggested that it might be better to press on, for she had an invitation to lunch at Gàradh and did not want to be late.

From Crioch, through Baile (a tiny hamlet where fishermen lived) and all the way to Gàradh, the road ran along the coast. The day became warmer, the sun still shone and Laura was almost sorry when she reached the great gates of the Gàradh policies and realised that this was journey's end. The gates were wide open, as though in hospitable welcome, and this impression was reinforced by the presence of her hostess waiting on the terrace to greet her.

'So this is Gàradh,' said Laura, when they had introduced themselves. 'It's indescribable. I expected something rather wonderful, but this beats anything I'd thought of.'

'You shall see it all when you've had your lunch. Did you have a good journey?' said her hostess, taking her into the house. 'Lunch will come to the table as soon as you're ready.'

Laura washed her hands and tidied her hair in a broad, low-ceilinged room to which Mrs Stewart showed her and from which a shy, smiling housemaid took her to the dining-room door. There was a fire in the room, Madeira wine on the enormous sideboard and a pleasant, homely atmosphere everywhere. Laura was very glad indeed that she had come.

After lunch there was a good cup of tea served in beautiful china and poured from a pot of Georgian silver. Tea, said her hostess, she greatly preferred to coffee after mid-day meals. After this they went into the grounds. From what she had seen when she had driven up to the house and while she had been standing beside Mrs Stewart for a moment or two on the terrace, Laura had realised that the policies were extensive, but she had not fully grasped what an acreage they must cover nor how truly superb were the seascapes and the natural scenery, even apart from the glories of the gardens themselves.

Across the sea-loch whose weedy tides slapped idly and in slow motion against the rocky walls rose the stern, dark outlines of the humped and massive Ben Caraid, and on the homeward side, running far out into the shallow water, was a long peninsula which formed part of the Gàradh estate. Gàradh was indeed a garden, a magnificent garden which had been contrived by the owner's grandfather on what had once been barren, heartless sandstone and patches of sour peat.

It was not ordinarily particularly enjoyable to Laura to linger among the treasures of gardening fanatics or to listen with patient courtesy while these poured out, in considerable detail and even more Latin, a wealth of information about their insignificant-looking plants, but this occasion was different. In spite of the details and the Latin nomenclature, Laura enjoyed herself. The very extensive garden had been romantically conceived, for all the soil had been transported to it from far, far away, earth had been banked and trees grown to protect it, and, by the time Laura saw it, it was, in effect, a miniature Kew.

To her right, as she peered with well-simulated interest at

Anacyclus Depressus, Cotoneaster Frigida Prostate, Leonto-
podium Alpinum and the rest of the fifty-nine species which
the rock-garden had on display, were palm trees and an
Australian tree fern, while in the opposite direction was a
group of northern pines. Between the two lay the house,
comfortable, large and built in Colonial style, to which
they returned at half-past four to what Laura called 'a
real Edinburgh tea.' After tea they went out again, for
the days were already long and the light good until late
evening.

'Come and see the rhododendrons,' said Mrs Stewart.
'Many are over, but we get some of them in flower, different
species and hybrids, you know, from April almost until the
autumn. We have some, indeed, which flower in February
and March.'

They left the house, passed beside the rock garden which
Laura had already seen and stood a while by the jetty and
a small boat-house to look across the sea-loch to Ben
Caraid's formidable cliffs and shadowed corries.

'It is a lovely place!' said Laura. 'I suppose it's not really
cold here, even in winter?'

'The trees and the banks give a great deal of shelter, and
the sea, this side, is warm, but we get snow, of course. I
mind well – four years ago last Hogmanay it was – I had
guests snowed up here for the best part of two weeks. Och,
that was a time! My son's friends, too, not folk of my own
choosing. One of them was the laird of Tannasgan. Did you
ever hear of Tannasgan?'

'No, I never did. Is it far from here?'

'Not so far. It's a wee island in a loch, a piece east of
Tigh-Òsda, ay, between Tigh-Òsda and Freagair. You will
have passed it on your way here. The laird is a strange
body and has not a very good name in these parts, but my
son had had business dealings with him and invited him to
stay a couple of nights to finish discussing the details. I did

not take to the laird at all, and there was I stuck with the poor man for a fortnight!'

'Talking of Freagair,' said Laura, 'if I'm to get there tonight I shall have to leave pretty soon, I'm afraid.'

'Ay, you'll not want to travel a single-track road in the dark. You'll not change your mind and bide here the night?'

'It's very kind of you, but I booked a room, so I'd better get back, I think. I *have* enjoyed it here.'

'You must persuade Dame Beatrice to bring you again before you both go back to London.'

'I most certainly will.'

They strolled on, past flowering shrubs and then, taking a steep little side-path, came upon an enormous and impressive bare rock.

'Torridon red sandstone,' said Mrs Stewart. 'If you'll look that way across the bay you will see the Torridon mountains.'

They returned by a détour to the house to collect Laura's bag and install her in the hired car. It was still broad daylight, but there was cloud coming up and Ben Caraid, never a friendly mountain, was looking ominous.

'It's going to rain,' said Laura.

'Ay, but you'll be well on your way before that. I wish you had been able to see the herbaceous border at its best, but that's not until July. The man I was telling you about, the laird of Tannasgan, gave me some rock plants, but I think it was my son's idea that he should, for I don't think the chiel would have thought of it for himself.'

They parted with thanks on the one side and a repetition of the invitation to 'come again and bring Dame Beatrice with you' on the other, and then Laura drove away from Gàradh and followed the only road, the coast road, back through Baile to the small resort of Crioch. Here she pulled in, got out of the car and took a stroll along the cliff-top.

There were very few people about, although a hotel of moderate size faced the sea. The tide was out and the sands were wet and shining, broken here and there by seaweed-covered rocks humped like glistening saurians lazily washed by tiny waves. It was a charming place.

Out to sea, and barely visible except to those who, like Laura, knew it was there, lay the Hebridean island of Lewis and, south-west and a great deal nearer, she could see the unmistakable outline of the northern end of Skye. She would have liked to descend the cliff by the rough steps which led to the sands, but gathering cloud and a glance at her wristwatch warned her that time was pressing, so she returned to the car and drove inland towards the road which ran alongside the waters of Cóig Eich, the Loch of the Five Horses, claimed (locally) to be the loveliest in Scotland. The name and the claim she had received from Mrs Stewart.

The way, before she reached the loch in its beautiful valley, wound upwards through pine-woods. Although here not strictly, perhaps, a single-track road, it was extremely narrow and the bends followed one another for mile after mile, so that it was unsafe to drive at any sort of speed. Alongside the water it was easier going, but the loch was often screened from the car by trees and on the opposite side of the road there were high banks, more trees and some bracken. It reminded Laura a little of the road alongside Loch Lomond, but it was lonelier, wilder and narrower.

Once past the loch, the view became more open, although the road itself was still narrow. Here Laura became aware that the fine weather was at an end and the clouds had won. The mountains she could see in front and to the right of her were standing starkly against a lowering sky and almost at once it began to rain. The landscape swam in a green haze and soon she was keeping to a road sheeted in the most relentless downpour. She dared not pull up, for she was by this time on a single-track stretch between high hills on the one hand and the shallow river, beyond which ran the single-line railway, on the other, so that passing-places could not be obstructed by a stationary car.

At last she approached the hydro-electric power station with its pipe-lines. The rain eased off a little and she was able to see that the little river had been diverted and the small, ugly loch into which it flowed had been turned into an even uglier reservoir. Then the rain came down again and blotted out everything. Fortunately Laura met nothing on the road until she reached Tigh-Òsda, the little hamlet with a railway station. It also possessed an hotel. At this, most thankfully, she pulled up, deciding to try to get a room there for the night and go on to Freagair in the morning. She wished she had not stopped at Crioch, or else that she had left Gàradh a little earlier.

Drawn up outside the hostelry was an empty estate-wagon, and just inside the covered entrance to the station stood a man and woman whose resigned expressions, as they stared gloomily at the rain, caused Laura to suppose them the owners of the vehicle. She got out of her own car and darted into the inn, but she had only time to wipe her shoes on the mat before a man's voice said :

'Losh ! You've a car !'

Laura turned and saw the man who had made one of the desolate-looking pair in the station entrance.

'Do you mean you've broken down?' she asked.

'Do I not ! And not a mechanic or a garage this side of Freagair ! I suppose you couldn't give my wife a lift home? I'd be eternally grateful if you could. You see, we've had a day out together and left the bairn with the baby-sitter. We promised faithfully to free the lassie by seven o'clock and it's a quarter to seven now. She lives in a wee clachan about two miles from our house, but, of course, she won't leave the wean until my wife gets in. It's ten miles from here and my wife isn't able to walk so far, especially in this awful weather. I'd go myself, but I *must* catch the up train, and it's due any minute. I have to get to Inverness.'

'All right,' said Laura, 'but I'll just need to reserve a room here first.'

'No, no,' said the man. 'It's an awful poor sort of place. My wife will gladly see you taken care of at our house for the night if you'll just run her along there. I'm much obliged to you for your kindness.'

Laura went back to her car and in a moment the wife had joined her.

'It's awful good of you,' she said. 'We telephoned Freagair, but there's only the one garage there and they said they had nobody to send. We tried the hotel at Crioch, but they said they had no facilities to deal with mechanical faults.'

Laura started the engine.

'You'll have to guide me,' she said.

'Well, it's the straight road towards Freagair and then we have a private lane and a bridge, turning off to the right and crossing a wee burn. I'll give you plenty of warning.'

So Laura found herself again upon the way to Freagair, driving in sheets of dark-grey rain on a single-track road with leviathan, dirty, green hills on her left and a broken-fenced morass on her right. The man had minimised the distance. It was nearer twelve miles than ten before she turned off. A gate had to be opened before the car could proceed bumpily forward on to the so-called drive – actually a causeway across a marsh – and this led to a rickety bridge. The 'wee burn' was a good thirty feet wide at this point, and Laura, driving over the narrow bridge with extreme caution in the pelting rain, half-expected the car to go through the rotten planking into the stream below. However, they crawled safely over and then had to negotiate a level crossing of the branch railway-line before they arrived at the house.

This was of fair size but appeared to be servantless except for the baby-sitter, and the woman used her own front-door key to let herself in. The fact of a front-door key in itself surprised Laura, who was accustomed to having her own Highland relatives keep open house to the extent of never locking up anything. An open-fronted shed formed the garage, it seemed, so Laura, left alone, drove into it, her headlights showing her the way. She switched off and went to the front door. Then she remembered that the baby-sitter would have to walk home in the teeming rain unless she was given a lift. Laura groaned.

'Come in!' called the woman. 'Kirsty is just leaving.' She switched on the light and in the hall Laura saw a tallish, round-faced girl wearing a raincoat, a head-scarf and gum-boots.

'I'd better drive you home,' said Laura. 'Come on.'

'No, no,' said the girl. 'It is pleasant with me to walk in the rain.' Without another word she passed Laura and stepped sturdily out into the elements.

'Let Kirsty be,' said the woman. 'She's independent and she'll take no harm. Come ben.' She led the way into a room where there was a pleasant fire burning in the hearth. 'Take off your things and draw up to the fire. The bairn's sleeping fine, and she's no trouble once she's off. Have you any luggage in the car? I'll go out and get it when we've supped.'

Laura's hostess was named Grant. After the meal the two women settled down by the fire, Mrs Grant observing that the washing-up could wait until the morning.

'I'm without any help in the house, as you see, Mrs Gavin,' she said, 'and the Dear knows I could do with it.'

'I suppose the local girls all move away to the towns,' said Laura.

'Och, it's not only that. It's the curse that's been put upon this house.'

'The curse?'

'I call it that. It's that wicked old wretch who lives on Tannasgan – or so I believe. He is harmful to this house.'

'Really?' said Laura, not attempting to divulge that she had already heard of the laird of Tannasgan. Mrs Grant, certain of a listener, continued :

'That old man is the devil himself. He can make anybody who is as simple as some of the folk in these parts believe anything he chooses to tell them. I cannot pin it down to him, and, if I could, I don't know what I would do about it, because he's so wicked and because he has influence. It goes ill with anybody who crosses him.'

'But why should he wish to do you harm?'

'Well, there are two reasons. It was dead against his wishes that the hydro-electric plant was established way back the other side of Tigh-Òsda – you'll have noticed the hydro-electric plant when you were after passing the loch of Cóig Eich? – it's a big ugly thing on the left of you along that road.'

'Yes, I didn't miss it, I must say !'

'Och, well, you see, my man has a very good job there, so the old devil has his knife into him.'

'But aren't other men working there?'

'Och, ay, but they're away to Crioch or maybe Fraegair and he has no hold over them. Besides, there's the second reason I mentioned. You see, he once made me an offer of marriage, but I was already promised to my man, and, in any case, I would have been terrified to have married on such an old warlock. So we're both in his bad books.'

'And too obstinate to move away from his neighbourhood?'

'You may say that. This house is my own, willed to me by my grandfather, who had it before me. What way would I let myself be driven off from what is mine?'

'Quite. But isn't it an awful bore to be without servants in a house of this size?'

'Och, my man gives me a hand with the rough. He's kind. And Kirsty will sit in when we both go out, although she takes good care to speir at me whether it will be both of us out before she'll agree to come ben the house.'

'Well, I'll do the washing-up before I go to bed,' said Laura, getting up. The conversation embarrassed her. There was something unreal about it.

'You'll do nothing of the kind! No guest of mine does a hand's turn here. I would be mortified to my death!' exclaimed Mrs Grant.

'What kind of a place is Tannasgan?' Laura asked.

'It is an island in Loch na Gréine, and Cù Dubh, as the people call him, lives in the Big House, *An Tigh Mór*. He keeps a wee boat and visitors have to use a special signal and then he brings the boat over for them. You'll see the same arrangement at other places just here and there about the Western Highlands.'

'You say he *brings* the boat over. Hasn't he servants, then? Can't *he* get them, either?'

'He has a couple, I believe, but he's all on his own and I heard tell that most of the house is shut up. He brings the boat over himself to see whether he wants a visitor. He mortally offended some of the local folk when first he came, because they went to call on him and were refused. I believe nobody signals now except the tradespeople.'

'Surely he doesn't row over to take in the shopping?'

'As to that, I would hardly know. I never go near the place if I can help it. Eh, but I'm glad to have company in the house this night!'

'When do you expect your husband to get back?'

'The Dear knows! He was for Inverness and then on to Edinburgh. That will be tomorrow. He doesn't know whether he'll need to go back and spend another night in Inverness, but I'll be hearing.'

She went on to give Laura a detailed description of the hardships of her own and her husband's life owing to the evil machinations of the laird of Tannasgan. Laura listened without much interest. Her day at Gàradh, spent mostly in the open air, her journey and now the warmth of Mrs Grant's fire and the heavy supper she had eaten, had made her sleepy. Her long limbs demanded a bed, and her general comment on the diatribe would have been that she thought the lady did protest too much.

Mrs Grant's tales of slights and petty tyrannies, of slanders and mischief-making were, however, apparently endless. She had an audience and was only too obviously prepared to make the most of it. It was two in the morning before the flow ceased and Mrs Grant proposed that they should retire for the night. She brought whisky and some brownish peat-stained water for a night-cap and then, when she had escorted Laura to her room, she said :

'I'll be bringing a can of hot water, so if you'll just give me the key of your car I'll get your luggage up to you.'

'Oh, please don't bother,' said Laura. 'I'll get it myself.'

'No, no! I couldn't think of that. You just get yourself ready for bed and I'll be along with it in two ticks.'

Laura handed over the car keys. In two minutes the hot water came and, before she had finished washing, her suitcase was deposited at the door and Mrs Grant said good night, adding :

'You'll not need to mind the wean if you hear her crying. She'll soon drop off again.'

Thankfully Laura fell into bed. It was a very comfortable bed and she was asleep immediately. In the ordinary way she needed very little sleep, but on this particular morning she did not wake until eight. The rain was over and the sun was shining. She did not know whether to get up or whether there was any prospect of early tea, but this problem was soon solved, for her hostess came in with a tray. On it were a large cup of very strong tea, milk, sugar and her keys. Breakfast would be in half an hour, she was told, and there was another can of hot water at the door.

Breakfast was porridge, kippers and thick slices of bread and butter, reinforced by bapps, scones and a home-made sultana loaf. Laura did full justice to it, thanked her hostess and hoped that her man would soon be home. There was no sign of the child, but this did not disappoint Laura, who was no baby-worshipper. She left the house – it was called Coinneamh Lodge on the direction-sign which fronted the road, she noted – at just after ten o'clock. It was a twenty-mile journey to Freagair and, as was her habit, when she had garaged the car she glanced at her mileage record.

Arithmetic was not Laura's strong point, but her memory was excellent and she had checked her mileage at Gàradh. According to her reckoning, the car had done thirty-two miles more than it should have done.

'Funny! So that's why my keys didn't come back until this morning!' thought Laura. 'Wonder where she went and what she wanted the car for? Dash it, she might have mentioned she was going to borrow it! I suppose her bringing it back was what woke me up this morning! Wonder whether the whisky was doped? I don't usually sleep like that!'

CHAPTER THREE

A Visit to An Tigh Mór

'Now who be ye would cross Lochgyle,
That dark and stormy water?'

Sir Walter Scott

THE girl in the hotel reception office at Freagair smiled sympathetically when Laura explained that she had been held up by the bad weather. She added that she would require her room that night, provided that it was still vacant, as she proposed to explore the countryside before returning to Inverness.

She was too early for lunch, so she bought herself a drink and, over that and a cigarette, she wrote a letter to Dame Beatrice describing her visit to Mrs Stewart at Gàradh and summarising her subsequent experiences.

Lunch over, she left Freagair in the hired car (which seemed none the worse for its extra trip), in quest of a place where she could park it and go for a walk. Before she left the garage she checked her petrol and discovered that Mrs Grant must have had a supply at Coinneamh Lodge, for the tank contained more than it had held when Laura had checked it at Tigh-Òsda before driving Mrs Grant home.

'Oh, well, that's something to her credit, and she certainly looked after me well. I wonder what on earth she *was* up to? Went back to Tigh-Òsda to make sure their van was all right, knowing that I was at hand to look after the kid, perhaps? I suppose the rain had left off when she went. I wonder when she *did* go? At about six, I should think. She'd hardly drive in the dark. She can't have had much sleep, anyway. Oh, well, she hasn't damaged the bus and she's given me lots of free petrol, so that's all right.'

She left Freagair by the road to Uinneag and parked the small car on the grass verge of a little, noisy stream which was racing through a wooded glen. It seemed possible to follow the course of the stream and, even if it proved necessary to return the same way, Laura reflected, the scenery would not look the same, seen from the opposite direction.

The grass verge soon ended, she discovered, and then the going became rough. Boulders, like passive grey sheep, were strewn all over the narrow valley and the birches grew so thickly that Laura welcomed the change when, some time later, she came out among pines. Here the little stream, still rippling, shouting and tumbling, wound freely, finding its way. Sometimes it narrowed between walls of rock, sometimes it broadened into shallow, brown, shining pools.

The going, beside the shallows and pools, was much easier, and after about an hour Laura sat down beside one of the pools and took out a cigarette. The trees here were not birches and pines, but slightly stunted oaks growing less than five feet from the water. The opposite bank was similar to the one on which she was seated, but the glen had widened considerably and beyond a hill, on whose lower slopes the deciduous trees were clustered, rose the high peaks of mountains. A little farther on, when she resumed her walk, she could see, on the opposite bank, a rough stone wall dividing neighbouring policies, but on her side of the river there seemed to be no obstacles.

In the next two or three miles the scenery changed again and the mountains altered their shape with the continual windings of the river. Laura found herself walking uncomfortably on shale, and on the opposite bank the pines reappeared, dwarfing the oaks and looking almost black

34

against their greenery. Occasionally thick bushes on Laura's side of the water hid the river from her view.

At last she came out upon a path and in full view of the mountains. There was bracken beside the path, and here and there, as the path mounted, there was heather among the boulders. A long, bare ridge of solid rock ran from the path down to the river, which, by this time, was churning its narrow way in the gorge below. A solitary Scots pine with a writhing trunk on whose smoothness the sun shone, was the only tree Laura could see, and the shadow it cast was a long one.

Laura glanced at her wristwatch. It was later than she had thought, but the sky was clear and she was thoroughly enjoying her walk. She made a mental note of the time and decided to give herself half an hour longer before she turned back. The path had been travelling steadily upwards for some time and she thought that the return journey would be speedier than the outward one.

Before the half-hour was up, however, her luck changed and so did the weather. The path went steeply downhill instead of up, then, for no obvious reason, it petered out as soon as it reached a clump of birches on a little knoll above the river, which here, having left the gorge and the boulders behind, ran shallow and clear, with low banks of dry pebbles dividing it into channels.

Beside the birch trees Laura paused to take stock. The sunshine had gone and a menacing little wind shivered in the delicate branches. The sky was ominously overcast and the river had lost all its colour. The mountains seemed suddenly nearer, and then down came the mist and blotted them out. Then it began to pour with rain. Laura took what shelter she could from the birches, but their attenuated branches and light, small leaves offered almost no protection.

'Oh, hell!' she said aloud, and, as though the infernal

35

archangel had heard her invocation and had decided to come to her aid, she saw, on the other side of the river, what she took to be a crofter's cottage. Faith in the traditional hospitality of the Highlands made up her mind for her. She was opposite a part of the river where it was safe enough to cross. She decided to seek sanctuary.

Still keeping within what little shelter she could get from the birches, she chose the likeliest fording place, where a long spit of shingle-shale almost cut the river in two. Here she faced the full of the teeming rain, slithered on the stones and stepped out into the water. At its deepest it reached to her knees and she found it difficult to keep her footing, but she was almost immediately in the shallows and soon reached the opposite bank. It was higher than the one she had left, but, with the aid of another spit of shingle – a small one this time – and a low-growing bush, she mounted the bank and, head down against the elements, battled her way towards the croft.

There was a stone wall to be surmounted, for there was no visible opening, and in climbing over this she tore her skirt. Then, when she approached the forlorn little dwelling, she saw that it was roofless. She saw something else, too. Because of the bends in the river she had not realised that she had almost reached the point at which it flowed into the loch, but there, in front of her, was not only the loch but a narrow road. What was more, as she came out on to the road through a gap in the stone wall which bounded the deserted croft, she saw that there was an island in the loch and against a black background of trees a big house on the island stood out eerily white.

'Pity it's on the island. I could have asked for shelter there,' thought Laura, pausing before she stepped out along the road in the hope – forlorn, she supposed – of coming upon a clachan. Suddenly a man's voice said, from just behind her :

'If it might be for the laird you are wishing, it is known to me that it is necessary to you turning the sign at the side of the small quay. There is a boat at the laird.'

Laura had not even seen the small quay. The man, a bearded figure in a stout anorak and fisherman's waders, pointed out where it lay to the left, about forty yards from where he was standing.

'Oh, thank you,' said Laura. Before she could say any more, the idiosyncratic stranger, whose pleasure it appeared to be to converse in a direct and unwieldly translation from the Gaelic, had made for the small quay and was operating what Laura, following him, perceived to be a large lantern, half of green glass and half of red.

'They'll never see that from over there,' said Laura, 'unless we light it, and I don't see how we can do that in this rain. Besides . . .'

'Is terrible this rain, but it is pleasant with me to ring the bell,' said the stranger. He swung the lantern round so that it showed green towards the loch and red towards the road and then took up a tarpaulin, which was pegged down by four large stones, and disclosed a handbell. This he swung vigorously until its harsh clamour violated the air. He put it back, replaced the tarpaulin and the stones, touched his dripping tweed hat and scrambled back on to the road. Laura, as wet as though she had fallen into the loch, looked across the water and saw a boat putting out from the island.

'Here's hoping!' she muttered, wriggling her feet in their squelching shoes. 'Now for the sacred claims of the way-farer!'

At this the rain eased a little and, as the boat approached the quay, she could see that it was a stout coble pulled by one man. She stood at the end of the quay and the boat-man, a huge, red-bearded brigand in oilskins and a sou'-wester, brought the boat round with the skill of long usage, reached over and gripped an iron ring.

'If you're for Tannasgan,' he said, in a voice which matched his frame, 'you had better get in.'

Laura's pulse quickened. It was a fantastic quirk on the part of Fate, she felt, to have brought her, in this roundabout fashion, to the lair of the ogre of An Tigh Mór. She stepped into the boat and, almost before she was seated, the boatman had released the ring, given a hearty push off from the side of the jetty, and was rowing, with short, powerful strokes, across the choppy water.

There was a boat-house on the island. Here the bearded man tied up and handed Laura out. The house was a mere thirty yards away. The man took Laura's wrist in a strong grasp and ran with her up to the front door, which was open.

'Come ben,' he said, and thrust her into the hall. 'Mairi! Mairi! To me here! We have a guest!'

A woman almost as tall as the man appeared from some lair off the side of the hall. She had the grim, almost mannish face of some elderly Scotswomen and was dressed in a black blouse of the type which used to be called a bodice, a black skirt to her ankles, and a starched white apron.

'Ye called?' she asked.

'I did that. Pop this water-kelpie in the bath-tub and then bed her with two hot bricks, a dram and a basin of broth. Dry out her clothes. She dines with me tonight. Send her down at three-quarters after eight and put out sherry on the sideboard and a bottle of champagne on the dining-table.'

Having given these orders, he pushed Laura towards the woman and went out by a door at the far end of the hall. The woman waited until he had slammed this door and then she relaxed her expression and grimly smiled.

'Dinna fash yourself,' she said, 'about that one. There's

them that think him a wee bit wrong in the head and his talk, times, is wild, but use him wi' sense and civility and dinna cross him, and he'll eat out o' your hand, as they say.'

'Do you come from Glasgow way?' asked Laura.

'Kirkintilloch. My man, too. Come wi' me. Ye're soppin' the floor.'

Three-quarters of an hour later, having soaked herself in a portable zinc bath which was so long and so deep that she concluded it had been fashioned to the individual specification of her host, Laura was between warmed sheets and also in the comfortable company of two hot bricks wrapped in flannel, a whisky toddy of almost frightening potency and a huge bowl of Scotch broth. Outside the bedroom window the rain still pelted down. Laura pulled a black woollen shawl more closely about her shoulders and breathed a short, heartfelt prayer of thanks for the situation in which she found herself.

She was left in peace until a quarter past eight, and had dozed off, when the housekeeper came in and informed her that she could not get her sodden clothes dry in such a short time, but that, although she had explained this, 'that one' was still determined that Laura should dine with him.

'What'll we do?' she enquired. 'He's a gey ill chiel to cross.'

'You had better lend me a pair of your man's breeks,' said Laura.

'Awa' wi' ye!' shrilled the housekeeper, highly diverted by this suggestion.

'Well, speir at the gentleman will he lend me his dressing-gown, then.'

To her amusement the woman took this suggestion with all seriousness, went off and soon returned with the garment in question. Laura was tall and well-built, but, even so, she had to gather up trails of the blanket-cloth from which the dressing-gown was fashioned in order to make a stately descent of the stairs.

The man, it appeared, (indeed, he stated it), preferred to take his meals in silence. Laura was allowed and even encouraged to converse with him while each of them drank two glasses of sherry, and then, as he offered his arm to her to conduct her from the sideboard to her seat at the table, he gracefully observed :

'And now, no more babbling until coffee !'

So they sat in complete silence at opposite ends of the table and consumed hare soup, boiled salmon, gigot of mutton followed by treacle tart. The man had changed his mind about the wine. Instead of champagne, two bottles of Clos de Vougeot had been placed upon the table, one beside Laura and the other at the disposal of her host. They were waited upon to the extent that a grey-haired man brought each dish in and put it on the table. Her host served it, carried Laura's plate to her, collected it when she had finished and then bellowed for Corrie. At this, the grey-haired man came in with the next course and took out the empty plates.

The dinner was a good one, beautifully cooked, and Laura, always a hearty trencherman, enjoyed it. At last the pudding plates disappeared and the man pushed back his chair and stood up.

'There's a kebbuk of cheese if you want it. If not, there's coffee beside the fire, and then you may loosen your wôman's tongue,' he said. 'Tell me, are there werewolves in your part of the country?'

'No. They live in the Hartz Mountains,' said Laura.

'They live in the Grampians; they thrive in the Cairngorms; they have been known at Leith and now they are here.'

'So is the basilisk,' said Laura, grinning.

'Do you tell me that?' He looked at her with a keen

interest which caused her to wonder whether he was something more than a mere eccentric.

'And what about the cockatrice?' she asked.

'But, my good lassie, they are the same creature! Where's your education? The crowned serpent hatched from a cock's egg, that's the basilisk – *basil,* a king, you ken. And the crown is like a cock's comb. I've seen it. I know.'

'Pardon,' said Laura, now convinced that she was in the presence of a madman. 'A slip of the tongue. I should have asked about the salamander.'

'I had one once as a pet, and a dear wee beastie he was until he fell into the fire – jumped into it, you might say. Then – losh! *There* was a blaze. It nearly had my house burnt down. One of these days I will show you. They love the fire, as you know. Born and bred in the secret, incredible heat of mid-earth, half-way to the Golden Gate – I mean to the Antipodes – is the salamander, and on fire he feeds. Ay, on fire he feeds and grows. Why, this one – Loki I called him – my ancestors came from Scandinavia, you ken – he grew like Yormungand.'

Laura, closely regarding the red beard and the tall figure of her host, had no difficulty in believing some of this.

'Then you come from the east coast or, possibly, the Orkneys,' she said. He looked pained.

'Not necessarily. Not necessarily at all. Is it unknown to you that the Vikings sailed as far west as Ireland? However, be that as it may, this salamander grew as big as a boa-constrictor that time the house was on fire and he was used to spitting – like this!' He leaned forward and expectorated into the heart of the glowing peat. 'Ay, and woe betide the chiel on whom he would be voiding his rheum. Wait until I shew you.'

He rose and went over to the sideboard, a massive affair in bog-oak on which the tray and the glasses which had held the sherry were still standing. There was a key in the cupboard drawer. He turned it and pulled open the stout door. Putting in a huge and hirsute hand, he took out a couple of small ornaments, placed them on the floor and then dived in for a couple more. These objects he brought to the table, which still bore its white, beautifully-laundered cloth.

'I say! They're nice,' said Laura. They were beautifully modelled, inches only in height and length, and they represented the fabulous creatures of which she and her host had been talking. They would have made wonderful chessmen, she thought. When she had sufficiently admired them the red-bearded man put them away, and then returned to his chair.

'Did you ever meet Shakespeare?' he enquired.

'Only once,' said Laura, 'and then I wasn't sure who it was.' Better humour the madman, she decided.

'Ay, meeting him on the Cam instead of on the Avon must have been very confusing. Yes, yes, your mind would have been confused,' he observed. Laura thought it was time to depart.

'It's confused now, too,' she said, 'because I'm most terribly tired. Will you excuse me if I go? I've had a long day.'

'Surely, surely, lassie. Up you go to your bed. How long are you staying?'

'I have to get back to Freagair,' said Laura. 'I am staying there at the hotel. I've booked a room.'

'Oh, never fash about that. You must stay a week here. I insist, now.'

'You're very kind,' said Laura, 'but . . .'

'Havers! Havers! Off to your bed. Breakfast will be at nine.'

'Good night, and thank you ever so much for your hospitality. I'll leave your dressing-gown on the banisters, shall I?' she asked, anxious only to be out of the house.

'That will be fine. Good night.'

42

She discovered, when she gained her room, that the rain had stopped and that a watery moon was riding in a sky half-clear, half-cloudy. Laura decided that her clothes would have been laid out or hung out in the kitchen and that in a house the size of An Tigh Mór there would be a back stair leading to the servants' quarters. Kilting the borrowed dressing-gown, which she was wearing over a petticoat belonging to the woman, and kicking off borrowed slippers, the property of the manservant Corrie, she set out to explore.

At the end of the long landing she found a door, and beyond it were the back stairs, as she had anticipated. She crept, barefoot, to the kitchen, found it deserted, as she had hoped, and groped around in the pale, thin moonlight for her clothes. They were not completely dry, but she decided that they were wearable. She carried them and her shoes up to her room. She retained the strong feeling that leave An Tigh Mór and the Island of Ghosts she must, and that forthwith. Laura, like Old Meg the gipsy, was tall as Amazon and brave as Margaret queen; nevertheless, the crazy owner, with his fixation on fabulous animals, his reputation, according to Mrs Grant, of being an implacable enemy, and his determination that Laura should extend her impromptu visit, drove her to take flight. She pulled on her damp and chilly garments, put on her soggy shoes and stuffed her stockings into a pocket. Then she hung the dressing-gown over the top of the banisters and crept downstairs again to the front door.

It was unlocked, but a light showing under the library door proved that the man had not gone to bed, so Laura decided to try the back door. This was bolted but not locked, so, with the utmost circumspection, she set about drawing back the bolts. As though to aid her escape, the sound of bagpipes came from the front of the house. Someone was playing a lament.

Laura got the door open, and, horribly uncomfortable in her damp clothing and sodden shoes, stepped out into the policies and round the side of the house. She was thankful for the moonlight. Without it she could hardly have found her way. She darted to the boathouse and there received a shock, for a man rose out of the shadows and demanded :

'Tell me where you are going !'

'Quick ! Don't stop me ! Help me row ! Doctor ! No time to lose !' said Laura. She climbed into the tub-like boat. The man hesitated. 'Come on !' she said fiercely. To her relief, he obeyed and they pushed out on to the loch. There was but one pair of oars and with these, using a short, stabbing sort of stroke, the man drove the clumsy boat across the water. 'Where's the nearest telephone?' asked Laura, as the boat reached the jetty and she stepped ashore while the man held on to a length of chain put there for the purpose.

'Three miles. Maybe I should go for you,' said the man. He pointed in the direction which Laura wanted to take; this to her relief.

'No, no,' she said. 'Better get back to the house. You may be needed.'

The man gripped her arm.

'What way would you be knowing a doctor might be needed? Tell me !' he said, in very low but fierce and threatening tones. Laura wrenched herself away.

'Get back to the house !' she said. She was brave enough and self-confident enough, but the whole adventure had been bizarre in the extreme and her damp clothes were making her chilly. Suddenly the piping, which sounded clearly across the lake, increased in volume. It skirled and screamed. It rose higher and higher. It sounded as though the piper had gone mad. Then it died down again to a sobbing lament and in a few moments it ceased.

The young man, who had been listening, poised like a statue in the moonlight, relaxed his stiff body.

'So that's all over,' he said. He reached out towards Laura again, but, deeming that discretion was the better part, she eluded him and ran. He began to call something after her, but he did not attempt to give chase and before he had finished speaking she was off the quay and on the very wet road. Hoping that this would prove a shorter way back to Freagair than the scrambling walk she had taken that afternoon, she pressed on, alternately running and walking, until she came upon the telephone that the man had mentioned. Here she hesitated, wondering whether to put through a call to the hotel, and had just decided against this, only hoping that the hotel employed a night porter so that she could gain admittance if and when she got back, when strong headlights indicated the approach of a car. It was coming up behind her. Laura stepped into the middle of the road, waved her arms and yelled. The car pulled up. It had not been going very fast on the single-track road. The driver put his head out.

'Give me a lift as far as Freagair, please,' said Laura. 'I got lost.'

'O.K.,' said the driver. He opened the door on the nearside. 'Hop in.'

'I'm a bit damp,' said Laura. 'I got caught in that rain.'

'This car won't hurt. You English, like me?'

'No, but I've lived most of my life in England and have lost my guid Scots tongue except when I employ it deliberately. Name of Gavin. My husband is a Detective Chief-Inspector at New Scotland Yard.' To unknowns from whom she accepted lifts on lonely roads, Laura always offered this piece of gratuitous information as a precautionary measure, for, although she was a match for most men, she preferred to keep unpleasantness and amatory enthusiasm at bay.

'Oh, really? My name's Curtis. I travel for Panwick, the shrubs and flowering trees people. Just come from Baile,

45

from the Gàradh estate. I was sent there to see whether the lady of the house, who's got those sub-tropical gardens, has anything she wants to sell when the time's right for transplanting.'

'Mrs Stewart? That's a coincidence. I was there myself a day or so ago,' said Laura. 'I'm glad I asked you for a lift. Isn't she charming? And aren't the gardens lovely?'

They talked of plants and gardens all the way to Freagair and, to Laura's relief, the young man asked no awkward questions. She found that she did not want to mention her strange and fortuitous visit to the island of Tannasgan and the big white house.

CHAPTER FOUR

Death of a Laird

'Safe in a ditch he bides,
With twenty trenchéd gashes on his head.'

Shakespeare

LAURA had to knock up the hotel to get in. There was no night porter. The manageress herself came down and unbarred the door.

'I'm right glad to see you,' she said. 'We guessed you had lost yourself and feared you were benighted again.' She felt Laura's sleeve. 'Losh, but you're wet! Out of your things and leave them outside your bedroom door. I'll put them in the drying cupboard and stuff your good shoes with paper. Did you dine?'

Laura thanked and reassured her, and had not been in bed five minutes when the manageress came up with a bowl of broth and a hot-water bottle.

'Do you take cold easily?' she asked. Laura again reassured her, supped the broth, then switched off the light and snuggled down, but not immediately to sleep. She needed very little sleep and her day had been an interesting one. She lay awake and thought it over. She had enjoyed her walk, in spite of the rain; she had enjoyed, in a different way, her visit to An Tigh Mór on Tannasgan, but she had no regrets about the cavalier fashion in which she had left the house. The laird was obviously crazy, and Laura had the normal person's horror of being in close contact with the mentally afflicted. The strangest part of the business was her encounter with the man at the boathouse, for she could

47

think of no reason for his having been there, apparently on duty, at that time of night.

At last she slept. In the morning she received her clothes, dried and pressed, retrieved the hired car and was off by noon. She still had three days' leave before she needed to return to Edinburgh, so she decided to leave Strathpeffer, Dingwall and Inverness out of her itinerary and return through Tigh-Òsda, stopping before she got there in order to revisit Coinneamh Lodge in order to tell Mrs Grant of her encounter with the laird of An Tigh Mór.

Mrs Grant was more than interested. She fed Laura on oat-cake and heather honey while they talked, and plied her with questions about the laird. At last she said:

'You have me puzzled. You say he made no trouble about taking you over in his boat? That he made you welcome? That you ate with him? That he wanted you to stay there a week? That he was red-haired and red-bearded and talked havers about creatures unknown to natural science?'

'That's so. He may be harmless, but he's rather more than a crank, and I have a superstitious horror of insanity, although I work for a psychiatrist, so I made my getaway, as I told you. It was horribly rude of me, of course, but I *had* thanked him for his hospitality before I went up to bed, and I shall write to him this evening from the hotel.'

'I cannot make it out. If that was wicked old Bradan – did I tell you I call him Cù Dubh? – Black Dog – he's a changed man. And if he's grown a beard it's the first time. And as for a kind heart – losh!'

'He may be more of a humanitarian than you thought. I was in a pretty fine pickle, you know – soaked to the skin and with no idea of where I could find shelter for the night, and miles from my hotel, and the dark coming on.'

'The Bradan I know would laugh to see a body in such a situation as that. No, no. There's something here I do not understand.'

Laura did not like to mention the secretive borrowing of her car, but she refused an invitation to stay to lunch on the plea that she must be getting along, and, passing through Tigh-Òsda, she followed the railway-line until it branched off to skirt Loch Carron, while she herself followed the road which led to the ferry. She took the car across and was still debating with herself when they reached the other side. She could take the little road to Kyle of Lochalsh and cross to Kyleakin on Skye, or she could take the opposite way and go by the northern shore of Loch Duich to Invergarry and Spean Bridge and finish the day at Fort William. In the end she compromised by opting for Skye.

She drove carefully off the ferry-steamer on to the quay at Kyleakin and then, instead of heading for Broadford, as at first she had thought of doing, she branched off south-wards, recollecting a *pension,* or guest-house, kept by two maiden ladies, sisters, at Isleornsay, on the coast. It would have been opened for the summer at the beginning of the month, although it was closed all the winter, but she had stayed there before and knew that although the only meat she would get would be boiled mutton, the beds would be aired and there would be a fire of peats in every room. So early in the season there would be no difficulty in finding accommodation there.

She was received with kindly courtesy and was conducted to her room. It was a turret chamber, well endowed with windows from which she obtained a magnificent view of the Sound of Sleat. Laura promised herself a morning walk along the coast to Armadale and perhaps as far as the Point of Sleat, from which she could get a view of the mountains of Rum and, northwards, the extraordinary outline of the Cuillin.

After breakfast, however, she changed her mind about walking the whole distance. A look at the map, and a swift computation of the mileage involved, persuaded her that, if she left the car at Isleornsay, she would have very little time for loitering to look at the coastal scenery, so she drove as far as Armadale Castle, the seat of the chief of Clan Macdonald, found a parking spot off the road, and walked on from there to Point of Sleat.

Beyond Armadale the road soon deteriorated, but from Point of Sleat the views were remarkably fine, and Laura, standing on the barren cliffs, could see, silhouetted against a pale sky, the mountains of Rum. What interested her more, however, was a man in a boat. He appeared from between two of the long, dark rocks below her and was standing up and propelling the boat by punting it along in the shallow water by means of a heavy pole.

Laura watched him approach the seaweed-strewn shore. His back was towards her, but something about him struck her as being slightly familiar. She did not want company, so she dropped down behind an outcropping of rock to be out of his view, but from where she could still keep an eye on him, for she was determined to discover who he was. She soon knew, for, as he shipped his pole and, letting the boat drift in, caught at a bit of iron piping which had been driven into the shingle, she recognised him. He was the curious character who had insisted upon her crossing the loch to take shelter on Tannasgan and who translated every sentence word by word from the Gaelic.

She kept him in view as he beached the boat and then lost sight of him as he crunched his way over the shingle. Her attention would have been distracted in any case, for a voice behind her said :

'I believe I have the honour, madam . . .'

Laura stood up and swung round.

'Good heavens !' she said. 'Yes, I believe you have. Aren't you the boatman from Tannasgan? I didn't see you so very clearly in the moonlight, but I'm sure I recognise your voice.'

'I *am* the boatman. I am glad to see you safe and well.'

'Yes, I got a lift, luckily enough. I must thank you for

helping me. Do you remember the laird's playing the pipes and how he stopped so suddenly?'

'The laird? The pipes? Of course! I'd forgotten. I was away to my bed after I had put you ashore. And now, what way were you leaving An Tigh Mór at such an hour? Very much surprised I was, to see you bob up at the boathouse.'

'Not more surprised than I was to run into you like that. It gave me quite a turn.'

'I suppose so, yes. But I was speiring at you what way . . .'

'Oh, I was literally running away. I think the laird must be mad. I went across the loch, in the first place, only to shelter from the rain and he wanted me to stay a week!'

'I can well understand that,' said the young man courteously. 'Did – did there seem anything – well – queer about the evening you passed there?'

'It was all a bit odd,' said Laura. 'The laird had been represented to me as a thoroughly nasty bit of work, but, although, as I say, he's obviously wrong in the head, he seemed quite a fellow-citizen.'

The man stared at her and then laughed, but before he could speak again, the other man reappeared.

'Do you know that chap?' asked Laura. 'He's the person who got me on to Tannasgan in the first place.'

'He did?'

'Yes. He hailed the laird with a sort of red and green lantern thing and a dirty great handbell.'

'I've never set eyes on him before,' declared the young man. Some small but interesting experience of Dame Beatrice's psychopathic patients caused Laura to believe that he was lying.

'Well, he's a long way from where I met him,' she remarked.

'I suppose you are thinking the same about me, but the fact is – well, never mind. You're not the only body who welcomes a wee holiday.'

He nodded to her and stalked away. The other man had disappeared. She strolled down to take a look at his boat, but it was the ordinary local type, broad and heavy, and it contained nothing but its own oars. She returned to her car and drove back to the boarding house.

In the early morning she ate porridge and kippers and after breakfast she paid her score, drove to Armadale Castle and took the mainland ferry to Mallaig. From there she dropped down to Arisaig and reached Fort William in time for lunch. She booked a table, although it was too early in the season for this to be absolutely necessary, and then went into the bar for a cocktail. Seated on a high stool at the counter was the man she had left on Skye, the man who had rowed her to the shore from An Tigh Mór. She could not be certain that he had seen her, but the moment she appeared he shot out of the door.

The hotel possessed two dining-rooms. They were connected by a wide archway, but, as it was early in the season and few guests were expected, this archway was blocked by a large screen. The head waiter showed Laura to a table by the wall. The dining-room was less than a quarter full and there was no sign of her boatman. He must have left by the hall door and gone straight out into the street.

While she was having lunch she debated which of two routes she should take and where she should spend the last night of her holiday. At Ballachulish she could follow the coast road southward towards Oban and then go by the Pass of Brander to Loch Awe and Dalmally, or she could drive eastward from Ballachulish through Glencoe and across the Moor of Rannoch to Tyndrum and Crianlarich. She remained very much in two minds during the whole of the meal and had come to no final decision when she paid her bill. In the end she decided to see what she felt like when she reached Ballachulish.

Here she had no difficulty in making up her mind, for

she realised that, so early in the year, the Pass of Glencoe would be free of trippers. The wild wastes of Rannoch had always exercised a strong fascination for her, so she turned eastward and was soon on the road through the pass. At Tyndrum she decided not to go on to Crianlarich, but to turn westwards to a village called Slanleibh.

It was easy enough here to get a room and the hotel was modern and pleasant. Laura garaged the car after she had been to the reception desk, unpacked, had a bath and put on a dinner gown, the first time she had worn one on the trip. Then she went into the large, beautifully-furnished lounge with its cocktail bar in a discreet alcove, and, picking up an illustrated weekly, sat by the fire.

After a bit, she walked up the three broad, carpeted steps which led to the cocktail bar and there, seated against the right-hand wall so that she had not been able to see him from her fireside chair, was her familiar, the Tannasgan boatman, respectably clad in a dinner jacket and smooth-cheeked from a recent shave. Laura ordered her drink and decided to take the bull by the horns.

'Hullo,' she said. 'You again?'

The man looked at her over the rim of his glass, and said :

'Let me buy you a drink. A dry Martini, is it?'

They went in to dinner together and sat at the same table. Laura was soon telling him about her unexpected holiday and describing her trip, but, obtaining no reciprocal information, she said, at a venture :

'Do you know some people called Grant who live at Coinneamh Lodge, not so very many miles from Tannasgan?'

'I do not, I'm afraid. What about them?'

'Oh, nothing much. They also sheltered me from the rain, that's all.'

'Oh, I see. Tell me, where do you make for tomorrow?'

'Oh, Edinburgh. I shall be on duty again the day after tomorrow.'

'On duty?'

'Yes, I'm a personal private secretary.'

She excused herself after dinner by saying she had letters to write and went up to her room. Here she saved her oath by writing a letter to her mother and sending her son a couple of picture postcards; then she sat at the window, looked at the view and decided that, in spite of the long drive to Edinburgh which faced her on the morrow, she would get up early and take a walk before breakfast.

This she did, but paused on the threshold of the hotel front door to look at the view and assess the weather. Before her, beyond the little river, rose the mountains, not threatening and dark, but scooped roundly out, with cup-like peaks, and against the mountain flanks the lower hills showed green. Near at hand, cattle grazed in a small paddock with trees in it, but away to Laura's right the distant peaks had bare and ragged outlines, threatening, and capped with purple cloud.

Laura shrugged, liking neither the clear outlines of the mountains before her nor the cloud behind the peaks away to the west, but she stepped out briskly and walked towards the main part of the village which lay in the direction of Loch Awe. Once past the post office she took a track to the left, a rough and stony road but one which, as she climbed, provided vast views of the mountains.

At breakfast, which she took as soon as she returned to the hotel, she glanced round the dining-room for her boatman, but he was nowhere to be seen. She concluded that he was breakfasting later, but when the waiter removed her porridge plate he produced an unaddressed envelope.

'The gentleman asked me to give you this during breakfast, madam.'

'What gentleman?'

'The one you dined with last night.'

'Oh, of course. Thank you.' She took out the letter. It was written on the hotel notepaper and was signed *A. D. Grant.*

If the need arises, please don't forget that you saw me on Tannasgan. Kindly enter the date in your diary before you forget it. You'll know why later on.

'Of all the cheek!' muttered Laura. 'Don't flatter yourself, my lad. Anyway, I don't keep a diary.' Then the signature struck her. 'Grant? Grant?' she thought. 'Oh, of course, *Grant!*' Then she reflected that there were thousands of Grants in the world and that it was probably only a coincidence that this one possessed the same surname as the acquaintances she had made at Tigh-Òsda. All the same, coincidence certainly had had a long arm on this holiday of hers.

Laura finished her breakfast, paid her bill and got out the car. It was nine o'clock and the weather was still holding up. It was raining over Ben More by the time she reached Crianlarich, but she had left the rain behind before she took a late lunch in Stirling, and from Linlithgow to Edinburgh the weather was perfect. She turned in the car at the garage from which she had hired it, flagged a taxi and reached the hotel in time for a bath and dinner. She was shown to her employer's table and told the waiter that she would wait for Dame Beatrice. She was still studying the menu when Dame Beatrice appeared.

'This calls for champagne,' said the black-eyed, beaky-mouthed, elderly, thin psychiatrist, 'but as neither of us cares for it much, we shall compromise with – let us see what we are eating and then I'll order.'

Laura asked how the Conference had gone and was told that Dame Beatrice was glad that it was over. Dame Beatrice then demanded a complete account of Laura's holiday and Laura described her rescue of Mrs Grant, whose car had broken down at Tigh-Òsda, her walk from Freagair in the pelting rain and her reception by the laird of Tannasgan.

'The laird of Tannasgan?' Dame Beatrice repeated. 'Do you know the name of his house?'

'Yes, of course. It's called An Tigh Mór, which simply means The Big House.'

'And you were to have spent last Tuesday night there?'

'Well, that was the idea.'

'But you slipped away by moonlight?'

'A moonlight flit describes it. But what,' asked Laura, '*is* all this?'

'All this is to explain my immeasurable relief at hearing that you did not spend the night there.'

'The laird suggested that I should stay a week! As he was obviously crazy, I decided that it would save argument if I skipped. But I still can't account for your eager interest in my ungrateful, uncivil act.'

'Simply that on Wednesday afternoon the laird was found foully and treacherously murdered.'

'Good heavens above! My guardian angel must have been working overtime!'

'Indeed, yes. Have you not been reading the newspapers?'

'Nary a single column.'

'Nor heard any discussion in hotel lounges?'

'No, I certainly haven't, but there's a bit more I can tell you about my doings which may interest you.'

She described her trip to Skye and her subsequent encounters with the man whom she had met in the laird's boathouse and who had rowed her across the loch, and her glimpse of the man who had sent her across to Tannasgan. She finished by telling Dame Beatrice of the mysterious note left for her at Slanleibh.

'Not, perhaps, so very mysterious now,' Dame Beatrice suggested.

'You mean he hopes I'll give him an alibi for the time of the murder? But that means he *knew* the laird had been murdered, and that looks like *guilty* knowledge, doesn't it?'

'Not necessarily. He may have read the papers.'

'How soon did the papers spread the news?'

'I do not know. The body was found at two in the afternoon on Wednesday last, and the local press, based on Freagair, I believe, scooped the story.'

'Who found the body?'

'The factotum named Corrie, whose duty it is to cycle into Freagair for the newspapers and the correspondence. The laird had a *poste-restante* arrangement, it appears. The man put his bicycle into the boat, rowed across, and found his employer's body lying in a barrel which had been partly submerged in the loch and prevented from drifting by being chained to an iron ring in the jetty.'

'Had he been drowned, then?'

'No. The man had been stabbed with a *skian dhu*.'

'Any trace of the weapon?'

'Well, the *skian-dhu* was still protruding from the victim's body.'

'Sounds like revenge.'

'It does, indeed.'

'Poor old boy! He seemed to me more than a bit crazy, but I hate to think of his coming to that sort of end. Are we – er – interesting ourselves in the affair?'

'There is no suggestion that we should do so. The police have the matter in hand.'

'Yes, of course. When do we go back to London?'

'There is no hurry. In fact, now that you have seen Gàradh and have made the acquaintance of Mrs Stewart, I should like to call there.'

'That's splendid. On the way we might look in on Mrs

57

Grant. As she lives not so far from Tannasgan, we might be able to pick up some local gossip about the laird's death. There are certain to be lots of rumours and perhaps some cast-iron facts which won't reach the ears of the police.'

'You are determined to involve us both?'

'Well, I didn't dislike the laird and I deeply dislike murder. What about it?'

'I see no harm in calling upon Mrs Grant.'

'Atta-baby! What's the matter with starting out to-morrow? As there's no hurry, we could go by way of Glasgow and Loch Lomond and spend a night at the Inversnaid hotel.'

'Whence you can walk to Loch Katrine and the Trossachs?'

'Don't suppose I shall bother. I love Inversnaid, and I'm not the only one. What about William Wordsworth, not to mention Gerard Manley Hopkins?' said Laura.

CHAPTER FIVE

At Inversnaid

'Degged with dew, dappled with dew
Are the groins of the braes that the brook treads through,
Wiry heathpacks, flitches of fern,
And the bead-bonny ash that sits over the burn.'

Gerard Manley Hopkins

APART from a rather messy pilgrimage along the shores of
Loch Lomond to some rocks known as Rob Roy's Cave, and
a steep and slippery climb up steps from the hotel past the
Falls of Arklet, there is no walk from the Inversnaid Hotel
except by the road through Glen Arklet and past the village
at the top of the hill. This walk Laura took very early in
the morning. She and Dame Beatrice had left George and
the Jaguar on the western side of the loch and had crossed
the water in the hotel launch on the previous afternoon.
They were to stay the night before making their leisurely
way to the north-west.

On Laura's left, as she climbed the winding hill, were
the lower slopes of Stob-an-Fhàinne, with a house here and
there well-screened by trees. On her right was the laughing,
sobbing, endlessly noisy Arklet Water as it cascaded turbu-
lently downhill to Wordsworth's Falls to crash impressively
into Loch Lomond. Bushes and bracken grew thickly on
the high banks, but whenever there was a gap Laura paused
to survey the leaping water. Her progress, because of this,
was slow and, looking at her watch when she reached the
little church, she decided that by the time she reached the
reservoir of Loch Arklet it would be as well to turn back.

In any case, the road to Loch Katrine was less interesting at this point.

She stood awhile by the loch, but it had been made too functional for natural beauty and was now part of the Glasgow waterworks (its size having been just about doubled for this purpose), so she turned and strolled back towards the village, through which she had passed before gaining the loch-side.

Just as she reached the post-office a man came up the hill towards her and, with a sinking of the heart, she recognised her boatman. He stepped purposefully up to her and barred her way.

'Oh, Lord! You again?' she said, with distaste, remembering the note she had had from him.

'Me again. You got the letter I left at Slanleibh?'

'Yes, I did, but I don't keep a diary.'

'I thought you might not, so I'll trouble you to sign a paper I've drafted out.'

'Look here,' said Laura, 'ever since that night you helped me cross the loch from Tannasgan you've been dogging my footsteps. I thought at first it was coincidence, but I know better now, and I am not prepared to sign anything for you. Furthermore, this nuisance must now cease. It's becoming something remarkably like persecution. I don't wish to be unkind, but I'm beginning to feel absolutely haunted.'

'You'll sign my paper and then I'll leave you alone.'

'I've told you I'll sign nothing. I understand your anxiety, but it's no business of mine.'

'You know that the laird of Tannasgan was murdered?'

'Yes, I heard in Edinburgh that he'd been killed by stabbing, and his body put into a barrel.'

'That's right. And when I go to the police with my story of how you skipped at dead of night from An Tigh Mór, what sort of position will you be in? No, no! You and I must stick together. Come, now. We go surety for each other.'

'Kindly get out of my way. I want my breakfast,' said Laura. She pushed past him, but he clutched her arm.

'You and I must stick together,' he repeated. Laura swung round. She was of Amazonian strength and fitness and of a high-mettled temperament. With her free hand she caught him a vicious blow on the nose and then wrenched herself away and strode off down the hill. She glanced back when she reached the first bend, but the man was making no attempt to follow her. He was mopping up the blood which was streaming from his nose.

Laura told Dame Beatrice the story at breakfast, and added that she hoped, most sincerely, that she would see no more of the young man. She wondered whether he had walked to Loch Katrine to take the Trossachs steamer. From Callander he could take a train and thus, although probably in a very roundabout way, get back to Freagair or as far as Tigh-Òsda, if he had decided to return to Tannasgan. From what he had written and from what he had said, however, she thought he was far more likely to avoid the neighbourhood of the crime and might make for Inverness or go back to Edinburgh, from where he must have followed her to Inversnaid.

Before she left the hotel again, it occurred to her to ask at the office whether a Mr Grant had booked in. She described him. The receptionist looked rather suspicious, Laura thought.

'A gentleman such as you describe booked in last night,' she said. 'His motor-cycle is still here. He came across with it in the launch while you were having your dinner. He was out walking the morn and has not yet been back for his breakfast, but his name is not Grant.'

'My mistake,' said Laura. 'I met him on holiday and thought I recognised him this morning. I was certainly under the impression that he told me his name was Grant.'

'His name is Campbell.'

'Ah, my hearing is not what it was.'

'Is it not? Och, well, maybe Campbell would sound like Grant to a Sassanach.'

Laura thought it best to ignore this insult to her Highland ancestry. She nodded in her turn and followed Dame Beatrice into the open air.

'Do you still want to put in the rest of the day here?' her employer asked, when Laura told her that the man, Grant or Campbell, had booked in at the hotel and had spent the night under the same roof as themselves. 'But perhaps the encounter has spoilt the place for you.'

'No, of course not. What do you yourself feel about it?'

'That, if you go off by yourself, I shall feel happier if you borrow a stout ashplant from the array which I noticed in the glassed-in porch.'

'By no means a bad idea, although I'm hardly likely to meet our friend on the slopes of Ben Lomond.'

'One never knows. You are proposing to climb, then?'

'On second thoughts, said to be best, I believe I'd like to leave here after lunch and make for Fort William, where we're booked for a bed tonight, so I shall give Ben Lomond a miss and take a scramble up the steps beside the falls and come back by road. But there's no hurry for that. The weather, praise be, is fine, so we might as well take a seat out here and meditate. I always like an after-breakfast cigarette.'

It was while she was enjoying this as they sat on an uncomfortable bench provided by the hotel, that Grant-Campbell came back for a late breakfast. Either he did not notice them (which was quite likely, because their seat was well below the level of the gravel forecourt of the hotel), or else he avoided looking at them, for he marched straight to the glassed-in porch and passed into the entrance hall.

Laura decided to stay where she was, in order to see what he did and where he went when he emerged. He did not keep her very long. After about thirty-five minutes he came out again and descended the rough flight of steps to board the hotel launch.

Laura earnestly hoped that they had seen the last of him, but this was not the case. He conferred for a short time with the two men who ran the launch as a ferry service, climbed the steps again, paused, and looked about him, then saw Laura. With a slightly exaggerated bow, which was intended to include Dame Beatrice, he asked whether he might share the seat with them. Laura scowled, but her employer gave the interloper an encouraging leer and moved up to give him room to sit down.

'A pleasant prospect,' she observed, waving a proprietory hand towards Loch Lomond. 'Are you staying here long?'

'I'm staying here as long as you do,' he replied. 'I'm in trouble and I need this lady's help. I don't know why she refuses it.'

'Possibly because she has not been told in sufficient detail why you solicit it. Should you not put all your cards on the table?'

'Should I? Can I trust you?'

'How do I know?'

'Well, I can't be worse off. I'm certain to be arrested, anyway.'

'Even if Mrs Gavin and I are able to succour you?'

'Oh, I don't know! I've been on Mrs Gavin's trail ever since the night I rowed her across the loch, hoping she'd consent to speak up for me when the time came. But women are flint-hearted, even when a man's life may be at stake.'

'But what makes you believe that Mrs Gavin *can* speak up for you, as you express it? Mrs Gavin, who is my personal private secretary as well as my young friend, has told me of her adventures, and nothing in her account, which, I am sure, has been of the fullest, gives me any reason to think that she can help you. What causes you to think she can?'

'Because,' said the young man, 'Cù Dubh was murdered just as I was tying up the boat to set Mrs Gavin ashore, so, if there is any trouble, it will be up to her to clear me.'

CHAPTER SIX

The Piper's Tune

'. . . of which this one
In chief he urg'd – that I should always shun
The island of the man-delighting Sun.'

George Chapman

'INTERESTING,' said Dame Beatrice. 'Pray go on.'

'I can do you the next bit myself,' said Laura, 'but we'd better have the revised version.'

The young man looked at her with loathing.

'It's no revised version you'll be getting, but the authorised account,' he protested, 'and you can check it against your own knowledge. Now, then!'

'My own knowledge isn't extensive,' said Laura, assuming a meekness she did not feel, but aware that Dame Beatrice did not want the witness antagonised beyond the point which had been reached. 'Carry on. We're all agog.'

'I went to Tannasgan in answer to a letter from my uncle.'

'Your uncle being the laird?'

'No, no, Mrs Gavin. My uncle is the man Corrie. He wrote that there was a job going at An Tigh Mór. As I was finishing my term at the University and needed to make a little money during the vacation, this was good news, so I happened along to present myself to the laird.'

'And got the job?'

'I was on trial for a fortnight. If I suited it, I was to stay until the laird could get a permanent body. If not . . .'

'And what were you expected to do?' asked Dame Beatrice.

'It doesn't matter telling you that, for the laird is dead and, in any case, I didn't carry out what he laid upon me and nobody can pretend that I did. My job was to sabotage, in any way that presented itself, the hydro-electrical scheme near Tigh-Òsda.'

'Did your uncle know the nature of this assignment?'

'No, no. He was as horrified as I was, when I told him what I was expected to do. However, we were agreed that the laird was mad to think of such a thing, and that there would be nothing I could do about it.'

'The laird was mad all right,' said Laura, 'but, as I believe I told you on Skye, I rather liked him.'

'It's as well that somebody did, then, for he was very short of friends, I'm thinking.'

'How long had you been on Tannasgan when Mrs Gavin called there?' asked Dame Beatrice. 'She does not seem to have seen you until you met at the boathouse that night.'

'A matter of two days, so, you see, apart from all else, I wouldn't have known the laird well enough to want to murder him,' the young man replied, ignoring the implication contained in her last remark.

'That's as may be,' said Laura. 'I've known myself to be in people's company no more than half an hour and I'd find myself wanting to murder them.'

'Ay, but that's only in a manner of speaking. You've never translated the wish into action. Now the laird surely *has* been murdered, and . . .'

'And you knew he was going to be. You've let that much out, haven't you? You told us that the laird was murdered just as you were tying up the boat to set me ashore. How did you know what was happening?'

'It was, first, the unearthly wailing and screaming on the pipes, and then the silence. The noise clearly told of the stabbing and the silence must have shown that he was dead.'

'All this sounds as though you may have been an

accessory before the fact. You knew he was going to be murdered?'

'I did not, then. It was after I had the news of his death that I put two and two together.' Young Grant sounded desperate.

'What were you doing down at the boathouse when Mrs Gavin was leaving the house?' asked Dame Beatrice.

'I was having a quiet smoke and I was wondering, to tell the truth, how I could keep my position and take the laird's wages without attempting to do the job I was to be paid for. Maybe it doesn't sound over honest, but I comforted myself with the thought that I could always lend my Uncle Corrie a hand about the place and so earn my money that way.'

'Who killed your employer? Do you know?'

'I could not hazard a guess. According to my uncle, there were plenty who did not like him, and it did not take me two days to find out the reason. He was a stubborn, self-opinionated, selfish old stot.'

'Was he a wealthy man?'

'That's not for me to say. He was a warm man, I think, but he kept just the two servants, my Uncle and Auntie Corrie. Still, they were on comfortable wages and the food was plentiful. They had no cause to grumble.'

'But you had no idea of the value of his property?' Dame Beatrice had taken over all the questioning and Laura retired into the background to wait until it seemed necessary that she should speak to the facts as she knew them.

'Property, is it? He owned the loch and its fish and the islands on it and, of course, the house, but you could buy the lot, I dare say, for a few thousands. If the laird was rich, it was not in land and water. No, no. He had some other ways of making money. My uncle was telling me that when he wasn't calling at the hydro-electric plant to complain, he was away to Inverness or Edinburgh on business and would be from home perhaps a week at a time, sometimes longer, but my uncle did not know what his business was.'

The association of the names of the two cities brought about another association in Laura's mind.

'You say your name's Grant?' she asked.

'It is, ay.'

'You did say you were not related to the Grants who live at a house called Coinneamh Lodge?'

'Coinneamh Lodge? No, I've no relatives living in such a place, so far as I know. And whereabouts would this Coinneamh Lodge be situated?'

'Oh, somewhere between Freagair and Tigh-Òsda, but nearer to Tigh-Òsda. You have to cross the river and the railway-line to get there. It's rather an isolated place, I should think. I wouldn't want to live there myself, but I may have told you that I spent the night there' – she had picked up a signal from Dame Beatrice that she was to go on talking – 'after I'd driven Mrs Grant home from Tigh-Òsda station after their station-wagon had broken down. I suddenly thought of it when you mentioned Inverness and Edinburgh and remembered that your name was Grant, the same as hers.'

'And why would Inverness and Edinburgh bring all that to your mind, Mrs Gavin?'

'Oh, because Mr Grant was going by train. He said that he was going to Inverness, but Mrs Grant told me he was going to Edinburgh, too. It just seemed a coincidence when you mentioned them.'

'Oh, hardly that! Apart from Aberdeen and Glasgow, where else would a business man go but to Edinburgh and Inverness?'

'I could tell you of quite a number of other places he might go to,' retorted Laura; but she was prevented by Dame Beatrice from embarking upon this recital, for, before she could even mention Perth or any of the prosperous towns and cities of the Lowlands, Dame Beatrice again took the floor.

'We have established, then, that you knew of a plan to murder the laird of Tannasgan,' she said, taking out a note-book and pencil. Off his guard, Grant gaped at her like a stranded fish and then began to stutter.

'Articulate clearly,' said Laura. 'You can't have it both ways. Either I can give you an alibi for the time the piping stopped – in which case you knew the murder had just been committed, *ergo* you knew it had been planned – or I can't. See what I mean? *If* the murder was committed while we were together in that boat, you didn't do it, but if it was committed at any time when we were not together – well, you can't come to me for an alibi, can you, however innocent you may be?'

'I think, Mr Grant,' said Dame Beatrice, 'that your best plan will be to tell us all you know.'

'I can't!' said the young man abruptly.

'You mean that the truth may involve your relatives, the Corries?'

'I don't know whom it would involve. I did *not* know the laird was to be murdered, *or* that the piping had anything to do with it. I found out afterwards – but I can't let you know how.'

'But, listen,' Laura urged him. 'If you knew nothing of what was to happen, why did you ask me in that wild sort of way how I knew a doctor might be needed? And why did you say, when the piping stopped, that *that* . . . whatever *that* was . . . was all over?'

The young man stared at her, then he smiled.

'I knew there was something I'd forgotten,' he said. 'If you knew a doctor was needed, you knew, *at that time,* more about the murder than I did! What do you say to that? By God . . .' he stood up and faced her . . . 'if you can queer my pitch, so can I queer yours! We stand or fall together, Mrs Gavin! What about it? You had better think it over. My position on Tannasgan was more regular than yours, you know!'

He climbed to the courtyard of the hotel, shouted to the men in the ferryboat and in a short while Laura and Dame Beatrice saw him manhandling a motor-cycle down the steep, precarious steps to the little quay. Several times it looked as though he might lose his footing, but he recovered it and the men received the motor-cycle over the side of the boat and stowed it away.

The young man returned to the hotel for a small suitcase not much larger than a big attaché-case, descended the steps again and, this time, went on board. The boat backed away, then turned and sputtered across the loch to a long wooden landing-stage on the opposite side. Here the motor-cycle was unshipped, the small case strapped on to the luggage carrier and the whole equipage was bundled along the landing-stage and, not without effort, thrust up the bank and on to the road. The last the watchers saw was that it turned to the right at the top of the bank and took the loch-side road for Ardlui.

'Thankful to see the back of *him*,' said Laura. 'Are you going to climb all those steps with me to look at the Falls of Arklet? Funny I should have mentioned going for a doctor as my reason for getting away from Tannasgan. Do you think he *will* blow his top and accuse me of knowing something about the murder?'

'I will climb with you and admire Mr Wordsworth's falls,' said Dame Beatrice. 'As to the rest – well, we shall see.'

'I shan't lose sleep, at any rate,' said Laura. 'Besides, there's always stout denial, an excellent and impregnable defence so long as one sticks to it. And there weren't any witnesses, you know.'

Dame Beatrice rose and they climbed to the courtyard

and crossed it to the foot of the steps which had been made beside the lashing, tumbling water. Dame Beatrice measured the ascent with her eye.

'We have a long way to go,' she said; but whether she referred to the climb up the rude stone steps beside the noisy and beautiful stream, or to the fact that the case of the stabbed laird of Tannasgan was only in its infancy, Laura did not enquire.

CHAPTER SEVEN

Auld Acquaintance

'They were great friends in a quarter of an hour:
and great friends they remained.'

M. R. James

As she had come by way of Rannoch and Glencoe, Laura
had expressed a wish to return to Tigh-Òsda and Gàradh
by the longer route out to Oban and so, by the coast road,
to Ballachulish and back to Fort William. She kept a sharp
look-out as the car took its dignified route through Dalmally
on the way to Loch Awe and the Pass of Brander, but
there was no sign of her motor-cycling boatman.

The evening and night which they spent at Fort William
passed without incident and in the morning Laura elected
to join a small party, led by a local guide, which was to
climb Ben Nevis. She had made the ascent once before, but
by the easier route from Achintee Farm by pony-track and
the long, rough, zigzag paths to the summit. This time the
party was to use these paths for the descent, but climbed
the huge, ugly mass by the tougher way up which followed
the Allt-a-Mhuilinn to the club-hut at the head of the glen
and then by a trackless route along the side of the mountain and then onwards and upwards between Cairn Mòr
Dearg and the summit.

Visibility at the top was particularly good that day. The
beautiful peak of Schiehallion stood out to the south-
east, distinguishable from the three Bens – Mor, Vorlich
and Lawers – by its remarkable symmetry and pointed
cone.

72

It had taken several hours to make the ascent, and Laura, who liked hard and strenuous exercise, had enjoyed it. The easier descent gave her time and a chance to do a little constructive thinking, and she pondered on all that had happened from the time she had driven Mrs Grant from the station at Tigh-Òsda to when she last had encountered her boatman at Inversnaid.

She had accepted Mrs Grant's personal reaction to the laird of Tannasgan, but she did not share it. There was a mystery because there was, somewhere, a discrepancy. The portrait which Mrs Grant had painted of an overbearing and meanly spiteful man, who used his position unfairly in order to make difficulties for people he did not care for, did not square with Laura's own impression of a hospitable eccentric, possibly mentally deranged to some degree, but definitely kind-hearted and obviously lonely. However, Mrs Stewart of Gàradh, whom she and Dame Beatrice were to visit, had not liked the laird.

Laura pigeon-holed these thoughts and reconstructed what had happened, apart from her encounters with Mrs Grant and with the laird. There was the rather odd business of the bearded stranger who, in arbitrary fashion, had called over the boat which had borne her, soaking wet, to the Island of Ghosts. He seemed to have taken it for granted that she was bound thither, and for no better reason than that they had met on the shores of the loch more or less opposite An Tigh Mór. He might have been a mere busybody, one of those irritating Helping Hands whose interference, so often, has nothing but nuisance-value, but Laura did not think so. Without possessing Dame Beatrice's trained psychological insight, she was intelligent when it came to summing people up, and, the more she thought of it, the more convinced she was that she had been sent to the Big House purposely. Then, was it another coincidence that she had seen him again on Skye?

Again she switched her thoughts, this time to the mysterious conduct of the boatman. She had been startled at meeting him so unexpectedly in the boathouse at that time of night, but had accepted his presence as one of the idiosyncrasies of the household. His subsequent dogging of her footsteps and his insistence upon her agreeing to furnish him with what seemed to be an alibi, together with his chameleon-like changes of speech and behaviour, added up to something remarkably like a man with a guilty conscience or else to a man who was afraid that, although he was innocent of any part in the murder, his presence at the Big House might implicate him. Laura could not help wondering how much he knew of the reason why the laird had come to his death in the manner in which this had occurred. A *skian-dhu* ! Romantic, she supposed, but horrible.

By the time she had turned these thoughts over in her mind and had built various theories upon them, the climbers reached the refreshment hut, where they stayed for a quarter of an hour. After this, Laura dismissed the murder and turned to the scenery. From a spur on the ridge which they reached a little later, they halted to admire the northern face of Ben Nevis, impressively different from the humped and uninteresting mass which is the usual picture of the highest mountain in Britain.

The precipices here were so steep that they seemed living giants literally pouring themselves headlong into the glen. The escarpments cut the sky-line in sharp silhouette and the crags looked monumental. Two enormous shoulders jutted out in strong support of the magnificence of the scene. The mountain dominated the light-blue sky.

As the party continued to descend, Laura thought she might suggest to Dame Beatrice, when she got back, that they should remain at the hotel another day and walk along

Glen Nevis, but by the time they reached Fort William she had thought better of it. She badly wanted to contact Mrs Grant again and obtain her reactions to the death of the laird, therefore to use up another day for the walk would be to put off this interesting encounter and would be a waste of time, she decided; so when Dame Beatrice enquired at what time they should order the car in the morning, Laura plumped for a nine o'clock start and they set off promptly at that hour for Inverness.

They stopped for coffee at half-past ten and, as they sat at the small table, Dame Beatrice said :

'What was it you told me about the appearance of the laird of Tannasgan?'

'Big, red-headed, red-bearded and with a wild and bright blue eye.'

'Yes. I shall be glad to meet your Mrs Grant.'

'Why, particularly?'

'I am most interested to find out whether, as you two seemed not to see eye to eye in the matter of the laird's nature and character, you are equally at variance in describing his looks.'

'Oh?'

Dame Beatrice said no more, but finished her coffee and led the way out. George was talking to the driver of a motor-coach which had pulled up for the coffee-break. As soon as he saw his employer, he nodded to the man and came back to the car.

'The driver of the coach-party tells me the Loch Ness monster has been seen again, madam,' he said.

'I bet it's gone again, too,' said Laura. 'Always my luck ! When was this, George?'

'Yesterday evening, Mrs Gavin, just before sunset.'

'Yes, she prefers the beginning and the end of the day when she decides to surface. Oh, well, it's just one of those things. Do you believe in her, George?'

George permitted himself a slight smile.

'You should hear some of the stories I've heard!' he replied. 'Skin divers who've gone down to look for her and never been seen again, and others who've come up, but can't speak of what they've experienced because it's *too* horrible, and others who've fallen out of boats and their bodies never recovered. It's all fairy tales, if you ask *me.*'

'Leaving all that aside – it may or may not be true, of course – what do you think yourself, George?'

'Well, Mrs Gavin, they never expected to find a live coelacanth, did they?'

Laura nodded, well pleased with this contribution from a fellow-believer, and, judging it best to leave matters in this satisfactory state, she joined Dame Beatrice, who was already established on the back seat of the car, and said no more. George slammed the door, took his seat at the wheel, and off they drove.

Inverness offered its usual impression of narrow streets, a broad shallow river, bridges, a modern castle and a general air of knowing that the city was the capital of the Highlands. After dinner they went out to see some Highland dancing. The dancers were children of tender years; in fact, the youngest was four years old, and, because of this, the belle of the ball. She danced sedately, in her own time and rhythm, with an engaging singleness of purpose, for she was, at times, completely divorced from the rest of the set. Whether she was enjoying herself it was impossible for the charmed and sentimental onlookers to tell, but her concentration and sense of heavy responsibility were there for all to see.

Laura and Dame Beatrice were discussing this child as they passed into the street on their way back to the hotel, when a young man raised his hat in response to Laura's quick look of recognition.

'Well, well!' she said, coming to a halt. 'Dame Beatrice, this is the kind-hearted and chivalrous gent who gave me a lift into Freagair that time I was benighted on my way back from Tannasgan. Mr Curtis, this is Dame Beatrice Adela Lestrange Bradley.'

'How do you do, Mr Curtis?'

'How do you do, Dame Beatrice?'

'I am grateful indeed to you for succouring Mrs Gavin.'

'It was a pleasure. You heard the news about what happened on Tannasgan after Mrs Gavin left?'

'Yes, and we are both very glad that she *had* left.'

'It might have been a bit awkward if she'd stayed, I suppose. Have you seen today's paper?'

'No, we haven't seen a paper since we left Edinburgh three days ago. Have there been developments?'

'Yes, the police have been questioning a man called Grant, a customer of mine. They must have some idea that he can help them, I suppose. They can't possibly believe him guilty! I know the chap well.'

Laura had a sudden inspiration. It arose from her previous uncomfortable feeling that her own and Mrs Grant's impressions of the laird of Tannasgan did not tally, and she also remembered the doubts expressed by Dame Beatrice.

'Was the owner of An Tigh Mór on Tannasgan also a customer of yours?' she asked.

'He was – and a more difficult, curmudgeonly, cheeseparing old party I've yet to find. I don't like losing customers, through death or for any other reason, but I can't say I'm sorry to think I'll never call on the owner of An Tigh Mór on Tannasgan again. When I think of that tonsured pink scalp with the fringe of red hair and the nasty little mouth always being wetted with that snaky tongue – I was always surprised it wasn't forked! – I know I can do very well without 'em.'

'I believe he wasn't generally liked in the neighbourhood,' said Laura, convinced now that she had never met him.

'*Liked?* He was absolutely loathed. Nothing was ever pinned on him, so far as I know, but I've heard that he was always playing dirty little tricks and doing people down. I *did* hear that he was pretty shady in other matters – bigger ones, too. Smuggling. This fellow Grant I mentioned . . .'

'Would that be the Grant who lives at Coinneamh Lodge, about a dozen miles this side of Tigh-Òsda? – a man with a wife and small kid?'

'No. This is a young chap who lodges with the postmistress at Crioch. She lets him do as he likes with the bit of ground she dignifies by the name of her 'policies.' He's a particularly keen gardener and always interested in our catalogues, although he doesn't buy very much from us because he hasn't much space.'

'Is he in his early twenties, with light-brown hair? And does he switch from fairly intelligible Scots to standard English, as the mood takes him?'

'That sounds like the same lad. Why, do you know him?'

'Well,' said Laura cautiously. 'I've met him once or twice. What were you going to tell me about him? Look, come with us and have a drink. Our hotel is not licensed, but the one next door is.'

'Grant's all right, you know,' said Curtis, over the drinks. His raised eyebrows seemed to demand explanations from Laura. She gave them.

'So, you see, I don't know what to make of him,' she added, at the end of her recital. 'He *may* be all right, but something has scared him, and, I should say, it's some sort of guilty knowledge that he possesses. Still, I can't possibly give him an alibi. I don't even know at what time the murder was committed.'

Curtis wagged his head and, swallowing the rest of his whisky, gazed into the bottom of the glass.

'This red-bearded old chap you met on Tannasgan,' he said, 'would be some sort of relation to the laird, no doubt. But I wonder where the other one was? He could have been dead by the time you arrived – at least, according to what I read in the papers.'

'Wherever he was, I don't think he was in the house, unless, as you say, he was already dead. You see, I saw quite a lot of the place, one way and the other, and I could have been certain that nobody was at home but myself, the Corries and this man whom I took to be the laird.'

Curtis shook his head again.

'I'm glad you got out of it when you did,' he said. 'It's an odd sort of set-up. How are the police getting on?'

'I've no idea,' said Laura, 'and, although I'm a Scot by birth, I've very little knowledge of legal procedure up here. I know they don't hold inquests in the English fashion, but that's about all.'

'You've had no visits from the police?'

'So far, none. I couldn't help them, anyway. But you were going to tell me about some trick or other that the laird had played on young Grant.'

'Yes, I was, but I'm not so sure about telling anybody else about it now. I don't suppose it would be considered enough to supply Grant with a possible motive for murder, but – well, murder has been committed and Grant was on Tannasgan, or may have been, at the time.'

'Yes,' agreed Laura, 'and, as I've told you, I've only his word for it that the killing was done while the pipes were skirling their loudest. Besides, if that were so, the piper could hardly have been the killer. You couldn't stick a man with a *skian dhu* and manage the pipes at the same time, could you?'

'I'm not an authority on piping or stabbing, let alone a

combination of the two,' said Curtis. 'Look here, it's my turn to buy a drink. If you're doubtful about young Grant, why don't you call at his lodgings in Crioch and talk to his landlady? I do assure you that the chap's all right, really he is.'

'Then why is he so keen on this alibi business?' asked Laura.

CHAPTER EIGHT

Married and Single Grants

'A strange, unlikely errand, sure, is thine.'
Matthew Arnold

'WHAT do you think of his idea of our calling on the post-mistress at Crioch?' asked Laura, when Curtis had left them and they had gone back to their own hotel. 'Any good?'

'I don't know, child. He certainly spoke in favour of young Mr Grant's character, but men are not always good judges of their own sex.'

'That's true enough. They are quick enough to spot a rotter, but they don't always recognise a criminal. However, I must say that the more we hear about the laird of Tannasgan, the more I have to admit that killing him doesn't necessarily come under the heading of committing a crime. And talking of Tannasgan . . .'

'Yes?'

'The description of the laird!'

'Yes.'

'Where does my red-headed, red-bearded bloke come in?'

'That, one would imagine, is a question for the police to answer.'

'Do you think I was on the wrong island? – that I didn't go to Tannasgan at all?'

'We shall soon know.'

'On the other hand, if I *did* go to Tannasgan and if I stayed the evening at An Tigh Mór, *where was the laird*? I certainly saw nothing of him.'

'It is a matter for deep thought.'

81

'I wonder whether the police are questioning the older, the married Mr Grant?'

'You say that he was not in his own home that night when you stayed there?'

'He went off by train. It makes one wonder whether he really did. I suppose most people in the neighbourhood know what the Grants thought about the laird. I only hope the police don't believe that they had a motive for killing him, because they're not the sort to do anything like that, I'm perfectly certain. I mean, I know they hated his guts, but, all the same——'

'Their dislike, even their detestation, of the laird hardly seems a sufficient motive for killing him, but, of course, we do not know the whole story. I look forward to meeting your Mr and Mrs Grant, I confess. We still have to find out why she borrowed your car that night or early morning while you were there. Of course, as she borrowed it when she did, that hardly amounts to a suspicious circumstance, nevertheless I have examined George's motoring maps and there is a marked similarity between the length of the journey from Coinneamh Lodge to Tannasgan and the extra mileage shown on the dashboard of your car. You remember telling me about that?'

'I see your point, but I can't somehow believe that Mrs Grant was up to anything very sinister. Still, if we call there, you can sum her up for yourself.'

'Yes, indeed. So we will by-pass Tannasgan on our outward journey, obtain what we can from Mrs Grant – and Mr Grant, if we should find him at home – and then we will visit the island, but not, I think, until we have paid the promised call on Mrs Stewart at Gàradh. I have advised her that we are in Inverness, and she will be expecting us. In any case, we must give the police time to leave Tannasgan and An Tigh Mór, so that we get a clear field for our own operations.'

'But, after all this while, there won't be anything left for us to find out, will there?'

'Time will show. I think, though, that the time has come for you to go to the police with your evidence, slight though it is.'

'You mean about my having been entertained that evening by somebody who was not the laird?'

'That, and the way you have been dogged, followed and waylaid by the young Mr Grant, not to mention his presence in the island boathouse that night. That, to my mind, especially taken in conjunction with his obvious anxiety that you should provide him with an alibi for the time of the murder, is a highly suspicious circumstance which the police might well investigate.'

'It occurs to me, though, that the scene of the murder doesn't lie within the boundaries of Inverness, but would be in Ross and Cromarty.'

'The Inverness police will know what to do, I imagine.'

On the following morning Dame Beatrice produced her own and Laura's credentials and Laura told her tale. It was taken down in writing, but no questions were asked and George drove her and Dame Beatrice out of Inverness on the road to Beauly at a quarter to twelve.

'They didn't seem particularly interested in my adventure,' said Laura, 'but I suppose that's because it isn't their pigeon.'

'They may pass the information on to Edinburgh,' said Dame Beatrice. 'I know very little of Scottish procedure in these matters. The point is that your story is on record. You can do no more unless or until they contact you again.'

They lunched in Strathpeffer and then drove through Freagair and so to Coinneamh Lodge, where Mrs Grant, previously apprised by telephone of their coming, was expecting them.

'Better weather than when I was last here,' remarked Laura, when the greetings and welcome were over and Mrs Grant had settled them in armchairs before a peat fire. Their hostess drew up a chair for herself.

'Kirsty will soon infuse the tea,' she said. 'I waited on you for my after-lunch cup. Och, ay, the weather's fine. I wish other things were as good.'

'We heard that the police had been bothering round,' said Laura. 'Did they come here?'

'I'll tell you all about it when Kirsty – ah, here she is. Thank you, Kirsty.'

Kirsty smiled shyly at the visitors, set the tray down and went out again.

'I see you've got some help in the house now,' said Laura. 'Is it permanent?'

'As soon as it was known that Cù Dubh was killed, Kirsty's mother came to see me. It is the only good thing that has come out of the business.' She poured out the tea and handed cups. 'I will tell you. Maybe' – she looked at Dame Beatrice – 'you can think and tell me what I should do. You see, the police believe my man knows who did it and is holding out on them. I'm so worried I don't know which way to turn. I'm not very sure that they don't suspect my man himself.'

'Why should they do that?' asked Dame Beatrice.

'He will not tell them where he was, or what he was up to, that night and early morning.'

'Has he told *you*?'

'He has not, then. All I ken is that he went to Inverness and was to go on to Edinburgh next day. I never speir at him what his business is, because I would not understand it if he told me.'

'His business would have to do with the hydro-electric project, no doubt?'

'Ay, it would be just that.'

'I don't see any connection with Inverness, though,' said Laura. 'Does he often go there?'

'Now and again, from Easter until the first snowfall. During the winter and early spring, not at all.'

'How long is he away from home?' asked Dame Beatrice.

'From the Friday, when he leaves work, until the Sunday night.'

'Always?'

'Always, except for his three weeks' holiday in September, and even then he's in a fever. "I wonder how they're getting on without me?" he'll say. I tell him not to fash himself, but he fidgets and fadgets until we're home.'

'Inverness? And Edinburgh?' said Dame Beatrice thoughtfully. 'Interesting. Do you think your husband would talk to *me*?'

'How I wish he would! Mrs Gavin here was telling me of some of your cases. I'm in fear of what may happen if he goes on refusing to give the police any information. If he would give them just one name of a body that would swear he was in Inverness that night, it would do, I think, but he'll not do even as little as that.'

'Why do you suppose he is being so secretive?' asked Dame Beatrice, with unusual bluntness. Mrs Grant's troubled eyes met hers.

'I have no idea,' she said, 'but I trust him absolutely. It's not a woman; I'm certain of that.'

Kirsty came in.

'I beg your pardon,' she said, 'but the wee *chridhe* is greeting. I think it is necessary to you going.'

'Excuse me,' said the wee *chridhe's* mother. She and the girl went out.

'Sounds like a love-nest to *me,* whatever she believes,' said Laura. '*She* may trust him absolutely, but I don't think *I* would.'

85

'It is much too early to judge him,' said Dame Beatrice. 'I wonder at what time he gets home this evening? Incidentally, it would have been on a Friday that you met him at Tigh-Òsda station, then?'

'Yes, and he'd taken a day's holiday, if you remember.'

'One would think he might have foregone his business in Inverness for that one weekend, then.'

'Yes. It can't be much fun for Mrs Grant being left with nobody but the baby for company from Friday night until Sunday night, however seldom it happens.'

'No, indeed. I wonder whether he *always* goes by train? They have a car, you say.'

'An estate wagon, yes.'

Mrs Grant came back, carrying the baby. Dame Beatrice put the question to her.

'Och, ay, he always takes the train,' she replied. 'You see, it's a single-track road from here to a mile or so this side of Freagair and he says he has enough of single-track driving to his work and back. The train is quicker. Besides, in a place like this, I'd be lost if I suddenly needed transport, and none was available, would I not?'

'Yes, of course.' Laura hesitated and glanced at Dame Beatrice, raising her eyebrows. Dame Beatrice nodded. Laura went on : 'Please don't be offended at what I'm going to ask you, Mrs Grant. I'm bound to sound blunt, I'm afraid, but I think it's fair to be.'

Mrs Grant's eyes very slightly narrowed.

'Bluntness is best, if it's something awkward,' she said. 'I don't like beating about the bush, so out with it, and I'll answer as best I can.'

'Right. What were you up to when you borrowed my car that night I stayed here?'

'Borrowed your car? But I did nothing of the kind, Mrs Gavin. What on this earth makes you think such a thing.'

'The extra mileage on the meter, for one thing.'

'Och, but you're mistaken. It's so easy to misread those things or to forget the previous reading.'

'That's not my experience, especially with a car I've hired. Besides, there's another thing.'

'And what would that be?'

'That my petrol tank had more petrol in it when I reached Freagair that morning than it had held when I reached Tigh-Òsda where I picked you up on the previous night.'

'Oh, that!' said Mrs Grant. She seemed at ease. 'Why, as to that, I gave your car a wee fill-up before I called you down to your breakfast. It was the least I could do, after your kindness in driving me home through all that down-pour of rain.'

Dame Beatrice decided that the time had come to change the subject. She had no doubt that Laura's car had been used, but there seemed no point in prolonging the discussion. She said :

'We're on our way, *not*, so far, in rain, to visit Gàradh. Do you know it?'

'Indeed I do, then. The Mrs Stewart who lives there opens the gardens once a week to visitors. She charges half-a-crown and gives the money to charity. It's a grand place and very wonderfully kept. I can't get my man to go, but as it is always on a Wednesday, I doubt if he would care to ask for the time off, even if he cared about flowers, which he does not. I myself go every year, though. We make up a small party and Maclean drives us there and back. This year I'll be able to take the wean. I used to leave her with Kirsty to mind her, but she'll be old enough to go with us this year. Have you a special permit, I wonder? The gardens will not be open to ordinary visitors today.'

'We have a special permit,' Dame Beatrice replied. 'And,

as our time is limited, I think we had better be making our way there.'

'I thought you intended waiting until her husband came home,' said Laura, when they had left Coinneamh and had bumped carefully on to the road for Tigh-Òsda and Crioch. 'Hadn't you some such idea?'

'Yes, but I have a better one. I want George to stop when we get to the hydro-electric power station. There is certain to be somewhere on their ground that he can park.'

'You are going to beard Mr Grant in his lair, so that Mrs Grant won't be present?'

'We shall see. You will remain in the car. Two of us will be an embarrassment of riches to the executives.'

She returned to the car at the end of twenty minutes and remained silent until they were in sight of the coast at Crioch. Then she said :

'It is all most interesting. They know only of the young Mr Grant who lives in the place we are approaching. He is a reporter on the *Freagair Advertiser and Recorder,* and it's his job to collect all the news of this part of the country and relay it to his office. He uses a motor-cycle for this purpose. The paper does not function in the extreme winter months, owing to the difficulty of supplying copies to its subscribers in time of snow, when many roads are impassable.'

'So he isn't the murderer, anyway,' said Laura. 'I'm rather glad. He's not a bad youth, although he's rather in favour of preserving a whole skin. But what price Mrs Grant telling me that her husband was employed at these works if he isn't?'

'I am hoping that young Mr Grant will be able to help us there. It may be a forlorn hope, however, and I think we shall need to find out, if we can, what, if he really goes there, the married Grant finds to do in Inverness and

88

Edinburgh. If he is not there in connection with the hydro-electric project——'

'A tall order, isn't it?'

'I do not think so. We have been in touch with the Inverness police, who, although taciturn, were polite, and that Conference I attended in Edinburgh brought me into some small contact with the Press. My connection with the Home Office was remarked upon, and the police, no doubt, read the papers. Besides, I am fortunate enough to know a number of people in Edinburgh. I think we may be able to conduct an unobtrusive investigation without much let or hindrance. I am not without a certain amount of——'

'Satiable curiosity,' said Laura.

The post office at Crioch was small and dark. Behind the counter was a small, dark woman engaged in checking some sheets of postage stamps.

'I've no picture postcards,' she announced, as Laura entered to a jangle of bells. 'Those you saw in the case outside are for advertisement, no more.'

Laura, thinking that to advertise a product which was non-existent was strikingly reminiscent of *Through the Looking-Glass,* asked for a five-shilling book of stamps and opened her handbag.

'You'll get separate stamps, as you're requiring them. I have no books of stamps. There's no call for them around here,' said the woman.

'Six threepenny ones and a dozen two-penny ha'penny ones, then,' said Laura.

'Very good. You might get a postcard or two at the hotel, if you're anxious for them.'

Laura received the stamps, paid for them and put them away.

'Thank you,' she said. 'Oh, I remember! I have a message for Mr Grant.'

'For Mr Grant?'

'Yes. From his editor in Freagair.'

'You'll need to write it down. He's away to Strathpeffer. There's a flower show. Does it need an answer?'

'Yes, I'm afraid it does.'

'Ah, well, here's a wee jotter, ninepence, and I can sell you an envelope for a penny. I keep stamped envelopes, but you've laid out your siller for stamps already, so you'll need nothing but a plain envelope the now. There's pens, unless you have your own.'

Laura had her own, and, in any case, had no intention of writing any messages to Grant until she had consulted Dame Beatrice, who, in accordance with plan, had just come into the post office.

'A pound of peppermint bullseyes, please,' she said.

'Do you need a whole pound of the peppermint cushions?'

'Yes, if you please.'

'Good for you. That's a very wholesome sweetie. Now some would be stuffing themselves with chocolates. I'm right glad to know you've more sense. There you are. That will be two shillings and eightpence.'

They took their leave. In fact, Laura had already gone out to the car before Dame Beatrice's purchase had been shot into a paper bag and paid for. Dame Beatrice placed the bag on the seat between them and Laura grabbed a handful of the sweets.

'Good old-fashioned stuff,' she said, approvingly. 'No luck there, though. Most unfortunately Grant isn't at home. He's covering a flower show in Strathpeffer.'

'Something of the kind was to be expected. Never mind. It may turn out for the best. If I read the postmistress aright, she will most certainly furnish Mr Grant with an unmistakable picture of yourself.'

'You think he'd recognise the description?'

'I do not see why not.'

'I wonder what you mean by that? Anyway, this message. What do I inscribe on this gosh-awful little writing tablet?'

'Nothing, child, unless you have something to suggest.'

'I could ask him again what relation he is to the other Grants, although I suppose we've had his answer to that. I could tell him that, now we know he's a cub reporter, we'd also like to know what he was *really* after when he squatted in the boathouse on Tannasgan that night. I feel that I must leave him a note. After all, I have spent tenpence on him and the stamp represents another threepence. When I've posted it we might as well have some tea at the hotel. Oh, yes! And if Grant's paper doesn't circulate during the winter, is *that* when he's had employment at An Tigh Mór?'

Laura, seated in the car with the ninepenny writing-pad on her knee, scribbled busily. Then she addressed and stamped an envelope and, jumping out of the car, posted the letter in the box outside the post office. She realised, when she had done so, that the sardonic eye of the postmistress had been watching her through the shop window.

It had been impossible to drive fast on the narrow road between Tigh-Òsda and Crioch, so it was half-past five when they left the seafront hotel after tea and seven o'clock in the evening when they reached the hospitable home of Mrs Stewart at Gàradh. Dinner was at eight, and the talk, as was to be expected, turned on Dame Beatrice's experiences at the Conference, news of mutual friends in Edinburgh and then Laura had to give an account of her adventures since she had left Gàradh after her first visit.

Coffee had been brought to the fireside – for, in Scottish tradition, Mrs Stewart kept fires burning all the year round, whatever the weather – when a maid announced that there was a gentleman at the door asking to speak with Mrs Gavin.

'That will be young Mr Grant,' said Dame Beatrice. 'Let us hope he has news for us.'

'Find out his name, Elspeth, and then show him in here and bring another cup and saucer,' said Mrs Stewart. The caller did indeed prove to be Grant. He came in with his motor-cycling goggles in one hand and gauntlet gloves in the other and apologised for troubling the company. Mrs Stewart sent him out to leave his equipment and his leather jacket in the hall and ordered him to return for some coffee. 'And now, young man,' she continued, when he had obeyed these instructions and was seated, coffee-cup in hand, between Laura and Dame Beatrice, 'I hope you have brought some interesting news. And it's of no use for you to imagine I shall go out of the room while you make your disclosures. I am consumed with curiosity, so drink your coffee and fire away.'

CHAPTER NINE

Young Grant's Story

'I reckon it's one of two things, 'Spec. Either
there come along somebody and done this devil's
job while I was fetchin' the poor toad his physic, or
else he done it himself.'

Eden Philpotts

YOUNG Grant accepted a second cup of coffee and in reply
to a motherly query from his hostess assured her that he
had had his evening meal. No one else spoke until he put
down his cup. Then Laura said:

'You *have* been a chump, you know. Now, what about
a first, Christian or baptismal name? The word "Grant" is
getting a bit confusing.'

'Me? Oh, call me Alastair.'

'I will, although I know it isn't your name.'

'Right, it is not, then. But I'm ganging warily because
you don't seem at all anxious to give me the alibi I'm
seeking.'

'I can't give it you. There's no proof whatever that the
laird was killed when the pipes ceased from skirling. Don't
be silly.'

Grant wagged his head and looked apologetic.

'I don't wonder you're mad at me,' he said. 'I suppose
I've made myself a fair nuisance to you.'

'Why have you come here?'

'In answer to your letter. Losh, but the old wife was
angry when the postwoman, Maggie McTaggart, handed
in your envelope! She always scrutinises the mail, does
Maggie, when she collects it out of the box. There's so

little of it, you see, because the people staying at the hotel have their own posting box and Maggie collects there, too, so if there's half a dozen letters with the postmistress that seems an awful lot.'

'Don't dodge the issue. Why have you come here?'

'Why, to have a crack with you. Why else?'

'Oh, cut out the witticisms,' said Laura. 'We don't mind trying to help you, but not if you want to be fresh. Now, then, tell us the tale and we'll do our best to believe you.'

'Very good. I do realise that I've made myself a great nuisance to you, but . . .'

'Cut the cackle, for goodness' sake, and begin.'

'Yes, well, to cut a long story short . . .'

'But we don't want you to cut it short,' said Dame Beatrice, giving Laura the cue to slip out of the ring. 'Please give us every possible detail. Begin at the beginning, illuminate and expand the middle and proceed at a decorous pace to the end.'

'Well, Dame Beatrice, the story begins in Edinburgh.'

'Eh?' exclaimed Laura involuntarily.

'The story begins in Edinburgh. I was standing waiting to cross the road when I saw an accident. Well, as you know now, I'm a reporter and, like all reporters, I'm always on the look-out for a story. That day I got one. I saw a man pushed under a car.'

Laura, in spite of her excitement, remained apparently calm.

'You did?' she said. 'When would that have been?'

Dame Beatrice intervened before Grant could answer.

'Tell us, please, Mr Grant, what you were doing in Edinburgh at that time.'

'Doing? Oh, you mean my reason for being there! Why, I was covering your Conference, Dame Beatrice. You may not know it, but all Scotland is interested – ay, intensely interested – in anything to do with education.'

'I was not speaking on education,' said Dame Beatrice mildly.

'Maybe not, but I was sent to cover the Conference and we regard such a gathering as educational.'

'I see. Please continue.'

'I managed to get leave from my editor to be in Edinburgh before the Conference was actually in session. I said I wanted to interview some of the notables in their hotels. What I really wanted – and he knew it, the douce man! – was to have a wee bit of a fling the way you can't get it in these parts. Oh, nothing I wouldn't care for my mother to know about – you can't get *that* sort of a fling in Edinburgh, anyway – but just to get to a theatre and walk with the crowds along Princes Street and that kind of thing, and maybe, over a dram, hear of a job on the *Scotsman*. Of course, I did some interviewing, too. I met two or three of the professors and psychologists and persuaded them to give me a few facts and theories that I could send back to Freagair to show that I was on the job, and it was when I was coming away from one of these interviews – with Signor Ginetti it was . . .'

'Ah, yes. The distinguished Italian alienist who thinks that apes are descended from men and that, in time, there will be no more human beings but a sort of *robot* world of intelligent but pitiless primates with neither religion nor morals,' said Dame Beatrice, amused.

'That's the laddie. Speaks very good English, too. I left him at something after six and I was waiting, with others, to cross the road to my bus stop . . . I was staying a bit out of the city for cheapness . . . when it happened. A big car came by, and a couple of men hurled another man clean in front of it. He didn't stand a chance, and neither did the driver of the car.'

'And you would recognise those men again?'

'I couldn't swear to them, but I think I would recognise them if I saw them. I never have seen them again and, of course, in the general consternation, they vanished. I recognised you, too, Mrs Gavin, when you turned up at the boathouse on Tannasgan that night. You were in the crowd waiting to cross that road.'

'Yes, I was,' Laura agreed. 'It shook me considerably. I didn't see *you*, though.'

'Well, you're more noticeable for a woman, being so tall and well-dressed and carrying yourself so well (if I may say so), than I am for a man. I'm only of average height and I was wearing the run-of-the-mill uniform of flannel trousers and tweed jacket. There was no reason for anybody to notice me.'

'Did you go to the police?' asked Laura.

'No, I did not. There was so little I could tell them and there was no proof of what I'd seen. I doubt whether anybody else was aware of what happened.'

Laura was about to speak, but Dame Beatrice dropped a lace-edged handkerchief, one of the code signs between them that Laura was to be silent. Grant bent and picked it up for her and the moment passed.

'This does not explain what you were doing on Tannasgan that night,' said Dame Beatrice.

'No, but I'm coming to that. It's all part of the same story. You see, one of the men who did the pushing was employed, as I well knew, by Cù Dubh himself, and I was fool enough to think that at An Tigh Mór I might be able to get a real scoop – an exclusive story good enough to qualify me for promotion to something a whole lot better than the *Freagair Advertiser and Recorder*.'

'This story to be connected with the murder you had seen committed in Edinburgh?'

'Yes. As I knew that this man was in the laird's employ, I thought a bit of blackmail might get me what I was after. I was, as Mrs Gavin has pointed out, every kind of a fool to think I could dent the hide of a man like that.'

'So what did you do, Mr Grant?'

'I did my job in Edinburgh and then, in the evenings, I went on my motor-cycle to the edge of Loch na Gréine to see what the chances were of getting into An Tigh Mór.'

'Not a difficult matter if you know what to do,' said Laura.

'Quite, Mrs Gavin. Well, I had no luck at all, to begin with. I turned the lantern; I rang the bell. Nothing doing, except that some old fellow cursed me across the water from the island bank and said that they were not expecting anybody and that I was to gang awa'. Which I did. But the following night was different. That would have been the night Mrs Gavin turned up.'

'Yes, possibly, but you must have got there later than I did,' said Laura. 'You weren't on the island when they brought me across to Tannasgan.'

'In the rain?'

'In the rain? I should say so!'

'I left Edinburgh at five, when the Conference rose – perhaps Dame Beatrice remembers? – and rode straight up to Inverness and on to Freagair and Tannasgan. I had turned the lantern and clanged the bell when I realised that the boat was tied up at the jetty, so I parked my motor-cycle and rowed myself across. Goodness knows why the boat was there. I suppose I pulled a fast one, taking it over like that, but I didn't hear any shouting, so perhaps the guest didn't turn up.'

'And when you landed on the island?' asked Dame Beatrice.

'Yes, well, thereby hangs a tale.'

'Aha!' said Laura. 'Give us a summary.'

'That's not so easy. I walked up to the house and reconnoitred. An old wife – well, not so old, really – came out of the door and speired at me to know what I wanted. I said I wished speech with the laird and, with that, she said I should call again on the morrow, as he always saw reporters the morn's morn.'

'How did she know you were a reporter?' asked Laura.

'I dinna ken.' He grinned. 'Maybe we carry the mark of the beast on us.'

'Well, what happened then?'

'It was then I heard the pipes. The sound came from a room, I think, which faced the loch.'

'Was there a light in it?'

'Never a light.'

'At what time would that have been?'

'Now, now, Mrs Gavin! You don't catch me like that.'

'So you never encountered the laird?'

'I did not. The only person I encountered, apart from the old wife, was yourself, when you were leaving.'

'Then why do you deduce that, when the piping ceased, the laird died?'

'It's the only thing to believe.'

'Is that so? I can't see the connection.'

'Can you not?' His expression was enigmatic. 'There is only one thing on which we ought to be agreed, Mrs Gavin. If I'm right, and the laird was murdered when the piping ceased, neither you nor I can have murdered the laird, can we? I seem to have said this before.'

'There's no proof about the piping, and there's nothing to show that the laird was on Tannasgan that night. I certainly didn't see anybody except the red-haired man, the servants and you.'

'Well, well! As I say, I did not see the laird either, but what does that prove?'

'I don't know, but I'm going to find out,' said Laura.

'And we're sticking together over all this?'

'Time will show,' said Dame Beatrice, before Laura could answer.

Loch Na Gréine

'Deep asleep, deep asleep,
Deep asleep it lies,
The still lake of Semmerwater
Under the still skies.'

Sir William Watson

'AND what are we supposed to make of *that* tale?' asked Laura, when young Grant had gone.

'What are your own reactions?' asked Dame Beatrice.

'Those of Sherlock Holmes and the dog.'

'Yes, I noticed that point. I suppose you would have been bound to hear the bell if he had rung for the boat to be brought over?'

'Absolutely. It's a fine big bell and rings out like the knell of doom and, whatever my shortcomings, I'm not hard of hearing. So the bell, like the dog, did nothing in the night. You know, we shall need to check that whole story with the Corries.'

'You would regard them as reliable witnesses?'

'I don't really know. She struck me very favourably, but one can't go by that. The point is whether their story fits young Grant's and, if it doesn't, we've got a platform from which to question him. Anyway, now that I know he's a reporter, I shall give up suspecting him of being the murderer.'

'Why should you do that? Did you not notice that there was another point on which his account of the evening differed from yours?'

'Was there? Let's see, now. Ah, I've got it! The piping.

According to him – let's see – he left Edinburgh at five, when the Conference rose, and went to Loch na Gréine on his motor-bike. It's – good gracious me! – it's a sheer stark impossibility!'

'Did you not realise that, while he was talking?'

'No, I didn't. I believe I was thinking of Inverness, not Edinburgh. So he actually had the crust to think he could persuade us that on two successive evenings he rode from Edinburgh at five and got to Loch na Gréine and across to Tannasgan before I left at about half-past ten. He must be crazy to think we'd swallow it.'

'But you *did* swallow it,' Dame Beatrice pointed out. She cackled harshly and Mrs Stewart, who had been a silent, interested listener while her fingers had been busy on the never-ending knitting of the Scotswoman, joined in with an appreciative chuckle.

Laura grinned and acknowledged the palpable hit, protesting, however, that she *had* spotted the lie about the time he had heard the piping and that when she had thought over young Grant's story she would have seen the light about the journeys from Edinburgh.

'What *do* you think happened, then?' she asked.

'He did ride to Loch na Gréine, that is certain,' said Dame Beatrice. 'My guess, for what it is worth, is that he spent the night somewhere *en route* and came to the island on the same night as you did. It will be interesting to find out why he told such an obvious lie, and we must interview the Corries, as you say.'

'If the police have been questioning them – and they must have done so – they may not be in much of a mood to confide in us,' said Laura. 'Mrs Corrie was a sweet soul so far as I was concerned, but I wouldn't put it past her to be very, very sticky if she felt like it. As for Corrie, I didn't hear him utter a word. All he did was to bring in the dishes at dinner and collect up as we finished each course. He might have been a deaf mute for all that I could tell.'

'Well, you assert, on no evidence at all (so far as I can see), that young Grant is not the murderer,' said Dame Beatrice, 'so who is your candidate? I gather you do not suspect the Corries?'

'Well, I don't know about *him*. And, somehow, I can't see my eccentric red-beard in the rôle. What do *you* think?'

'I have no idea, but I look forward to meeting him. Let us hope that he is still at An Tigh Mór.'

The following two days passed pleasantly and talk of the murder was shelved. Dame Beatrice sat on Mrs Stewart's broad terrace above the rock gardens and gazed at the sea and the mass of Ben Caraid, or read Professor John Dover Wilson on *What Happens in Hamlet*. Laura was carted round the gardens, again in remorseless and systematic fashion, by her hostess, and heard a great many more Latin names than she expected to be able to remember, but the sea and the mountains which surrounded the gardens were satisfying and soothing, and her hostess's gentle voice and Edinburgh speech were music in the ears of one who had lived long in southern England.

The murder of the laird of Tannasgan was not mentioned again until they were ready to leave Gàradh. Then Mrs Stewart said :

'I suppose, Beatrice, nothing will satisfy you until you've had a finger in the Tannasgan pie, but, if you'll take my advice, which, from a lifetime of knowledge of you, I am perfectly sure you will not, you will keep away from An Tigh Mór. Everybody knows there's a curse on the place, and although, the Dear kens, I am not a superstitious body, there are things better not meddled with, and what has gone on in The Big House will be one of them, I'm thinking.'

'If *I* took your advice, *Laura* wouldn't,' stated Dame Beatrice. 'She regards herself as a heaven-sent investigator of crime and thinks that Tannasgan is her especial province.'

'Well, well, if you'll not take my advice, at least have a care of yourselves.'

'We always do that,' said Laura. 'I take care of Mrs Croc. and she takes care of me. Besides, she always totes a small gat on these little expeditions of ours. It scares me stiff. I can't abide firearms, but I suppose it would be a very present help in time of trouble.'

They did not call in at the post office, but at Crioch Laura swam. Miraculously the weather still held up. There was a clear, almost Greek, light over the beautiful bay and a shimmer on the level, wet sands. The water, to Laura's powerful, vigorous body, did not even strike cold. When she was dressed they had coffee in the hotel lounge before they took the turning for the Loch called Cóig Eich, the Five Horses, and the winding hilly road to Tigh-Òsda and Tannasgan.

This time they did not follow the rough path to the bridge and the level-crossing which led to Mrs Grant's house, but continued on the single-track road to Loch na Gréine, the Loch of the Sun, the Tom Tiddler's Ground on which the island of Tannasgan formed a base. It was the second time that Dame Beatrice had seen the loch since the murder, for they had been obliged to pass very close to it on their way from Freagair to Coinneamh Lodge, but on that first occasion she had obtained only the most cursory view of the waters of Gréine as the car carried her past the little stone jetty from which Laura had embarked for the island.

George drew up on the verge to take the car off the road, and Dame Beatrice and Laura got out and walked to the jetty. Dame Beatrice looked at the iron ring in the stonework and then walked to the end of the tiny pier and gazed across the loch to the island and its house.

'Nothing much doing, by the look of things,' said Laura, joining her. 'Have you seen the apparatus for summoning a boat?'

'We might make use of it, I think,' said her employer. 'Will you operate it?'

Laura did this and then rang the bell. They waited for five minutes by Laura's wristwatch and then she tried again, but again there was no response from the island. They could see two rowing-boats in the boathouse and this was too much for Laura. She went back to the car, retrieved her wet swimming costume, sheltered behind a convenient bush and, a couple of minutes later, was in the water.

George also had left the car, deeming it his duty to act as bodyguard, and he and Dame Beatrice stood on the bank and watched Laura's progress. As usual, she swam fast, on a powerful freestyle, and they saw her scramble out and then get into the smaller of the boats.

'I'll just immobilise the car, madam. Mrs Gavin took her towel out,' said George. 'I hope she isn't being rash,' he added.

'So, indeed, do I. I realised her intention, but she is a law unto herself, of course. Do you wish to visit the island, George?'

'I have studied such accounts of the murder as have come my way, madam, and have listened to the conversations in public houses, and I feel a certain amount of curiosity about the affair. It *is* a little bizarre, madam, don't you think? We have never been involved in anything quite like it.'

'I would not have missed it for the world, George. Well, Mrs Gavin seems to be getting away quite safely.'

Laura pulled the heavy boat across the loch and George held on to it as soon as it reached the jetty. He tied up. Laura dried herself and dressed, then she and Dame

103

Beatrice, followed by the chauffeur-henchman, stepped aboard. George courteously relieved Laura of the oars and they were soon across the water and tying up in the boat-house of the Island of Ghosts.

'You saw no sign of life, I suppose?' asked Dame Beatrice, when they had negotiated the planking and were standing on the lawn.

'No sign and no sound,' Laura replied. 'I expect the place is deserted. Let's go up to the house and have a look-see.'

As one who was acquainted with the *terrain,* she led the way. The front door was wide open.

'It hardly looks as though the place is deserted,' remarked Dame Beatrice. 'It is almost as though visitors are expected. One would expect the front door to be closed, if not bolted and barred.'

Laura agreed and then added :

'I hope the police aren't still in charge. It will queer our pitch properly if they are.'

'A policeman would be on duty at that door,' said George, a slight distortion of his uniform indicating the presence of a heavy spanner in one of the deep pockets. 'By your leave, Mrs Gavin, I'd better go in first.'

'Oh, rot, George!' retorted the Amazon. *'Women and children first!* You ought to know that.' She produced a bit of bicycle chain. 'Wonderful what you can learn from the Teds. I am armed and well prepared. Together we can defend Dame B. from all the slings and arrows of outrageous fortune. Come the four corners of the world in arms and we shall shock them.' At this point she tripped over the step. Dame Beatrice produced a small revolver from the capacious pocket of her skirt. 'And God defend the right,' concluded Laura piously, picking herself up and dusting herself down. 'For goodness' sake, put that thing away, Dame B. It gives me goose-pimples in the small of my back. I never did care about gats, as I told Mrs Stewart a while ago.'

She led the way to the dining-room door, turned the handle without a sound and then suddenly thrust the door open. The room was tenanted. Seated by the empty hearth was her red-bearded friend. Beside him on the table was what had been a bottle of Scotch. It was now merely a bottle which, no doubt, retained the aroma of Scotch, and the stertorous breathing of the sleeping man gave sufficient indication of where the contents of the bottle had gone.

'What d'you know!' said Laura, under her breath; then, in a whisper to Dame Beatrice, 'Think he's alone in the house?'

Dame Beatrice motioned to her and they crept back to the hall.

'I think we must either wake him or return to the jetty,' she said, when they were away from the dining-room door. 'We can hardly explore the house under these circumstances. I had anticipated either that it would be empty, or else that we should encounter someone to whom we could explain ourselves, even though the someone turned out to be a policeman.'

'I should judge,' said Laura, 'that the citizen in there is so far under the influence that, even if we did wake him, it might not be the easiest thing in the world to explain ourselves to him. *In vinas veritas* is all very well, but in my experience a superabundance of alcohol is apt to impair the intellect and stimulate little but the wrong reactions. Look here, how would it be if we rowed about on the loch for a bit? I'd like to see what the other side looks like.'

'It would be taking a liberty, of course, but, as we have already put ourselves in an equivocal position, I think it cannot do much to darken our offence. Perhaps though we ought first to find out whether your friend *is* alone in the house.'

'Well, I know where the kitchen regions are, so, swinging my bicycle chain in the approved fashion, I'll go along, shall I, and take a gander around?'

Without waiting for an answer, she walked down the hall and through a green-baize door at the end of it. She came back almost at once and reported that nobody seemed to be about.

'Did you try the kitchen door?' asked Dame Beatrice.

'Locked, but neither bolted nor barred, so the Kirkintillochs *may* have gone shopping.'

'The . . . ?'

'Oh, the old wife told me they came from Kirkintilloch. Their name's Corrie. And that's another funny thing. If Mrs Grant's description of the laird was correct, the Corries aren't a bit the kind of servants you'd think he'd engage, nor would they be likely to stay if he did. They're really decent people.'

'I think, you know, that people take the work they can get. Now I will give one more glance at your sleeping friend and then we will take to the boat, if that is what you would like.'

The red-bearded man was still asleep, so down to the boathouse they went.

'Unless you wish for my services at the oars, madam, I suggest I stay here and apprise you with three short blasts on my police whistle if the gentleman wakes up, or strangers approach,' said George, who appeared to be enjoying himself. Dame Beatrice agreed to this plan, but asked whether he would not be bored if they left him by himself. After all, he was one of the party.

'Thank you for inquiring, madam,' he said, 'but I have my pocket sketching block and a soft black pencil. The views are extensive and imposing, and the air is clement. I shall do very well indeed.'

So Dame Beatrice and Laura left him, and Laura soon

had the boat out on the loch and was pulling round to the blind side of the house. As she rowed past the white, windowless façade, she could see that the loch broadened, and when she had rounded the house, and come to the back of it, she could also see that Tannasgan was not the only island in the loch; it was merely the largest. From where she was, four stony outcroppings, one thickly wooded, came into her view. On the further shore of the loch rose the high, bare slopes of Ben Dùn which she had seen from the opposite side, and with their backs to the lower slopes of the mountain and their suspicious, inquisitive gaze fastened on the boat and its occupants, were a dozen or so of wide-horned, shaggy, Highland cattle.

'A picturesque group,' remarked Dame Beatrice.

'Highland cattle always look so young for their age, and Ben Dùn is a fine chunk of Lewisian Gneiss,' said Laura. 'Learnt that at College and I've always been proud of knowing it. Nevertheless, the mainland, at the moment, does not attract me, so what about exploring that island with the trees on it?'

'A childishly pleasant idea. Pray manoeuvre us thither.'

The loch was shallow close inshore to the wooded islet, and Laura paddled cautiously to the land. They tied up to a tree and, Laura leading the way, followed a rudimentary path which began at the water's edge and disappeared into the woods.

'Made by the police exploring all avenues, I expect,' she said. 'Wonder what they expected to find? You'd think they would have stuck to Tannasgan. I suppose it didn't yield any clues.'

Dame Beatrice offered no criticism of this view, and they continued to follow the little path as it wound in and out among the trees. Laura very soon changed her opinion.

'It wasn't made by the police. It's more like a bit of landscape gardening. It's been worked out. It makes the woods seem ever so much bigger than they are,' she said. She realised another thing, too, and gave voice after about another hundred and fifty yards of motiveless perseverance. 'Makes you think of *Three Men in a Boat*,' she observed.

'In what way?' Dame Beatrice demanded, interested to learn whether Laura's deductions coincided with her own.

'You know – the maze at Hampton Court.'

'I see that you recognise the silver birch we are coming to.'

'That, and the clump of heather in the shape of a half-moon, and the cotton-grass in that circular swamp and the little trench where peat has been dug.'

'Amazing! I had not realised quite how observant you must be.'

'I'm going to take a chance and see whether I can cut the cackle and get to the centre. You'd better stay here. I'll yodel if I'm lucky.'

'Very well, child.' Dame Beatrice was quite capable of a little rough walking, but she was prepared to respect and encourage Laura's pioneering spirit, and remained where she was to await Laura's call.

This came even sooner than she had expected. Laura had plunged through a tangle of undergrowth and was able, almost immediately, to announce that her iconoclastic plan had worked out. She yodelled happily. Dame Beatrice followed the trail and, in the clearing which formed the centre of the maze, came upon an extraordinary and most unexpected sight.

Laura waved a large and shapely hand.

'Welcome to Battersea Park,' she said. 'What do you think of the monumental masonry?'

Dame Beatrice inspected the inanimate tenants of the clearing. They made a strange addition to the living vegetation of birch and pine.

'Let us look more closely at these petrified fauna of another and more picturesque age,' she suggested. 'Let us inspect these phenomena of the imagination of mediaeval man.'

They inspected them. All were fabulous beasts rendered crudely but powerfully by the hand of some amateur sculptor.

'I observe the basilisk, the gryphon, the werewolf (at the moment of changing from man to wolf – very clever, that!), the salamander and the gorgon,' said Dame Beatrice, after she had studied the exhibits in silence. 'I wonder why the salamander is in pieces and is covered in what looks like soot?'

'I wonder whether he carved them himself?' said Laura, ignoring the work of some iconoclast.

'Our slumbering red-beard?' suggested Dame Beatrice.

'Yes. I told you about his fixation on fabulous animals, didn't I?'

'Yes, indeed you did. The discovery of this very permanent-looking stonework raises the question of whether An Tigh Mór was really the dead laird's home – or, rather, whether the house we have just vacated *is* An Tigh Mór. I shall be interested to talk with our friend when he is able to carry on a conversation. Some of your suspicions may be justified.'

After a further study of the group, which was carved in Portland stone except for the basilisk, which, owing to its serpentine shape, was of bronze, they were about to find out whether the path continued among the trees on the other side of the clearing when they caught the sound of George's police-whistle. They returned to their boat and were soon on the return journey to Tannasgan. George was at the boathouse to meet them, his heavy spanner in his hand. Taller by a head, and leaning on a *cromach,* the red-bearded man stood beside him and helped to pull the boat in. Laura stepped ashore and held out a hand to Dame Beatrice.

'Well, well,' said the tenant of An Tigh Mór. 'To what will I be indebted for this honour?'

Laura gravely introduced him to Dame Beatrice as 'my host and benefactor of some days ago, of whom I told you.'

'Is Malcolm Donalbain Macbeth my name,' said the man. It was a statement and, Laura felt with some reason, an *alias*.

'That's a very fine *cromach*,' she said, indicating the walking-stick.

'Ah, but the *callant* here has a spanner,' said Macolm Donalbain Macbeth. 'Up to the house with you, till you tell me what way you stole off like a thief in the night when I was after offering you hospitality for a week.'

'Dame Beatrice wants a word with you first,' said Laura, grinning. 'We only waited until you woke up. Is the whisky out of you?'

He took no manner of offence at this blunt question, but led the way to the house.

CHAPTER ELEVEN

The Big House Again

'There sometimes doth a leaping fish
Send through the tarn a lonely cheer;
The crags repeat the ravens' croak
In symphony austere.'

Wordsworth

'Now,' said Macbeth, when they were seated in a well-furnished room whose windows overlooked the loch, 'what will be your business with me?'

'The death of the Laird of Tannasgan, whose house this was,' Dame Beatrice replied. He looked at her out of his very bright blue eyes and puffed out smoke from the pipe he had filled and lighted.

'What had you to do with the laird?' he asked at last.

'Nothing.' Dame Beatrice gave back look for look.

'Then his death will be none of your business.'

'I do not endorse that opinion.'

'Your reason?'

'Mrs Gavin here, my secretary and close friend, may have been in this house, or, at any rate, in this neighbourhood, when the murder was committed. What is more, she has been followed and accosted by a man who was here at the same time as herself. He wants her to give him an alibi for the time of the murder – or thereabouts – and has made a considerable nuisance of himself.'

There was another interval of silence. Macbeth, his eyes now veiled, puffed away. Dame Beatrice waited. Laura, who had received no cue, stared at the carpet.

'You wish me to say that I am prepared to co-operate

with you?' asked the red-bearded man at last. 'I'll need to give thought to that. I was bidden here by the laird. Did you ken that I was his cousin?'

'No, that is news to me.'

'And I am his heir.'

'I see. That could mean that you had an interest of a selfish kind in his death.'

'It could. Well, now, I hold to my opinion that you are meddling, but if it will rid me of your company to speir at me what I know, then speir away.'

'You have been questioned by the police?'

'I have that.'

'With what result?'

'They went away very discontented. I was just no help at all.'

'Deliberately?'

'No, no. There was nothing helpful that I could tell them. They speired at me where had the laird been, if, as I told them – and it's the truth – he was away from home all that day. I told them that I was not in the laird's confidence. Then I had to give an account in detail of my actions from the time I came to Tannasgan until the time of the death.'

'Did you tell them that I was here for part of that time?' asked Laura.

'I did not. The death was nothing to do with a young lass like yourself.'

'Very chivalrous of you to say so, but wouldn't it have been wiser to have mentioned my visit? It's going to be a bit awkward for you if it comes out now – perhaps for me, too.'

'Havers!' He gave the word all the contempt in the world.

'I don't think it's nonsense,' said Laura. 'You see, I thought it as well to go to them and give them a full account of what I did and where I went that evening. I told them that I was here, and that you gave me food and shelter. Of course, I didn't know your name, but I described you and the others, so, even if I were willing to keep quiet about it, I shouldn't be able to now. If they question me, it's bound to involve you.'

'I see that. There's the fellow who followed you and spoke to you, of course.'

'And the other fellow, who gave me a lift to Freagair that same night. He knows I was here. He can confirm my story. And there's the first fellow, the one who got me on to the island.'

'Ay.' He continued his furious puffing while he pondered. 'I would advise you to communicate with the police and get them to deal with him. A man like that might be dangerous.'

Laura decided to change the subject.

'It *was* you playing the bagpipes that night, I suppose?'

'Your supposition is perfectly correct. Did you like my playing?'

'Well, it was a useful cover while I got away from this house. In any case, I always like the sound of the pipes.'

'And now,' said Dame Beatrice briskly, 'what about this account you're going to give us of all that took place on Tannasgan and at An Tigh Mór on the day that Mrs Gavin turned up on the shore of the loch? You were good enough to take her in and give her food and shelter, but on that same night your cousin was killed and his body put into a barrel.'

'Och, that!' There was another long silence, then he said, drawing his thick brows together, 'In a barrel was where he belonged, the drunken stot! Whisky Johnny should have been his name. But his death and the manner of it is the business of the police, and neither themselves nor you will get any more out of me than I'm prepared to tell. And what I dinna ken I canna tell, now can I?'

'At least tell us one thing,' said Laura.

'And what would that be?'

'*Is* this Loch na Gréine? – and is this house An Tigh Mór?'

He looked at her and put on a crafty smile.

'You must just please yourself,' he replied. 'Maybe they are – and maybe they're not. And now, if you'll just excuse me, I have work to do.'

'Will you allow us to borrow a boat to cross the loch?'

'Ay. Tie up on the other side and somebody will be back to bring it over. How did you get here?'

'I swam and then I rowed back for the others.'

'You did? I kenned you were a braw lassie as soon as I set eyes on you. You swam, eh? Well, well, I'll no insist that you swim back.'

With this he leaned back in his great armchair and closed his eyes. Laura glanced at Dame Beatrice and they walked to the front door and joined George who, spanner in hand, was keeping guard under the front windows. He seemed relieved to see them.

He rowed them across the loch and handed them out on to the little stone jetty. Soon all three were in the car. He turned it, with infinite care, on the rough grass and on to the road, and Laura, who was on the right-hand side of the back seat, glanced out. On the other side of the water stood a man, but it was not Macbeth. For a moment Laura could not place him, then it came to her who he was. She was about to draw the attention of Dame Beatrice to his presence, when he ducked into the boathouse and was lost in the shadows.

Dame Beatrice, who missed nothing, had noticed him, however.

'So there was one more person on Tannasgan than we realised,' she said. 'I wonder whether the manservant Corrie was in the house after all?'

114

'That isn't Corrie,' said Laura. 'Corrie is older and shorter than that. No, that's the young man I told you about – the one who met me in the rain and rather – well, it was a nerve, really – insisted on sending me over to Tannasgan. He was on the mainland side then, of course, and worked the signal and rang the bell to bring the boat over. I had no notion that he was actually connected with the place, though. I assumed he was out for a walk and had been caught in the storm, like me. In fact, I think, looking back, that I imagined he was going to cross the loch, too, and try to get shelter, but, when he walked off, I suppose I concluded he had a place of his own near at hand, or else was so wet that he couldn't get any wetter.'

'I wonder what, if any, his part is in the drama? Everything in this little adventure seems more than a little odd.'

'Absolutely off-beat.'

'This new friend, I must say, intrigues me. I wonder whether it was chivalry, or something much less admirable, which caused him to expedite your first visit to An Tigh Mór?'

'Goodness knows! Anyway, there doesn't seem any doubt that he believed I would be received and warmed and fed – unless he expected me to take shelter in the boathouse. However, old Macbeth took care of all that. You know, in spite of the battiness and the guile, I believe that old man possesses a sense of humour.'

'Indeed? It may be a macabre one, though, don't you think?'

'Oh, you're thinking of the body in the barrel, but there's no evidence yet that he put it there.'

'I agree.' There was silence while both stared ahead, engaged in thought and surmise, then Dame Beatrice added, 'This furtive young man we've just seen interests me very strangely. He is quite a new factor in the case.'

'The nigger in the woodpile, you mean? We've nothing whatever to go on in suspecting that, though, have we?'

'No. All the same, I am glad I caught a glimpse of him.'

'Would you know him again, do you think?'

'Certainly I should. I saw him quite distinctly.'

'You know, Mrs Croc., the more I think about it, the more certain I am that he had some ulterior motive in sending me over to Tannasgan that evening. By the way, where are we going next?'

'Back to Mrs Grant. There are points which she must clear up.'

'Such as which island really *is* Tannasgan?'

Dame Beatrice did not reply, but gave George directions. George eased the car on to the single-track road and they went westwards, and slightly north, on the way to Mrs Grant's lonely and cut-off house. Nobody was at home.

Laura ceased hammering on the front door and tried the handle, but the door was locked.

'Stymied,' she observed. 'Now what do we do?'

Dame Beatrice was saved from the necessity of replying by the arrival of a station wagon driven by a man whom Laura recognised as the passenger to Inverness whom she had met in the rain at the station. It seemed at least three months since she had seen him. He pulled up behind George, who was still in the driving-seat of Dame Beatrice's car, and got out, raising his tweed hat with a smile of recognition.

'Hullo,' said Laura. 'We came along hoping for a chat with your wife, but she seems to have gone shopping or something.'

'No, no, she's away to her mother in Dingwall. Did you want her for anything in particular? I have to thank you for driving her home that bad night.'

'I was the lucky one. She put me up,' said Laura. She glanced at Dame Beatrice. 'This is Mr Grant. Mr Grant, Dame Beatrice Lestrange Bradley, my boss.'

They acknowledged the introduction and Laura received

a slight nod from her employer which she interpreted as an indication that she was to carry on the conversation. Before she could do so, Grant spoke, producing, as he did so, a latch-key.

'Do please come in,' he said, and opened the door. 'I hope my wife has left us a fire.'

This, it appeared, was the case. A good fire was glowing red in the dining-room and a basket of peats and a scuttle of coal stood one on either side of it. Grant tossed his hat and driving-gloves on to a chair, advanced to the fire and put coal on it.

'And now, do you sit down while I find the whisky,' he said. He produced whisky, a syphon and a decanter. 'Maybe ladies would prefer sherry?'

Laura accepted the whisky, Dame Beatrice the sherry. Their host joined Laura and solemnly wished them good health.

'And now,' said Laura, 'we came to ask a question of Mrs Grant, but I expect you can answer it. You'll have heard of the death of the laird of Tannasgan?'

'I have that. Nothing else is talked of around these parts. We get little excitement hereabouts as a rule.'

'Well, I've been mixed up in it all.'

'You don't tell me!'

'I have, in a way.' Briefly she told the story of her adventures after she had left Mrs Grant for the first time. She concluded by saying, 'So, you see, we're wondering whether the island we've just left *is* Tannasgan, or whether the dead laird used to live somewhere else and was murdered on his cousin's estate.'

'That,' said Grant, 'is very easily settled. There is nothing I need attend to at the moment, so why don't we go along and see? From your description I would say that you have certainly been across Loch na Gréine and on Tannasgan, but there's nothing like making sure. Shall we go in your

car? Then your man can show me where it is you want
to take me.'

'Certainly,' said Dame Beatrice. 'George knows the way.'

Grant nodded and then asked :

'*What* did you say yon man calls himself?'

'Malcolm Donalbain Macbeth.'

'Oh, ay. That will be a pseudonym, no doubt.'

'It seems rather more than likely.'

'A red-headed, red-bearded man?'

'Yes, and of pretty hefty build and about five foot ten
in height,' said Laura. 'An odd bod in many respects, but
likeable, I thought. Drinks whisky, sometimes to excess, and
has a fixation on fabulous beasts.'

Grant finished his drink and poured himself another.

'I don't know him,' he said. 'Let me give you a wee drop
more whisky.'

'No, thanks.'

'Then some more sherry for you, ma'am?'

'No, thank you.'

'Right. Then let us be on our way. It's curious I am
to see this island of yours.' He drank off the dram he had
poured for himself and heaved himself out of his chair.
'I'll not trouble to fasten the door, although the lassie who's
to look to me has a key.'

A point occurred to Laura. The servant was no longer
afraid to be left with her master while the wife was away
from home. So much was clear, but the significance of it,
if any, eluded her. She led the way to Dame Beatrice's car
and addressed the stocky chauffeur.

'Back to that island, George. We're taking Mr Grant to
vet it for us, to make sure it really *is* Tannasgan.'

'I shall have to move my bus,' said Grant. 'It's blocking
your man's way out.' He climbed into the station wagon
and backed it as far as the bridge. In the ooze of the river
bank he brought it out of the way of the other car. George

reversed until he found room to turn, picked up Grant and drove cautiously on to the narrow, winding road.

They were soon at the landing-stage opposite Tannasgan. Here Grant leaned back.

'Yon's Tannasgan and this is Loch na Gréine,' he said. 'You were not deceived. And the Black One was found chained to the jetty, his body in the water, was he not? Well, well! It's a strange thing, that.'

Laura turned round.

'Not in the water. In a barrel in the water,' she said. 'By the way, what were you doing in Inverness? And why didn't you come home when you were supposed to? Your wife seemed terribly worried about you.'

If she expected to surprise or discomfit Grant, she was disappointed. He half-closed his eyes and answered :

'Well, do you see, I was kidnapped.'

Laura found this incredible.

'But Inverness isn't Chicago,' she protested.

'No, no, Inverness isn't Chicago,' he agreed, 'but kidnapped I was, although not held to ransom. I was released in Tomnahurich Street after being blindfolded before we left the hotel!'

'What hotel would that have been, I wonder? I know Inverness pretty well, you see, so I'm interested.'

'The one I always use when my business takes me to Inverness. Maybe you wouldn't dignify it by the name of hotel, but it's a most respectable place, or so I always thought. That has been my reason for staying there. However, after I had had my dinner that night, three gentlemen came up as I was drinking my coffee and asked me, with civility, would I make a fourth at bridge. I was willing and went with them to a private sitting-room they'd hired.'

'In the hotel?'

'Certainly. It was a room on the second floor, but I did

119

not take note of the number. Well, we played for a couple of hours and I won a few shillings – the stakes were very low, otherwise I would not have played – and then they sent down for drinks and the drinks came up with a bit of a sour face on the waiter because it was late, and the next thing I knew was that I woke up in broad daylight with a splitting headache and a bad taste in my mouth, to find one of the villains at my bedside with a gun in his fist.

' "You'll stay in this room and we'll have your meals sent up," he said.

' "Like hell," I told him.

' "Keep your good health," he said, fingering the gun in a meaningful kind of way. "We don't want to hurt you."

' "But what's the idea?" I asked. He shook his head and said he'd be hanged if he knew, but he had his orders. I thought it was something of a shady deal connected with my work and I was to be kept out of the way until it was through. That gave me something to think about. I asked him what was contemplated. He didn't know, or, if he knew, he wouldn't say. I asked him whether it had anything to do with the hydro-electrical work I was engaged on. He said it might have, and then, again, it might not. He was only a hired gun and did as he was told and didn't ask questions.'

'Didn't you – couldn't you reach a bell or anything?' asked Laura.

'I could not, without the risk of having a hole blown in me. The fellow seemed amiable enough, but he had an eye like that of a very dead fish and a mouth like a bit of steel cable. I wasn't prepared to take chances. He must have known that the thought of trying to escape had crossed my mind, though, for he advised me not to try any funny business – those were his words – because the hotel people knew I'd been carried up to bed dead drunk the night before, and had been told that I'd had a nasty knock on the head at work and wasn't fully responsible for anything I did or said.'

'He didn't mention that the laird of Tannasgan had been murdered?'

'He did not. Anyway, how could he have known? Inverness is a long way from Tannasgan.'

'No,' said Laura thoughtfully, 'he did not know, and the chief reason, apart from what you say, is that it hadn't happened as soon as that. What did you do when they released you?'

'Nothing. They escorted me down the stairs and I paid my score at the desk and then all three of them came with the car into which they pushed me and when the car stopped they just told me to get out. I did that, and waited until the car had turned the corner into Ardross Street and then I went to our Inverness office to transact the business I'd come to see about and told them the tale. I could see that they didn't believe a word of it.'

'Not surprising, I suppose,' said Laura, who did not believe a word of it either. 'Well, if this is Loch na Gréine and that's Tannasgan, we might as well drive you home.'

'Which is your own way?'

'Oh, we shall go back to Crioch. Our plans were uncertain,' said Dame Beatrice with deliberate vagueness.

'Drop me there, if you please. I have business to see to in Gàradh. I can get a lift from people I know in Crioch.'

'He wanted to know where we were staying, I think,' said Laura, when they had parted from him at double gates which opened on to a gravel slope leading up to the terrace of the hotel. 'What did you make of his kidnapping tale?'

'Enough to feel inclined to go to Inverness tomorrow. I wonder whether he has told the police of his experiences?'

'His alleged experiences. It remains to be discovered what he actually *did* do after I left him at the station that first wet night. I suppose he did go to Inverness? If you ask me, he's a pretty fishy customer and I don't like him very much, at that. Did you notice that he referred to the hydro-electric works again, as though he really *has* got a job there, whereas we jolly well know he hasn't?'

'Yes, I did notice it. Very significant, child.'

'Can we believe that the island we showed him is Tannasgan?'

'No, but we can purchase a map in Inverness.'

'Have to be one of those six-inch things, then, to show anything so small. That is, they'll show it but will they name it? I don't know about roses by any other name, but islands are a different matter, and the motoring maps don't show Tannasgan at all. They don't even show Loch na Gréine, because I've looked. And I'll tell you what,' added Laura. 'I'm beginning to think that there may have been more people on Tannasgan, the first time I was there, than we wot of.'

CHAPTER TWELVE

Discoveries and Theories

'My virtue, wit, and heaven-help'd counsels set
Their freedoms open.'

George Chapman

IN Inverness, two days later (for they did not leave Crioch until the late afternoon, which left no time except for dinner when they arrived in the capital of the Highlands), Dame Beatrice and Laura began their search for the guest-house in which Grant claimed to have been held prisoner. His story, on the face of it, was farcical, but, as Laura pointed out, if he had not been held by the three men, he must have been engaged in some activity of which his wife (presumably) knew nothing.

Laura had formed her own opinion of Mrs Grant, however, and observed darkly to Dame Beatrice that she jolly well betted that, if Grant had been up to n.b.g., then Mrs Grant knew all about it.

'As I sum her up,' she added, 'she isn't the woman to have the wool pulled over her eyes. She was clever enough with her smooth words when she had borrowed my car without leave. She's as deep as Loch Ness, if you ask *me*.'

'Well, now,' said Dame Beatrice, as they crossed one of the suspension bridges which linked the islands of the River Ness, 'after this pleasant constitutional (which it was a very good idea of yours that we should take), where do you suggest that we begin work?'

'You first,' said Laura. 'I bet you've got a cut-and-dried plan.'

'Well, I thought we might try working back from the railway station to Tomnahurich Street and then rely on rule-of-thumb, so to say.'

'Fine! I can't pretend it was just what I was going to suggest myself, because I hadn't got further than exploring the possibilities of Ardross Street, into which he claimed that the car turned after the men had booted him out of it. Of course, I have to keep reminding myself that he may not have been speaking a word of truth all the way through. So – the station, by all means. Let's get back to the east bank and pick up George and the car.'

At the railway station, Dame Beatrice's first move was to purchase a copy of British Railways' holiday guide to Scotland. She observed, as she sat in the car and turned over the pages, that it was remarkably good value for the money. Having admired the volume, she looked up in the index the list of hotels and boarding-houses in the city. Laura peered over her shoulder and observed that it would take them 'weeks to inquire into that lot.'

'We can reduce the number we need to inquire into,' Dame Beatrice pointed out. 'I shall begin by supposing that Mr Grant's story is substantially true.'

'How can we reduce the number? I mean, obviously we can knock out the big hotels, but that still leaves an awful number of places where he might have stayed.'

'Not so many as you seem to think. The three men were staying in the house; so was Mr Grant; so were the proprietor and, possibly, his family.'

'Ah! I get it! Number of bedrooms is of the first importance. What's the minimum number we should look for, do you suppose?'

'I am inclined to begin with the maximum number, (as given in this excellent publication) and work downwards to my minimum number, which is three, for the proprietor would not advertise the accommodation he reserves for himself, his family and any domestic helpers. I am, in fact, more inclined to plump for a minimum of four, as men have a prejudice against sharing a room, except with a woman. Then we can leave out any establishment which offers a service technically known to the advertisers as B.B., for, if Mr Grant was telling the truth, all his meals were sent up to him.'

'In other words,' said Laura, 'Grant was lying, so all we shall be doing is wasting our time.'

'Oh, I don't know,' said Dame Beatrice. 'Something may transpire. What we propose to do is really no business of ours, anyway, and it is always interesting to behave abominably.'

'Yes, so it is. Well, we seem to have ironed out quite a number of these establishments, and that's a comfort. Where shall we begin?'

They began and ended at the first boarding-house to which they applied. Grant was well known there, was well spoken of and had stayed for three days (unusual, this) during the dates in question. He had business interests in Leith and used the boarding-house as a *pied-à-terre* before setting off by rail for the Edinburgh seaport.

It was impossible to doubt the sincerity and good faith of the landlady, neither did she appear to take it amiss that she was questioned. Dame Beatrice's story of a favourite nephew was accepted without difficulty or comment, and Grant's home address was readily supplied and proved to be the correct one. Anything less like the haunt of thugs it was impossible to imagine, and, apart from his wild story, Grant appeared to be a respectable citizen.

'So he *was* up to n.b.g.,' said Laura, as they went back to pick up the car. 'Where do we go from here?'

'To the police, child.'

The police received them with courtesy and an understandable degree of aloofness. They had no knowledge of Grant and pointed out that any further enquiries had better be made in Dingwall, the county town of Western Ross. Dame Beatrice, however, thought otherwise.

'Before we go to the police in Dingwall,' she said, 'we shall add up our assets. Now, it seems to me that we have five suspects. That is to say, I am counting the married Grants and the Corries as one each, not two. In spite of what you say about Mrs Grant, the wives may have nothing to do with their husbands' secrets, although I have a feeling that there you are right.'

'The Corries?'

'We can scarcely leave them out. They were employed – or so we suppose – at the time of the murder and must surely know something about it.'

'I like the Corries,' said Laura. 'I feel positively certain they're all right. It's only a hunch, of course.'

'And, as such, has some claim on our attention, but we cannot dismiss them at present. I also have a hunch – considerably more far-fetched than yours, I may add.'

'Spill?'

'Let us first name the rest of the suspects.'

'Young reporter Grant? That tale of his struck me as containing a fair quantity of baloney. What did you think?'

'That what he said was the truth, but not the whole truth. However, now that we know where he lives, and what he does for a living, we can see him later. I do not consider him a vital link in our chain of evidence.'

'He saw murder committed in Edinburgh.'

'And knows the guilty party. So much is evident. There remain the mysterious young man who arranged for the boat to take you on to Tannasgan that night and, of course, our extraordinary acquaintance Malcolm Donalbain Macbeth.'

126

'What about motives? Yes, I can see what the last-named could have been up to. He inherits.'

'If he does! We have his word for it, I know, but I should wish for confirmation of that.'

'Why should he say he does, if he doesn't? It's a most dangerous ploy. The police always think the lowest motives are the strongest. Does he *want* to be convicted?'

'He is a strange character and a most intriguing one. I revert continually to thoughts of his absorbing interest in fabulous beasts.'

'Oh, he's quite crazy, wouldn't you say?'

'Like Hamlet, only north-north-west, I fancy. He knows a hawk from a handsaw. However, let us see what possible motives for murder we may attribute to the rest of our suspects.'

'All right,' said Laura, grinning. 'Keep yourself to yourself, but it ain't very sociable, you know. What about the married Grants?'

'There are two possibilities, if not more. The laird may have uncovered what Mr Grant, whose story of the kidnapping – a misnomer, surely? – we have no longer any reason to believe . . .'

'We never did believe it! Kidnapping and general skullduggery in Inverness! It doesn't make sense!'

'The laird,' pursued Dame Beatrice patiently, 'may have found out what Mr Grant *really* did in Inverness and (if his wife is to be believed) in Edinburgh, too, and Mr Grant may have been sufficiently concerned about this to wish the laird out of the way.'

'If wishes were horses . . .'

'In Mazeppa's case, of course, they were. Did you ever have to learn those fearful verses?'

'Don't think so. Anyway, you think the laird was a blackmailer?'

'Well, I mentioned a while ago that I had what you call

a hunch. It may seem far-fetched, but did it never occur to you that Mr Macbeth (for want of his real name) was trying to find out from you, that evening you spent on Tannasgan, whether the names of fabulous animals had for you anything more than a slight academic interest?'

'Good heavens, no! I just thought the poor old red-beard was bats.'

'Did you? You have an excellent verbal memory and, I am pretty sure, you reported your conversation with him *verbatim*. I have my notes.'

She produced a small, black-covered book and studied it thoughtfully.

'*Verbatim*? Well, I wouldn't be surprised,' said Laura. 'The whole thing was more than a bit *outré*, if that's the word I want, so I wasn't likely to forget anything that was said. But what's your idea?'

'Vaguely, that the fabulous animals represent some kind of code.'

'Whatever for?'

'That is what we have to find out. Cast your mind back to the evening in question, and I will read out what you told me of what passed between you and Mr Macbeth. But, first, were you not a little surprised when you were welcomed, dried, warmed and fed?'

'Well, after what Mrs Grant had said about the laird, I suppose I was, although Highlanders are always hospitable. But, of course, I was so horribly wet and cold that I was only too thankful to get into the house, and when the old boy actually welcomed me, in his odd sort of way, all my critical faculty left me.'

'Not altogether. You knew that it would be wise to leave Tannasgan instead of waiting until the morning. Well, now, this is what you told me. I give it in the form of a dialogue. I may add my own comments if I see fit.

128

Macbeth: Are there werewolves in your part of the country?

Laura: No. They live in the Hartz Mountains. (An equivocal answer, if he was trying to pump you.)

*Macbeth: They live in the Grampians; they thrive in the
Cairngorms; they have been known at Leith and now
they are here.'*

Laura: So is the basilisk.

Macbeth (interested to a degree which makes Laura wonder
whether he is rather more than eccentric) : *Do you tell
me that?* (Did you not think that there was something
in your answer which caused him to deepen his suspicion that there was more behind your unexpected visit
than he had supposed? No, don't answer now. Just
think it over.)

Laura: And what about the cockatrice? (And it was with
this question that you really put the cat among the
pigeons, I think. He thought you were one of the
cognoscenti or else had been sent as a spy. The same
sort of thing happened a moment later. Do you remember?)

Laura (continuing after he has explained that the basilisk
and the cockatrice were one and the same creature) :
I should have asked about the salamander.

Macbeth (speaking, I think, allegorically) : *I had one once
. . . until he fell into the fire . . . There was a blaze! It
nearly had my house burnt down . . . Half-way to the
Golden Gate – I mean the Antipodes – is the salamander.
Ay, on fire he feeds and grows . . .* (At this point he was
quite certain that you knew what he was talking about.
Now, does nothing strike you as significant?')

'The mention of Leith and the slip of the tongue about
the Antipodes,' said Laura.

'The mention of Leith I am taking to be a deliberate
attempt to test you. The Antipodes reference I am inclined

to leave for further investigation. The other was no slip of the tongue. The Golden Gate, if I am right, meant something other than a geographical location. I think it referred to money.'

Laura knitted her brows.

'Down in the forest nothing stirs,' she said. 'Ought it to?'

Dame Beatrice waved an apologetic claw.

'All will be gay when noontide wakes anew the buttercups,' she said. 'Meanwhile, what of our other suspects?'

'Well, we *have* mentioned the Corries, but you know what I think about *her*.'

'Like you, I think we may forget Mrs Corrie as a suspect, although I still wish to talk with her. You did remark once, though, I believe, that the Corries did not seem the kind of people who would have consented to serve a man such as the laird.'

'No. In a way, though, Mrs C. seemed quite the type to look after the loony Macbeth. I thought her simple and dignified and kind, and no end fond of a joke.'

'Just so. Well, the only reason for her to have murdered the laird would seem to be that she was tired of his ways and preferred those of his successor.'

Laura laughed. 'Could be,' she said. 'Well, who's next?'

'Young Grant wanted his newspaper scoop so badly that he murdered the laird and then reported the death.'

Laura laughed again.

'That rabbit? Oh, rot, whatever you may say. We agreed, long ago, I thought, that, liar though he's proved himself to be, he isn't a murderer.'

'I am not convinced that I fully associated myself with that opinion. What was he doing on Tannasgan?'

'I should say that he'd got reason to hope for some sort of scoop – that part of his story may be true – and had the horrors when he found out that he might have let himself in for being suspected of murder. He was in a panic all

130

right, following me about all over the place like that. Don't you think so?'

'I shall call upon the editor of the Freagair local newspaper,' said Dame Beatrice. 'In fact, we might make it our next assignment.'

'Well, we didn't get much out of Ye Ed., did we?' said Laura, an hour or two later.

'Only that young Mr Grant, although permanently employed as a reporter, is allowed to act as a freelance when the editor has no particular assignment for him; only that the editor's is father's friend and, for that reason, he a person of some importance on the paper; only that he receives an expenses allowance out of all proportion to his salary——'

'Ye Ed. being his father's friend would account for that, I suppose. It's his way of giving him an allowance which doesn't actually come out of his own pocket. Quite an idea, in a way. Wonder what the other reporters think of it?'

'I doubt whether there are any other reporters, child.'

'Ye Ed. is his own newshound? How dashed improper! I thought they always sat glued to a swivel chair and wore a green eye-shade and got all hectic because they'd got a blank half-column or their advertisers weren't kicking in the dough at the appointed time.'

'From what I gathered, the editor covers all the purely local or Freagairian excitements, sometimes accompanied by a photographer, but that young Mr Grant has a roving commission, over a wide area, but no photographer.'

'There's an office boy, anyway. Did you see him? – a freckled, intelligent-looking kid of about fifteen.'

'The son of the editor, I understood.'

'You seem to have understood a whole lot more than

131

I did. You think the kid is left in charge while father is out nosing around for news? Is that the set-up?'

'It may be. You know, young Mr Grant was not reporting our Conference *all* the time he was in Edinburgh.'

'Well, he said he liked crowds and the bright lights and soft music, so I expect he went to the pictures and did himself well at the best restaurants and all that kind of thing.'

'I think he may have spent some of his time in Leith, child.'

'How that place is beginning to crop up! What's its importance in this tangled history?'

'What is its *general* importance?' asked Dame Beatrice. 'Or did you never study geography?'

'Shades of Cartaret Training College and the ghost of one Tweetman, whose jogger notes I inherited from one Cartwright! Remember? Oh, no, you weren't in on that one. Leith is the port for Edinburgh, not that that bit of information was in Tweetman's notes, those being of local importance only. Leith – my Uncle Hamish used to point in its direction when I was a child of tender years and during those times when he used to instruct, inform and entertain me on the heights of Edinburgh Castle. And talking of Edinburgh, what about that bit of young Grant's story?'

'The death of the man in the street?'

'I told you at the time that it was murder.'

'He seemed quite sure of it, too. It must have startled him when he recognised you as the woman who had made one of the crowd with him at that time.'

'Once seen, never forgotten,' said Laura smugly. 'But what did you want me to tell you about Leith?'

'Leith does not quite fit in with my ideas and yet it has been mentioned. What I am in quest of is something smaller, less important and populated by people who can emulate the three wise monkeys – people, in short, who are conservative, inbred, not particularly interested in strangers, can mind their own business and——'

'Newhaven,' said Laura. 'My uncle took me there once to have a special fish dinner. It's a fishing port just west of Leith and the fish dinners there are quite something. The population are all descended from Danes and Dutchmen and keep themselves to themselves. They don't care to marry anybody from outside and their women are enormously tough and strong. They seem to be a community quite on their own. How will Newhaven suit your book?'

'So beautifully that I regard you with reverence, my dear Laura.'

'It's Uncle Hamish you should regard with reverence. There's nothing about the environs of Edinburgh that he doesn't know. What do we do? – dash to Newhaven and put the inhabitants in a panic? I really doubt whether we could.'

'I feel sure we could not. Neither would it be desirable. We need not even go to Newhaven at present – if, indeed, at all.'

'Pity! I could easily manage another of those fish dinners. What next, then?'

'Next we find out the significance of the fabulous animals and supply the authorities with a code. To do this we shall need a digest from Lloyds' Register of Shipping.'

'I begin to see daylight – at least, I think I do. You mean that each of Macbeth's fabulous beasts represents a ship?'

'That is my theory, and, of course, it is nothing *but* a theory. I may be hopelessly wrong.'

'And these ships use Newhaven as a base?'

'If I am right, these ships bring sugar and coffee from a self-governing island, and, so far as anybody on this side is concerned, they are owned by a reputable and honest trading company whose name we shall learn in due course.'

133

'How do we get hold of Lloyds' Register?'

'We do not. I write to a friend of mine who sees a copy yearly upon publication. He is one of Lloyds' underwriters and will thoroughly enjoy playing detective for us.'

'And while he's doing that?'

'We return to Tannasgan and endeavour to track down and interview the Corries. There may be considerable importance in what they tell us.'

'*If* they tell us anything. As I say, I don't feel sanguine about getting them to talk, especially after the police have had a go at them – several goes, in fact, if I know the police. That reminds me! I'd better write to his grandparents and find out to what extent my son Hamish has wrecked the home and how soon they want to get rid of him. Gavin, bless his heart, is still happy with his barracuda and won't be back in harness for another week.'

'His grandparents will probably refuse to part with your son.'

'What a hope! Anyway, you've now put me wise about Macbeth and his fabulous beasts. The very fact that I'd forgotten for the moment that the basilisk and the cockatrice are one and the same creature means that there are sister ships . . . the reference to the salamander, a lizard which is always connected with fire, means that a ship got burnt out . . . I say, do you really think so?'

'It is only a theory and may be wildly wide of the mark. It gives us something to work on, that is all.'

CHAPTER THIRTEEN

Story told by the Corries

'Heard the rivulet rippling near him,
Talking to the darksome forest.'

H. W. Longfellow

IRRATIONALLY to Laura's surprise, the lantern and the bell on the mainland were answered at once. The boatman was Corrie, whom she had known previously only as a waiter at table. Also, to her astonishment, he spoke.

'You're welcome. Maybe you can speak up and save us all this anxiety.'

'Right,' said Laura. 'All aboard!' She handed Dame Beatrice (who needed no such assistance) into the broad-beamed rowing-boat. 'And how's the laird?'

'He does well enough in his grave.'

'Oh, come now! You know perfectly well that I was speaking of the one who calls himself Malcolm Donalbain Macbeth,' said Laura, stepping into the boat.

'He's awa' to Dingwall.'

'Did he do it? Did he kill the laird?'

'I dinna ken. Maybe he did, and maybe he did not.'

'Fair enough. What is your own opinion?'

'I have given it to you. What will be your business this time at An Tigh Mór?'

'You'll find out when we get there,' said Laura, matching her tone to his. He dug the short oars into the calm waters of the loch and soon was tying up on the other side.

'Come ben,' he said, leading the way to the house.

'Is your wife at home, Mr Corrie?' asked Dame Beatrice, addressing him for the first time.

135

'Ay.' The front door was open. 'She will be speaking to you in the dining-room. Mr Macbeth said to be always keeping a fire in the dining-room, for he didna ken when he would be coming back.'

He showed them into the dining-room and drew an arm-chair a little nearer to the fire for Dame Beatrice. She and Laura seated themselves and in a moment Mrs Corrie came in and stood between them and the enormous dining-table.

'Well, well!' she said, grimly smiling at Laura. 'Such a to-do when the laird came down to breakfast and I had to report that you were missing.'

'Yes, it was very ungrateful of me to sneak off like that after all his kindness – and yours. But I had to get back to Freagair, to my hotel, you know. I didn't want to be reported to the police as a missing person,' said Laura, improvising with some success. Mrs Corrie wagged her head in sympathetic agreement.

'Police!' she exclaimed. 'We were swarming with them after they discovered the old laird's body. Police all over the house and all over the policies. They rowed themselves about on the loch and they searched the wee inch with the trees on it – ay, and every nook and cranny on the other rocks that stand up out of the water.'

'Ah, yes,' said Dame Beatrice. 'I wonder what they made of the statuary?'

'They speired at us about that, but we could tell them nothing. My man had seen the strange beasties, but I had not. Those were here before our time, and that's as much as we could say.'

'Mr Corrie told us that Mr Macbeth had gone to Ding-wall. Did the police take him there?'

'No, no. He went of his own will to make a statement and to see a lawyer.'

'And he went – when?'

'Corrie took him across the loch the morn.'

'Today?'

'Ay.'

'How much do you know about the death of Cù Dubh?'

'Well, there's mony a mickle mak's a muckle, as they say. Things were adding up. There was the visit of the young laird.'

'Not a chap who translates his sentences from the Gaelic into literal English?' asked Laura.

'That same. Dinna tell me you are acquainted with him!'

'Considering that he was the man who got me on to Tannasgan in the first place, and that I saw him on Skye a day or so later, I think I may claim that I've met him.'

'Deary me! Did it come to you that you should visit at An Tigh Mór, then?'

'No, it most certainly did not. I was terribly wet and this man was near the little quay and insisted upon turning the lantern and ringing the bell.'

'Ay,' said Corrie. 'I heard it, but the laird insisted that himself should take the boat over. "I ken well who it is," he said, "and I have a thing or two to say to him," he said. "It is not he who is the heir to Tannasgan, but myself." And with that he ordered me to the kitchen to help with the dinner, and himself rowed the boatie over the loch to bid the visitor come ben.'

'He must have had a surprise when he saw *me* there,' said Laura.

'Surprise? You couldna surprise that one gin you were putting a charge of dynamite in his breeks! No, no, he was not surprised. Said he to me whiles you were to your bed and he was waiting on his dinner, "The poor-spirited clarty gowk! He sends a lassie to speak for him!" Those were his words, mistress, and that is what he thought.'

'So the man who signalled for the boat was the laird's son?'

137

'Disinherited.'

'And you think he killed his father?'

'Him? No, no, mistress. He hasn't it in him to kill anybody.'

'What do you know of some people named Grant who live this side of the hydro-electric power station?' asked Dame Beatrice.

'Grant? Ay, Grant.' He stopped to think. 'Would that be the Grant who lives at Coinneamh Lodge?'

'It would.'

'Ay.' He spent more time in thought. 'I canna tell you anything about him.'

'Can't, or won't?' asked Laura.

'I canna. Aiblins he killed the old laird; aiblins he didna. There was nae love lost between them.'

'Oh? How do you know that?'

'I dinna ken. It might be something I overheard. The old laird kenned something about Grant that was no to his credit.'

'Such as?'

But Corrie shook his head.

'Who fashioned those curious animals on the little island with the trees and the maze?' asked Dame Beatrice.

'The fabled beasties? I dinna ken. All I ken is that they used to travel.'

'Travel? Travel where?'

'To Leith.'

'What for?'

'For advertisement, so I was told.'

'Who told you? The laird?'

'Ay. I had to row them, two at a time it was mostly, across the loch to meet Grant from Conneamh Lodge wi' his motor van and tell him the wee shop in Leith was doing badly again and needed a window-dressing to attract customers. That was all. When I had handed over whichever of the beasties I had been given, I would walk in for the laird's letters and then row myself back here.'

'What do you know of another man called Grant? – a reporter on the *Freagair Advertiser*?'

'I'd like fine to skelp that young limmer!' He turned to Laura. 'You'll mind the day you turned up here and the laird brought ye ower the loch the way my guidwife could warm ye wi' a hot brick to your bed?'

'Yes,' said Laura. 'I've blessed her ever since.'

'Ay. Well, I had orders to tak' the boat over to the other side before dinner and give a message on the public telephone that's on the road to Freagair.'

'Do you remember the message?' asked Dame Beatrice.

'Ay.' He glanced at her sharply. 'But I've told all this to the police. What way would you be speiring at me as well?'

Dame Beatrice had been expecting this question and she replied without hesitation :

'The young Mr Grant, the reporter, is expecting to be questioned by the police. Mrs Gavin is in the same predicament. Both were here round about the time of the murder. If the police question Mrs Gavin, naturally she wants to know exactly where she stands. Of course, she possesses no guilty knowledge, but we want to be sure that the police will accept that as a fact. We are asking you for help.'

'Ay.' He stroked a craggy chin. 'I can tell you all I ken, but it willna help Mrs Gavin ower much, I'm thinking. The old laird might hae been still alive while she was here, and I couldna swear she didna kill him.'

Laura was speechless, but Dame Beatrice appeared to take only the most casual interest in this damaging statement.

'Oh?' she said. 'How do you know that he might have been alive while Mrs Gavin was here?'

'I was telling you about that reiver of a young Grant.'

'Oh, yes. You rowed across to the mainland and went

139

off to telephone, leaving the boat tied up, and when you came back . . .'

'Ay. When I came back it was across on the other side.'

'So you turned the lantern and rang the handbell?'

'Na, na. Naething o' the kind. That would have vexed the laird. I whustled.'

'You——?'

'He whistled,' said Laura.

'Ah, yes. And what happened then?'

'Then my guid wife left her cooking and brought the boat across. A rare cuddy she called me, but I pointed out that not the biggest gowk in Scotland would leave his boat the wrong side o' the water. It was then she told me o' this young journalist frae the Freagair paper, and how he was wanting speech wi' Mr Macbeth, but Mr Macbeth – wouldna see him but had gi'en orders that when I was home I was to throw him into the loch.'

'Which order you were prepared to carry out because he had pinched your boat and left you high and dry,' said Laura. Corrie's grim face creased into a smile.

'I was fully prepared to gie him the length o' my tongue, but it's ill to maltreat the Press, and I was considering what best to do, when the laird came out of the dining-room and speired at me what I had been hearing on the telephone, for I had felt bound to tell him what my orders were.'

'Now you said you thought the old laird was still alive while Mrs Gavin was here,' said Dame Beatrice. 'May we return to that point?'

'I hae na left it, mistress. Ye gie me no time. I ken verra weel that the old laird was alive while Mrs Gavin was here. It was himself that I rang up on the telephone.'

'I see. You are certain, I suppose, that it was his voice you heard?'

'It was that, then. I had to ring him up to find out whether he wanted a car to be ready for him at Tigh-Òsda railway station and, if so, at what time. He did wish a car and he told me the time the train should be in.'

'So, having rung off, you telephoned the garage for a car. *Is* there a garage at Tigh-Òsda? I don't remember one,' said Laura.

'There's no' a garage, but the station-master obliges when he kens the person who wishes to hire.'

'Oh, I see. Hm!' said Laura, meeting Dame Beatrice's understanding eye. 'Would you say he "knows" the passengers who regularly travel by train from his platform?'

'Certainly. There's no a great deal of passenger traffic at Tigh-Òsda, for maist o' the workers at the hydro-electric works use their own cars, although the station was built for them when the hydro-electric scheme was first planned. There's the mail frae the wee post office at Crioch that a bicycle-laddie brings and puts on to the train, and there's the mail frae Tigh-Òsda itself, although there wouldna be a muckle of letters there, for few in the village write mair than once a year to their relations in Canada. Ay, and them that are putting up for the night at the hotel – for such Ian Beg chooses to call it – are bagmen wi' their samples, puir bodies that are mair like tinklers or pedlars, to my mind, than the sort you would find in a city.'

'So you booked the station-master's car for the old laird,' said Dame Beatrice patiently. 'For what time in the evening was it booked? Can you remember?'

'For half after nine, the way I would be able to wait at table on the laird and Mrs Gavin here, and the guid-wife would be able to prepare a supper for the old laird, the way he would no' be compelled to eat up the remains of the gigot which was served at dinner.'

'I see. So the old laird arrived at An Tigh Mór at soon

141

after ten, I suppose. Did he give the usual signal for the boat to be brought across for him?'

'He did not. I had orders to have the boat on the other side to meet him, the way he wouldna be kept waiting, so at ten o'clock I went to the boathouse and rowed across. He showed up in the station-master's car after a bit – Ian Beg, the porter, driving – and I took him back to the boathouse and he stepped ashore and we brought him up to the house.'

'Did you see anything of young Mr Grant in the boathouse? I ought to tell you that he was there when Mrs Gavin decided to leave the island for Freagair.'

'I didna see hide nor hair of him.'

'I wonder where he got to?' said Laura. 'You say you went up to the house with the old laird?'

'I did that.'

'And actually saw him go in?'

'I helped him along the path and up the steps. He was fou.'

'How fou?' asked Laura.

'Verra fou. He was telling me that the Devil was after him and that he wouldna have any supper. He was going to play on the pipes and frighten the Devil away. That is what he said. Ay, those were his very words.'

Laura again caught Dame Beatrice's eye.

'And did he play on the pipes?' asked the latter.

'He did that. Well enough it was at first, but he finished wi' such a skirling ye would have thought the Devil had snatched the pipes from him and was piping his soul to damnation.'

'Are you certain it was not Mr Macbeth who was piping?' asked Dame Beatrice. 'Mrs Gavin, I think, put the piping down to him.'

Corrie looked undecided.

'I couldna say. The laird was in the mood,' he replied.

CHAPTER FOURTEEN

Story told by the Grants and Others

'And up from thence, a wet and misty road . . .
Clouds of white rolling vapours fill the vale.'

Matthew Arnold

'WELL,' said Laura, when Corrie had rowed them across the loch and they were back in the waiting car, 'something to think about, definitely, wouldn't you say?'

'Say on,' said Dame Beatrice, as George let in the clutch, and the car, in spite of the rough ground at the roadside, moved sedately on to the highway. 'You have comments to make?'

'Haven't *you*? There's one thing, surely, that sticks out a mile and a half.'

'Indeed?'

'Of course. The business of the Grants and my car.'

'Recapitulate.'

'As though you didn't have both episodes at your fingers' ends!'

'You make me sound like one of the Norns, child.'

'Well, so you may be, for all I know. And that's not intended to be flippant. No, honestly, though, let's face the facts.'

'Willingly. Say on.'

'Well, how truthful do you think the Corries are?'

'Possibly truthful and probably trusting, child.'

'Meaning that they trusted Cù Dubh?'

'And ourselves, you know.'

'Yes, well, if we accept (and, like you, I do) that Corrie

was telling the truth, why did the Grants ask *me* to drive Mrs Grant home, that first night I came back in the rain from Gàradh, when they must have known they could hire the station-master's car?'

'There are two possible, and, I venture to think, obvious explanations.'

'Oh?' said Laura, belligerently. '*I* can't think of even one. Oh, yes! Of course I can,' she added, altering her tone. 'You mean that the station-master's car was already on hire.'

'Exactly, and what is so satisfactory is that it will be a simple business to find that out.'

'Maybe not as simple as you would think,' said Laura, grinning. 'I don't suppose for an instant that the station-master keeps any records of the hire of his car. A Highlander wouldn't, you know. It isn't that he wants to dodge the tax-collector, but simply that he has very little sense of time and is just too lazy, anyway, to bother. Besides, he probably doesn't think of payment for hiring out his car as being part of his income. He'd tell you – and he'd believe it – that he only does it to oblige, and that, as he had to pay for the car in the first place, it is not the business of anybody else how he uses it.'

'I see,' said Dame Beatrice. 'I must show him my notebook.'

Laura made a rude, hooting noise, well aware that few, if any, could read her employer's cryptic shorthand, Dame Beatrice's own invention. Dame Beatrice sedately explained that she would produce the notebook and read aloud to the station-master certain dates and times.

'Well, all right,' said Laura. 'There may be, as I say, this probable explanation of why the Grants couldn't hire the car. But what else had you thought of? You said the other explanation was also a possible one. Expatiate.'

'They had your car free of charge, child.'

'Oh, I see. Yes, but, against that, Mrs Grant put me up for the night and fed me jolly well, you know, and she more than replaced the petrol.'

'There is usually food in a house, dear Laura. The production of ready money in order to cope with an unforeseen situation is another matter.'

'It's still all a bit odd, you know,' said Laura, moodily.

'An understatement, I feel.'

'So we go and see the station-master?'

'Yes, indeed. He may not remember whether his car was on hire that afternoon and evening but he will most certainly remember whether Mr Grant did, or did not, travel by train to Inverness that day.'

'Good enough. Have you decided who killed Black Dog?'

'Oh, yes, of course, child. That was fairly obvious from the beginning. The police know, too. Their trouble is the same as ours – lack of proof.'

'Well, who did it, then?'

'Suppose you tell me what you think.'

'Mr Grant Senior, assisted by Mr Grant Junior, in which case they must be related, and I don't believe they are,' said Laura; but she spoke doubtfully. 'The name is a common one and, although I know they live fairly near to one another, I don't see that that makes them either relatives or fellow criminals. It's just a hunch I have, that's all.'

'What else makes sense, my dear Laura?'

'Well, there's Macbeth. He must come into the picture somewhere. I just can't fit him in. I can't see him as a murderer, though. And then, what about the disinherited son? We simply must regard *him* as a suspect. You know – revenge and all that.'

'But there is nothing to suggest that he was on Tannasgan when the murder was committed.'

'But is there anything to suggest that he wasn't?'

'I think there may be, but of that I am a little uncertain.'

'Yes? How do you mean?'

'Nobody has mentioned that he was there. To particularise, you did not see him, Macbeth has not suggested that he was on the island and the Corries cannot have thought that he was there.'

'It wouldn't have been too difficult for him to have hidden himself from all of us. However, I still think the Grants know most about what happened. Oh, well, now for the station-master at Tigh-Òsda.'

The station-master at Tigh-Òsda proved to be a cautious, softly-spoken man who received them in his primitive little office behind the booking-clerk's den, offered them seats and asked what their complaint was.

'We have no complaint whatever,' said Dame Beatrice. 'We are hoping for information.'

'You cannot understand the time-tables, maybe?'

'Nothing of that kind. I am sure they are as clear as British Railways can make them. Our enquiries, in short, are connected with a Mr Grant who lives at Coinneamh Lodge, about a dozen miles from here.'

'Ay?' said the station-master. 'I know Mr Grant very well as a passenger to Inverness.'

'You do? That is helpful, then. Would you remember a Friday at the end of last month when there was a deluge of rain, severe even for the Western Highlands, when Mr and Mrs Grant left their station wagon or estate car here because it had broken down?'

'I mind it very well. This young lady here' – he nodded at Laura – 'was good enough to drive Mrs Grant home.'

'That is so.'

'How do *you* know?' asked Laura. The station-master pointed to the windows on either side of the little room.

'*That* way I can keep my eye on the platform. *That* way I can see who comes in from the road.'

'Oh, of course. Well, I spent the night at Coinneamh Lodge, as the weather was so atrocious, and, some time during the time I was there, my car vanished. It was returned – I mean, I've got it back all right – but it was a hired car and I was responsible for it, so I'd rather like to know who had it. All I can think of is that somebody who knew the Grants also knew that they owned a station wagon and went to Coinneamh Lodge to borrow it. They found my car in the shed, so borrowed that instead.'

'Did it suffer damage, then?'

'Well,' said Laura, treading on delicate ground because she did not want to tell a direct lie, 'it certainly wasn't quite in the same condition as when I left it, and judging by the mileage figures and the – er——'

'The petrol consumption?'

'—I just wondered whether somebody – it would have to be two people, actually – used it to reach the station here so that one of them could catch a train.'

'What would be the latest time you could be sure it was safely housed at Coinneamh Lodge?'

'Well, I didn't go to bed until well after midnight, and I should have heard it being driven away, I'm sure, or the door being slammed, or something. From what I can work out, it was taken away some time between about two o'clock and six in the morning.'

The station-master fished out a time-table.

'You may see for yourself, mistress, that there is no train leaves this station after the one Mr Grant catches at eight-fifteen when he travels to Inverness during the clement months of the year. The earliest morning train does not go out until nine-five.'

'Well, anyway, thank you for telling me,' said Laura. 'I just thought it *might* be somebody who wanted to catch a train.'

'Does Mrs Grant have no suspicion who might have

helped himself to the loan of it? Coinneamh Lodge lies a long way off the road.'

'She seems to have no idea.'

'Well, well, I'm sorry you were in trouble over a hired car. That would be sorely vexing for you, yes, and expensive, too.'

'Talking of car hire,' said Laura, 'I think somebody told me that there was a car here at the station. Is that so?'

'It is, indeed.'

'But the Grants took shelter in the station entrance instead of having it take Mrs Grant home. That seems odd to me. After all, they couldn't have known that I was coming along, could they?'

'No, no, they could not.'

'I only stopped because I had made up my mind I would have to find a bed at the hotel.'

'Yes, I see. That was a fortunate thing indeed for Mrs Grant.'

'If you don't mind my asking, *was* the station car on hire that evening?'

'My mind is not clear about that. Ian Beg may know.' He went out and returned with a thin, very shy young man whom he introduced as, 'This will be Ian. He issues the tickets and does the portering and holds the train if there should be those on the road wishful to ride on it. Now, then, man Ian, put your thoughts to the wet Friday Mr Grant's estate car broke down and himself pushing it with his wife at the steering. Do you mind the Friday I mean?'

'I do so, Mr Murray.'

'Well, now, was our own car away?'

'It was not, then.'

'It was not? Did Mr Grant speak of wishing it on hire for his wife to get home?'

'He did not.'

148

'I suppose,' said Laura, 'that, if he had driven his wife home in it, he would not have been able to get to Coinneamh Lodge and back in time for the train?'

'That would be the way of it.'

'You mean, then,' said Dame Beatrice, giving Ian a friendly leer which obviously frightened him very much, 'that Mrs Grant was absolutely dependent upon some friendly motorist coming along and offering her a lift?'

'It would be like that, yes, indeed.'

'Was it a likely thing to have happened? I should have thought that this was rather a lonely road.'

'Anybody would give anybody a lift on such a night,' said Ian.

'How many passengers do you usually expect on the evening train?' asked Laura.

'Och, it might be as many as fifteen, times it would be two.'

'Well, that doesn't exactly sound like a London rush hour. Couldn't you have offered to drive her home yourself? Surely, when she was in such difficulties, and had to get home to her baby to free the baby-sitter, Mr Murray here would have looked after the train for you?'

'Ay.' Ian appeared to lose himself in thought. 'Och, ay. There is something in what you say. Only, you see, our car was suffering from a defective clutch, righted on the following morning.'

Laura wanted to laugh, but knew that this reaction would deeply offend the young Highlander.

'Oh, I see,' she said. 'But you told us that Mr Grant made no enquiry about hiring the car. I quite understood when you said that he himself had no time to take her home because of missing his train, but couldn't he have suggested that, for once, you yourself could have taken her? – before he knew that the station car was out of action, I mean.'

'He could not. He would be knowing that not for anyone would I enter the policies of Coinneamh.'

'Why not, then, Mr Beg?'

'It is clear to me that you have not the Gaelic,' said Ian, shaking his head. The station-master rose and, courteous to the last, showed out Dame Beatrice and Laura.

'Well,' said Dame Beatrice, when they were in her car and clear of the station, 'I am stunned by the way in which you dominated that interview. I offer congratulations, and rejoice that the mantle of Elijah should have fallen upon Elisha to such excellent effect.'

Laura grinned.

'We've found out what we wanted to know, anyway,' she said, 'so a truce to the leg-pulling. We know Grant went by train that night, but, if that lad Ian is right, we can't be at all sure that it *was* Mrs Grant who borrowed my car that early morning. And yet who else could it have been, and what about that crack of my not knowing the Gaelic? I do know what Coinneamh means. It means *Meeting.*'

'Does it, indeed?' said Dame Beatrice. 'Well, now for the Grants, for, as Mr Peachum indicates in *The Beggar's Opera,* matters must not be left where they are.'

As it happened, both Mr and Mrs Grant were at home. So was the baby. The first sounds which greeted the visitors were those of a screaming child.

'Temper,' said Laura, pounding vigorously upon the door.

'Teething, perhaps?' suggested Dame Beatrice, whose children were a good many years older than Laura's little son. The door was opened quietly, and yet dramatically, by a girl of about seventeen.

'Yes, please you?' she said. Dame Beatrice enquired for Mrs Grant and was informed that she and her husband were both at home. As this exchange was taking place, Mrs Grant came into the hall. She greeted Laura first and then looked a little doubtfully at Dame Beatrice before she led them into the dining-room. Grant stood up and said :

'I take it you're interested in the papers.'

'To some extent,' Dame Beatrice replied. 'At the moment I am much more interested in Newhaven.'

She allowed this name to sink in, but it was evident from his demeanour that it had touched no chord in Grant.

'Newhaven?' he said at last. 'And what will Newhaven have to do with it?'

'Well, that is just what I'd like to know,' said Dame Beatrice briskly. 'Come, now, Mr Grant! Admit that your story of the kidnapping was a fake.'

Grant glanced at his wife and then grinned.

'A fake?' he said. 'Well, well, perhaps the less said about that the better. I was hard pressed. You see, there are a number of people who think I may have killed the laird. Maybe you are one of them.'

'One of many?'

'Ay. You remember reading about the loss of a ship called the *Saracen*?'

'Do you not mean the *Salamander*?'

Grant looked startled.

'I see that you know it all,' he said. Dame Beatrice, pleased at the result of a shot in the dark, shook her head.

'Oh, no, Mr Grant, I do not. I wish I did,' she said. 'Why did she blow up?'

'I dinna ken. Christie, some tea for the ladies.'

'You don't know?' said Dame Beatrice, as Mrs Grant went out of the room. Mr Grant's face darkened.

'It was listed as "an unfortunate incident" in our official files, but it was sabotage,' he said. 'I have no doubt about that. My only brother was lost when the *Salamander* or, when she was in Scottish waters, the *Saracen,* blew up.'

'If you know it was sabotage, you must have some idea of who was responsible.'

'An idea is not a proof, Dame Beatrice.'

Dame Beatrice wagged her head in acceptance of this view.

'Very true,' she agreed, 'so I will not press for your opinion.'

'Oh, you are welcome to my opinion. I think Bradan arranged it all.'

'Why should you think that?'

'He believed we had an informer aboard that ship. You see, our trade would not bear too close an inspection.'

'Really?'

'I shall say no more about that.'

'I cannot blame you. The cargoes which came back to this country . . .'

'Were innocent enough. Ah, here comes Christie with the tea.'

'I soon found out that you were not employed on the hydro-electrical project,' said Dame Beatrice conversationally. Grant laughed.

'You did that! Ay, it was not a very effective smoke-screen that I put up there.' He handed over the cups of tea as his wife poured them out. 'But I dinna fash myself about that, as some people say.'

'Of course not. Well, it is very kind of you to have us here and give us tea when our object – I will not mince matters – is to find out, if we can, whether one or both of you slaughtered the laird of Tannasgan.'

Laura gasped at hearing this frank statement, but Grant laughed again and turned to his wife.

'Did you hear that, Christie? What will folk think of next?'

'We have found out why you were stranded at Tigh-Òsda station,' Dame Beatrice went on. 'The station-master's car was out of action owing to a faulty clutch.'

'Even if it had not been out of action it would have

been of no use to us,' said Grant. 'Nobody at the station would have been willing to leave his work to drive Christie home, and I could not have done it myself for fear of missing my train.'

'How long had you been at the station when I turned up?' asked Laura. Grant considered the question.

'About a quarter of an hour, I would say,' he replied.

'Ah,' said Dame Beatrice. 'By the way, who *did* kill Mr Bradan?'

Grant put down his cup.

'I have told you that my brother went down with the *Saracen.*'

'You have, yes.'

'*If* I had killed Cù Dubh, that would have been my reason.'

'But you didn't kill him?'

'I did not. Consider the facts. Here am I, an honest poor man, the Dear knows, tied in partnership with a scoundrel. Oh, ay, Bradan was a rascal all right. Now he's dead – murdered. But, mistress, he was my bread and butter, ay, and my cake, too. What way would I wish to lose all that? Forbye, I'll tell you this : what we were doing was against the law. So much I am well prepared to admit. What I am not prepared to admit is that it was sinful.'

'You do not think of gun-running as being sinful?'

'Woman, if they hadna got the stuff from us, they would only have bought it elsewhere!'

'Sophistry!'

Grant grinned again. He might be a villain, thought Laura, but he was a likeable one.

'Maybe,' he said. 'But the gun-running was a bit of an afterthought. It was the moonshine trade that brought in the dollars first of all.'

'Rum?'

'Ay, rum. There was nothing difficult about it. We took

153

out coal, potatoes, pig-iron – that kind of innocent stuff – and we sold it. We had regular customers out there, and it was a good business. Bradan, to give the man his due, had a good head on his shoulders. Then all we had to do was to buy rum in the islands and work it to the 'dry' places, pick up a cargo of sugar and cotton and land it in a perfectly legitimate way at Leith (or maybe Newhaven) and that's all there was to it.'

'Interesting. And the *Salamander,* of course, was not engaged in the innocent pursuit of rum-running.'

'You ken very well that she was not.'

'Now, Mr Grant, you have been comparatively frank with us, and I realise that this is a story which you can hardly tell to the police.'

'And you?'

Dame Beatrice indicated her cup of tea.

'It is not for me to cast – what is the rest of it, Laura?'

Laura, who had been studying the tea-leaves in the bottom of her cup before relinquishing it to Mrs Grant, looked up.

'I prefer not to call the police swine, Dame B.,' she said, with affected seriousness.

'No, no. I was not thinking of asking you to do so. We cannot think of pigs and our dear Robert at the same time,' responded Dame Beatrice in a similar tone.

'Casting bread upon the waters doesn't fit.'

'You know, you're not trying,' said Dame Beatrice, giving a harsh cackle which had the curious effect of quietening the baby in the next room.

'Casting nasturtiums? Care to the winds? A clout before may is out? The runes? The lie in someone's teeth?'

'Dear, dear! I had no idea that I should provoke all this! Anyhow, Mr Grant, I shall not betray you to the police under any circumstances except one.'

'Well, I didna murder Bradan,' said Grant.

'And the kidnapping story?'

'I willna talk about that. It was all in the course of business. I had to make contacts. It had naething at all to do with Bradan's death except that I had to shoulder some of his work.'

'But this would have been *before* his death, would it not?'

Grant gave her a very odd look.

'Maybe it would,' he said. 'We had reasons, and that's all I'm prepared to say.'

'I see. Mr Grant, I ask for no names, but do you know who killed Mr Bradan?'

'I wish him well, whoever he was, although he's cost me my cake, if not some of my bread and butter.'

'That is not an answer, you know,' said Dame Beatrice gently. Grant passed his cup to his wife for more tea.

CHAPTER FIFTEEN

The Meaning of Coinneamh

'Up jumps old Peter, and, heaving the regelashuns
away, yells, "Damn all the nonsense! Heave the
body overboard." '

Harry Lander

'*Meeting*,' said Dame Beatrice, referring to the English
rendering of Coinneamh. 'If so, I wonder why Mrs Grant
was willing to put you up for the night? I wonder how she
ever contrived to persuade a baby-sitter to stay in the
house? I wonder how much Mr Macbeth knows about the
Grants, and how much of that knowledge he has never
disclosed?'

'Golly!' said Laura. 'What hare has poor Ian at the
station started now?'

'In what sense, dear child?'

'This Coinneamh gag. Are we talking of witchcraft, do
you think?'

'Of one kind of witchcraft, no doubt. We now know that
we are talking of the kind of witchcraft which (to coin a
phrase and alter it just a little) has been running guns and
butter in the same ships.'

'As for Mrs Grant putting me up for the night, I am
pretty sure that she may have wanted the use of a car in
the early hours of the morning and saw how she could get
it. But I may be wronging her hopelessly about that. Anyway, where do we go from here?'

'Oh, back to Tannasgan.'

'To confront Macbeth with our new knowledge, such as
it is?'

'To invite his co-operation, as I see it.'

'Some hopes, if you ask me! I shouldn't think he'd ever given anybody any co-operation in his life!'

'We shall get it, provided that he has returned safely from Dingwall. I shall challenge him, and I am fairly certain that he will pick up the gage.'

'Don't forget to be quick on the draw with that lethal little gat of yours, then,' said Laura. 'Sheriff,' she added unnecessarily.

Dame Beatrice cackled and her car drew in to one of the passing-places to let through a car coming from the opposite direction.

'That was our friend Macbeth,' she said. 'Did you see him?'

'Good Lord! We ought to follow him up,' said Laura, 'but I don't see how George can turn on a road as narrow as this.'

'There is no need for us to follow him,' said Dame Beatrice. 'It will be much better to meet him on his own ground. We will await him at An Tigh Mór.'

Arrived on the shores of Loch na Gréine, the car drew in on to the grass verge and Laura got out. Macbeth, it seemed, had rowed himself ashore, for the boat was tied up to the jetty. George opened the car door for Dame Beatrice and then led the way to the boat, handed in his employer, waited for both women to seat themselves and then untied the boat and pushed off from the jetty.

'Wonder whether the Corries are still in possession?' said Laura, when they reached the boathouse. 'Oh, well, we shall soon know.'

'Do you wish me to accompany you to the house, madam?' asked George. Dame Beatrice patted the pocket of her skirt.

'Not this time, George, thank you,' she replied. 'I think you had better stay here in case the owner of the house comes back and needs the boat. If you hear the sound of a shot, you may come to our rescue.'

'Very good, madam.' He watched them as they walked towards the house, for the boathouse had wooden planking on three sides and the door was at the back and had been left open. Laura went up to the mansion and hammered on the door. It was opened by a police-sergeant.

'Well, I'm blessed!' said Laura, her marriage to Detective Chief-Inspector Robert Gavin having freed her from the average citizen's awe of the police. 'I thought you lot had finished here a couple of weeks ago!'

'Gin ye'll step inside, ladies, the Inspector would be glad of the favour of a word wi' ye. We spied ye from the window,' said the policeman, holding the door wide open and standing aside. 'He'll be in the dining-room. That is the door, on the right there.'

They entered the dining-room and a tall inspector of police looked round and then stood up.

'I am very glad to see you, Dame Beatrice,' he said gravely. 'This saves me the trouble of running you to earth. It seems you have been travelling half over Scotland since your Conference ended.'

'Yes, Mrs Gavin and I have had some enjoyable journeys,' said Dame Beatrice. 'Inspector . . . ?'

'MacCraig, of the Edinburgh police. Please to sit down.'

They took chairs and he seated himself (uncharacteristically in the presence of witnesses) in the chair which he had been occupying when they came in. This caused him to face the window.

'As Mrs Gavin remarked to your sergeant at the front door, we thought you had left this house for good,' said Dame Beatrice.

'Ah, well, you'll note I'm from Edinburgh. Now, we have in our files a story which Mrs Gavin told to one of our men on point duty about a man being deliberately

158

pushed under a car and killed. Well, very recently that story has received confirmation from a reliable source and it ties up, we fancy, with the murder of Mr Bradan of this house, whose body, as you well know, was found stabbed and in a hogshead or barrel which had contained rum.'

'Not whisky,' said Laura. 'Most unpatriotic.'

'No, it wouldn't have been whisky,' said Dame Beatrice.

'What causes you to say that?' asked the inspector.

'There is a good deal of symbolism mixed up in this business, Inspector. You saw the significance of the fabulous beasts, of course?'

'I am not aware that they had significance, Dame Beatrice. See here, now. We ken very well that you and Mrs Gavin have interested yourselves in this queer business. We know, from her own report to the Inverness police, and also from another source, that Mrs Gavin was in this house for some hours on the night when Mr Bradan was killed, and we also know of your connection with the Home Office and that Mrs Gavin is the wife of a C.I.D. officer at present on so-called leave. We have heard from Detective Chief-Inspector Gavin. He is not spending *all* his time fishing for barracuda, as Mrs Gavin, I take it, knows perfectly well, or you and she would not be chasing murderers in Scotland.'

'I have no idea what you're talking about,' said Laura. 'I've heard only once from my husband since he went on leave, and that was before Dame Beatrice went to Edinburgh for the Conference.'

'Did you not think his leave was an extended one?' The inspector watched her closely.

'I hadn't thought much about him at all. He's never been a good correspondent and he has a very busy couple of years' work behind him, so I took it for granted that he would get a fair amount of leave and would simply let me know when he was coming home.'

'Ah,' said the inspector. 'Well, well!'

'You are making me very curious, Inspector. What *is* Gavin up to, then? Is he on a job?'

'He is that, then. But since he has not told you anything about it, I must respect his confidence.' His ordinarily grave face creased suddenly into a smile. 'All the same,' he added, 'by the time Dame Beatrice and I have put our heads together and maybe pooled our ideas, an intelligent lady such as yourself will know how many beans make nine.'

'Am I allowed to ask whether it was a young newspaper reporter named Grant who confirmed my story of the street murder in Edinburgh?'

'It was. He also told us that you were here that night and that you could give him an alibi for the time of the murder of Mr Bradan.'

'But I can't, as I've told him myself, and this is for the good and sufficient reason that I haven't any idea of the time when that murder was committed.'

'There was a mention of the skirling of pipes.'

'But there's not necessarily any connection between that and the time of the murder, is there?'

'As a matter of fact, there may well be a connection. At the enquiry – as you know, we do not hold inquests as they do south of the Border – the evidence was carefully edited for the Press, and trouble was taken for some details to be scamped if not suppressed, notably the limits of time between which the death may have taken place, and the fact that the barrel in which the body was found had contained rum. Now, young Mr Grant is very ambitious, or so he told us, and there is no doubt that he wanted a scoop for his paper big enough to allow him to try for a job on an Edinburgh journal. He not only saw the Edinburgh murder committed. He also knew by sight one of the two men who committed it.'

'Did they also recognise *him*?' demanded Laura.

'He thinks not. He lives at Crioch, you see, and works in Freagair, and there is nothing to connect these men with either place. Except that he is a reporter and so gets to find out a good deal about local affairs, I do not suppose he would have known either of them. Unfortunately he cannot name the man. He knew him by sight, but not by name.'

'Could he describe him?' asked Dame Beatrice.

'Not very well. The description would have fitted a thousand men – maybe a hundred thousand. There was nothing in it that would help us.'

'I see. Of course, he may not have *wanted* to describe him very clearly.'

'What would you be meaning by that, ma'am?'

'That the man may have borne the same surname as Grant himself. Just a while ago, Inspector, you suggested that we pool our ideas. I have one in particular which I am prepared to present to you. I am wondering whether the man involved was the Grant who lives at a house called Coinneamh Lodge, between here and Tigh-Òsda.'

'Any relation, would you say, to young reporter Grant?'

'I doubt it very much. But there is a psychological angle here. Either one betrays a person of one's own name with a certain amount of enthusiasm – a revenge reaction, let us say – or one cannot bear to bring the clan name into disrepute. In the case of young Mr Grant, I think he would take the latter view.'

'It might well be. I shall see him again and put the point to him. Of course, he may be telling the truth when he says that he cannot name the man. Only one thing troubles me. The laird of Tannasgan is dead : murdered. What way is it that this Grant of Coinneamh Lodge is still alive? The murder of Bradan must have been an act of revenge. There can be little doubt of that. What way, then, has Grant escaped the murderer's hand?'

'Because he murdered Bradan, perhaps,' said Dame

Beatrice. 'That is, if you are right, and the murder was an act of revenge for the loss of the *Saracen*.'

'Do you tell me that? Where is your proof?'

'There is no proof that a court of law would accept. The psychological proof would lie in the remark which you yourself have just made. *If* Bradan's death was an act of revenge, then Grant could not possibly have escaped the murderer's vengeance either, unless he himself is the murderer.'

'That sounds logical, I admit. We ourselves have had strong suspicions of Mr Bradan's son, but I am bound to admit that we have nothing on him at present.'

'Is it not true that his father disinherited him?'

'He says so, and as we know that Bradan was a wealthy man it seems likely that the laddie got his own back on him.'

'What about Macbeth?' asked Laura. 'He seems to be the heir. Wouldn't he have had a pretty strong motive for murder? – to obtain possession, I mean.'

'Well, there, you see, Mrs Gavin, you're the strongest witness we've so far found in his favour.'

'I have sometimes wondered whether the laird was killed on Tannasgan,' said Dame Beatrice, 'or on the mainland.'

'The Island of Ghosts!' said Laura. 'It sounds a sinister sort of name to *me*. Just the place to expect murder.'

'There was once a monastery where this house stands,' said the inspector, 'but Norsemen from the Hebrides wrecked the place at the end of the eighth century, so I have read, and murdered the monks. That is the story and it goes on that the island has been haunted ever since.'

'Good heavens!' exclaimed Laura. 'So it wasn't Macbeth I fled from that night, but the ghosts! I *knew* there was something queer about this place!' She looked over her shoulder fearfully and gasped to find a black-clothed figure standing just behind her shoulder.

'Will I infuse the tea?' asked Mrs Corrie.

'Ay, Mrs Corrie,' replied the inspector. 'Ladies can always do with a tassie and so can I. You were saying, a while back, Dame Beatrice, that you have sometimes wondered whether Mr Bradan was killed here.'

'I do not see how he can have been, and yet I cannot see how he could not have been. There is the *skian-dhu*, of course, but one cannot imagine even such an eccentric as Mr Macbeth entertaining Laura as he did, and asking her to extend her visit, if he had contemplated killing his cousin while she was in the house. Besides, unless the Corries were in collusion with Mr Macbeth and knew where the laird had been (we'll say) incarcerated, why did Laura obtain no inkling of his presence and why did the young Mr Grant fail to obtain the interview that he wanted?'

'Since you have interpreted the facts so far, ma'am, perhaps you know where the killing took place?' said the inspector, smiling. Dame Beatrice shook her head.

'I might hazard a guess,' she said, 'but it would be nothing more.'

'Well, now!'

'Tell me, first, whether the police know where it took place.'

'We do.'

'Then I will suppose that he was set upon in or near Inverness (since Edinburgh would have been too far away) and murdered on the wooded island where stand the carvings of the fabulous beasts.'

'What brought you to that conclusion, I wonder? You mean that he ran into some sort of trouble in Inverness, but was actually murdered on Tannasgan?'

'I did tell you that it was only a guess. One other thing that I know, however, is that Mr Bradan had interests in or near Edinburgh and that those interests were in shipping.'

'How did you come to that conclusion?'

'The fabulous beasts, Inspector.' True to her half-given promise, she did not mention Grant's regular visits to Inverness and Edinburgh.

'The fabulous beasties, Dame Beatrice?'

'Your men – no, I suppose it would have been the men from Inverness or Dingwall – must have seen them when they first searched these islands and rocks, and you appear to have seen them, too.'

'Oh, ay, I've seen them, of course.'

'Well, they must have had *some* significance. Not one of them, so far as I am aware, figures in Scottish legend.'

The inspector wrinkled his brow.

'What way did you get on to shipping?' he demanded. Dame Beatrice advanced her theories, bolstering them by describing the activities of herself and Laura. 'So you thought maybe Mrs Gavin would be in trouble because she was in this house on the night of the murder,' the inspector observed, when she had concluded her recital.

'It took a little time to work out my theories,' said Dame Beatrice blandly, 'and we were not helped by the persistence with which the young reporter Grant dogged Mrs Gavin and waylaid her with requests for assistance in establishing his alibi. There was no doubt that *he* thought the murder was committed here. Once I had realised that he was in earnest about this, I began to wonder whether he was in any way responsible for the disposal of the body.'

'You did, ma'am?'

'Well, a mixture of the dramatic and the macabre is often a feature of the minds of his age and sex; then, he needed his scoop; then – and this, I think, Inspector, may be of the first importance – being a journalist and, as we know, an ambitious one, he may have found out something about the activities of Mr Bradan and he may even have come here in the first place to blackmail Mr Bradan into using his influence to obtain him a post in Edinburgh. Now, do please tell us what our dear Robert Gavin has been up to when he has not been fishing for sharks or whatever it was.'

The inspector studied his shoes.

'Well, well,' he said. He hesitated for a few seconds. 'Ah, well,' he added in a tone of resignation, 'fair's fair, I suppose, so – you'll not be letting a word of this go further?'

'Well, I did mention the loss of the *Saracen*,' said Dame Beatrice.

CHAPTER SIXTEEN

The other Side of the Herring-Pond

'Far under shore the swart sands naked lay.'

George Chapman

'PITY it was Inverness and not Edinburgh,' said Laura, 'because in Edinburgh, according to my Uncle Hamish, there would be two chief possibilities. The Castle Esplanade is one, but, in this case, I should say, a most unlikely choice because I simply don't think you'd dare to risk attacking anybody there, even at night. The other one I'm thinking of is the Grassmarket, where, after 1660, they brought Covenanters to be hanged. What about the Grassmarket, Inspector?'

'Unfortunately, although I appreciate your knowledge of Scottish history, we know Mr Bradan was attacked in Inverness, Mrs Gavin. Well, now, about your good man.'

'He might have told me he was on a job. What is it? – piracy on the high seas, gun-running, smuggling?'

'Perhaps a bit of everything. He went to Florida as the guest of a millionaire whom he'd helped at some time, it seems.'

'Saved his kid from some kidnappers who had followed the family from the U.S.A. to London at the time of the Festival of Britain in 1951. We seem to be haunted by kidnappers all through this business, don't we?'

'The millionaire seems to have taken some time to repay his debt, then,' said the inspector, ignoring the question.

'Oh, no,' said Laura earnestly. 'He was always badgering us to go. I was the one who stood out. I didn't think I'd fit in with a millionaire's environment and, until this Edinburgh Conference turned up and we *thought*' – she looked accusingly at Dame Beatrice – 'we *thought*, I repeat, that I would be needed to aid and abet, Gavin refused to go alone. Anyway, this time, when the invitation came, I insisted that he accept it. I think the prospect of the fishing clinched it, you know.'

'You don't care for fishing, Mrs Gavin?'

'Salmon and trout, yes. Barracuda, sharks and tunny, no. I feel they're above my weight.'

The inspector looked at her long limbs and splendid body and shook his head admiringly.

'Anyway,' he said, 'from the reports he has sent back to New Scotland Yard and they have passed on to us, it was not so very long before your good man was fishing for something other than barracuda. Maybe you'll mind a letter you wrote your young son, with marginal illustrations?'

'Oh, Hamish, yes. I've written to him a number of times since we've been up here – picture postcards mostly – and I did send him some rather exaggerated drawings of the fabulous animals——'

'Ay, those that are on the small, wooded inch with the maze, and which Dame Beatrice believes are symbolic.'

'Yes. I thought he might be interested. I wrote him a short legend connected with each one.'

'You did, so? Well, the wee laddie, it seems, was so pleased with the drawings and the old tales that he must send the letter to his daddy, with strict instructions that it was to be returned. Well, your good man has an alert mind and a seeing eye, and he was intrigued to notice that running between a Florida creek, where the fishing party was in camp, and, apparently, somewhere in the West Indies, were three tramp ships named, respectively, *Basilisk, Werewolf* and *Gryphon*.'

Laura looked at Dame Beatirce and raised her eyebrows.

'I suppose Detective Chief-Inspector Gavin was struck by the coincidence,' said Dame Beatrice non-committally.

'You may say that, ma'am, especially as he had had the *Scotsman* and the London papers flown out to him so that he could keep in touch with events at home. There was a wee paragraph copied from the *Freagair Reporter and Advertiser* which bore out what Mrs Gavin had written to her laddie and which gave the locality of the inch on which she had seen the models of the fabulous beasties.'

'Young Grant's report to his local paper, of course,' said Laura.

'Well, Detective Chief-Inspector Gavin is a very canny man and the coincidence of the names seemed to him so striking that he sent word to London and suggested that Scotland Yard might like to contact the Customs and Excise people, or possibly Lloyds, and find out a little more about these sonsie wee craft. It did not take long to discover that no boats under these names were registered with Lloyds.'

'No, but these are,' said Dame Beatrice, delving into the pocket of her skirt and producing a small black notebook. 'Of course, it may be fortuitous that the first two letters in each name correspond with the first two letters in the names of the boats in question, but there is another coincidence which, I think, may well be worth noting. Did our dear Robert obtain any impression of the tonnage of the boats he mentions?'

'He did. He points out that he is only estimating the tonnage, but it seems that he is well acquainted with boats of all kinds . . .'

'The Clyde,' explained Laura. 'He spent a lot of his boyhood at Dumbarton and Greenock.'

'Aha. Well, before you show me your list, mistress, I'll quote you what Mr Gavin has to tell. Here it is : *Basilisk,* about nine thousand tons, diesel driven, type made on the Clyde in about 1938. *Werewolf,* about the same size, steamship. Probably built a little earlier – say in the early 1930s. *Gryphon,* motor-ship, modern, about four thousand five hundred tons. All ships appear to be well-found. Captains and crew drink together but are unsociable with other people ashore. Suggest may be engaged in illicit liquor trade or gun-running. (Always chance of revolutions in these latitudes.)'

'Hm!' said Laura. Again she glanced at Dame Beatrice. 'Did your man at Lloyds give any more help?' she asked her.

'I think so. Will you give us your conclusions first, Inspector?'

'No, no, ladies first, Dame Beatrice.'

'Well, from the list supplied to me, I have formed the theory that when these ships are in British waters they may be called by rather different names. I have a footnote here which my friend provided in answer to a question I particularly asked.'

'And that would have been?'

'What had happened to a ship, probably based on Leith, whose name began with the letters *SA.* Well, as it happened, my informant at Lloyds was able to inform me that a ship based on Leith, whose lawful trade appears to have been that of a collier, blew up and burnt out in the Gulf of Mexico two years ago. She was called the *Saracen.* She blew up, with all hands, and the cause of the explosion was unknown.'

'What was the amount of the insurance?'

'That I did not ask, but as my informant did not mention the matter, I take it that the insurance was adequate and the premiums not abnormally high, and that the underwriters had no proof or even suspicion of sabotage.'

'Sabotage,' said the inspector thoughtfully. 'What gared you think of sabotage, ma'am?'

'Simply that I cannot see why a cargo of coal, destined, it appeared, for Montevideo, should blow up at all. A fire, of itself, I could understand, but an explosion in such a ship sounds rather unlikely. Of course, I am biased by the fact that I believe these murders to be connected in some way with these ships which camouflage their names as soon as they are on the high seas. Then,' she added thoughtfully, 'we must get rid of that *skian-dhu.*'

'That what?' cried Laura. 'But that and the barrel of rum are the most picturesque touches in the whole thing!'

'We must get rid of the *skian-dhu,*' her employer repeated. 'It is a red herring so far as I can see.'

'Now how on earth do you know that, ma'am?' demanded the inspector. 'I ken well that you're a distinguished member of the medical profession, but you did not even see the body, let alone perform a post-mortem on it! We've been keeping very quiet about the other injury, but there's no doubt whatever that we believe the knife-wound was the death wound, ay, and the murderer must go on thinking so, too. But what way . . . ?'

'Well, I confess that, in the beginning, I was as much in the dark as the rest of the public. It was something Laura said which made me think that the stabbing might be a gesture on the part of somebody who wanted the murder to appear an even more dramatic business than it was.'

'Good Lord! That young ass Grant!' said Laura. 'But what pearl of great price fell from my lips to put you wise about the knife-wound?'

'When it was known that it was an empty cask of *rum* in which the body was found. Do you not remember asking . . .'

'Whisky! Of course!'

'And, of course, if the *skian-dhu* had any place in the matter, it *ought* to have been connected with whisky. Rum goes . . .'

'With a cutlass and not with a *skian-dhu*,' said Laura, slapping her hand on the arm of her chair. 'Well, Inspector, what do you say about that?'

The inspector's smile replied to her, but he spoke as well.

'About that, Mrs Gavin, all that I can say has been said already. "There's a chiel amang us taking notes." I congratulate you on your logic and your powers of deduction, ma'am,' he added gallantly, addressing Dame Beatrice. 'Of course, whatever activities are going on in the West Indies, South America or Mexico (or anywhere else, for that matter), is not our business at present. No, no. But what *is* our business is murder.'

'Well, you've got two murders on your hands, then,' said Laura. 'There's the man who was pushed under a car in Edinburgh and now the laird of Tannasgan.'

'I doubt whether the incident in Edinburgh was intended to result in death,' said the inspector. 'You couldna guarantee that the man would be killed. I am inclined to look upon it as a disciplinary action. It was intended to frighten and maybe punish somebody who was threatening to sell out to the police. I must look up the files. They may well cast a good deal of light.'

Laura and Dame Beatrice were about to take their leave when there came across the water the loud sound of a bell.

'Somebody coming,' said the inspector. He glanced out of the window. 'Now, why ding the bell? Corrie is there with the wee boat. Ah, it is Mr Macbeth. It might be as well if you were not in evidence, ladies. Gin you would just efface yourselves, maybe . . .'

Dame Beatrice and Laura effaced themselves, the former at the bend of the stairs and the latter in the kitchen, and both heard the front door flung open. Macbeth's voice cried violently :

'Will you not bring that young man's heart to me on a siller dish and with cresses heaped around it !'

'Well, now, Mr Bradan,' Dame Beatrice heard the inspector's soothing voice respond, 'what way is it that you're speiring after Mr Grant's youthful heart?'

'Bradan? I am not Bradan! What gars you call me a salmon? I was born a Scot, like yourself.'

'Come, come, now! Something has vexed you. Did you not get what you wanted at Tigh-Òsda?'

'I did not. You might just as well arrest me for my cousin's murder and have done with it. Who am I, to protest my innocence?'

'You may protest your innocence with all the voice you have, man. It was a good day you had when you invited Mrs Gavin – you mind her, do you? – to stay to dinner that time.'

'Mrs Gavin? And who may *she* be?'

'She will – ah, well, maybe you had better see her, for she's here again.' He called loudly, 'Come, if you please, Mrs Gavin, for a word with Mr . . .' He hesitated.

'Grant,' said Macbeth. Laura slipped noiselessly out of the kitchen, glanced up the stairs, received a confirmatory nod from Dame Beatrice and presented herself in the dining-room doorway.

'Well, well,' said Macbeth. 'So the water-kelpie has come ashore again !'

'Unicorn on leash,' said Laura, advancing with a smile.

'Unicorn?' He looked puzzled. Laura waved a large and shapely hand.

'One of the fabulous beasts *not* on display,' she said. 'What *did* happen to the salamander, by the way?'

'Not by the way, but on the sea. Burnt out. I managed it myself to spite Cousin Bradan, but that he never knew.'

172

'Nonsense!' said Dame Beatrice, suddenly entering the room. 'You knew nothing about it until you heard that it had happened. Now tell us about the bagpipes.'

'The bagpipes? Oh, yes. Well, what about them?'

'Why were they played on the night Mr Bradan died?'

'Do you know about salmon?' asked Macbeth.

'Indeed I do. Their life-story has been a study of mine for many years.'

'And of mine. Well was he called Bradan, good Gaelic for Salmon. He was spawned in the Spey, gravitated – I call it that because of the very strong pull – to South America, returned to his native river and has fouled it ever since. Now all that he held is mine.'

'Yes,' said Dame Beatrice, 'but could he really bear to disinherit his only son?'

'His *only* son, say you? Well, but, mistress, what about Grant of Coinneamh?'

'I see,' said Dame Beatrice. 'And what about the young Mr Grant who lives at Crioch post office?'

'Oh, that one,' said Macbeth. He waved a hand, imitating Laura's gesture. 'That would be a collateral branch, maybe. A clansman, ay, but nothing – I would say nobody – to signify.' He was extremely drunk.

'But the bagpipes! You *must* remember the bagpipes? Mrs Gavin heard them and so did this young Mr Grant.'

'Ah, so that's the limmer you mean? I ken him well. He was a rare nuisance here, speiring after the laird. I was telling him I was the laird, but he would none of it. He said he would be claiming squatter's rights until the laird came home, so I bade him go squat in the policies, for I would not have him in the house.'

'Yes, he squatted in the boathouse,' said Laura. 'I nearly fell over him when I left An Tigh Mór that night. A fine old fright he gave me, because, of course, I wasn't expecting to find anybody there. Still, he made up for it by rowing

me across the loch, and it was then that we heard you playing a lament on the pipes.'

'Me? That was no me.'

'Corrie, then?'

'No, no.'

'Don't tell me *Mrs* Corrie plays the pipes!'

'It was no Mrs Corrie, although, between you and me,
mistress, I do not believe they twae are married.'

'That's as may be. Well, there was nobody else on the
island at that time, was there?'

'Nobody but the Great Silkie of Sule Skerrie.'

Laura stared at him.

'Oh, well,' said Dame Beatrice, rising, 'whoever played
the pipes knew that Mr Bradan, or Salmon, was dead.'

But Macbeth was not to be drawn. Laura got up, too,
and the inspector opened the door for them and followed
them into the hall. Here he jerked his head towards the
room they had just vacated and significantly tapped his
forehead.

'And you know he did not kill his cousin?' murmured
Dame Beatrice.

'Impossible that he committed the deed with his own
hand, but less certain that he was not the head of a con-
spiracy to make away with him.'

'Is there any possibility that Grant of Coinneamh is Mr
Bradan's son?'

'None in the world, ma'am. We know a good deal about
that Mr Grant. We know that he has shipping interests
and we know the names of the ships and that one of them,
the *Saracen,* as you already know, blew up and was written
off as a total loss.'

'Sabotage, do you suppose? – or done to collect the insurance money?' asked Laura.

'There was no reason at the time for any suspicion, Mrs
Gavin. She was not over-insured and she was a well-found

174

ship, so far as we know. No, no. It was just one of those things and the case is too firmly closed for anybody to reopen it now, even if there seemed any reason for doing so.'

'What happened to the officers and the crew?' asked Dame Beatrice.

'Unhappily, all lost. I would say they never stood a chance of surviving.'

'I suppose it would be possible to obtain a list of their names?'

'Certainly.'

'I should be grateful if I could be furnished with such a list.'

'You're not suggesting . . . ?'

'It is a long shot, Inspector, but, as I think you will agree, we still do not know for certain what motive the murderer or murderers of Mr Bradan may have had for what they did to him.'

'Motive?'

'Well, self-interest, in one form or another, is seen to be a motive in most cases of murder, is it not?' asked Dame Beatrice. 'But in this case I would postulate revenge.'

CHAPTER SEVENTEEN

Following the Death of a Salamander

'Treason has done his worst: nor steel, nor poison,
Malice domestic, foreign levy, nothing,
Can touch him further.'

Shakespeare

THE list of names and addresses, supplied to Dame Beatrice at her hotel in Slanliebh two days later, at first offered no hope of providing any clue to the still mysterious death of the laird of Tannasgan. It transpired that most of the crew of the lost collier *Saracen* had been Lascars and that of the captain and three officers (the third officer, so-called, was an apprentice), only one was a Scotsman. This was the second-mate, a man named Baillie. Dame Beatrice decided to try his wife first.

The address was that of a street in Glasgow; this to the surprise of Laura, who insisted that the man must have lived in Leith. Dame Beatrice confirmed the address with the inspector and in due course George drew up the car in front of a quiet, respectable house in Govan.

The door was opened by a quiet, respectable woman who confirmed that her name was Mrs Baillie. She asked Dame Beatrice and Laura in, and produced strong tea, bannocks and shortbread.

'Ye'll be from the police,' she said. 'I had word.'

'Full marks for the inspector,' said Laura. 'That's going to save a lot of explanation.'

Dame Beatrice picked up the cue. They had rehearsed several openings to this conversation on the way from Slanliebh.

'We are conducting an enquiry into the destruction of the collier *Saracen,* which was lost somewhere in the Atlantic five years ago. As you know, I have no doubt, one of the owners has been found killed. The circumstances seem mysterious and the motive for the murder rather obscure. Did your husband ever express any opinion as to the nature and scope of his employment?'

Mrs Baillie sipped tea and thought over the question.

'Nature . . . and scope . . .' she repeated, with long pauses. 'Well, maybe he did. I mind well him saying that, once he had his master's certificate, he could be very sure of a command. It is not all those who hold a master's certificate that can get a ship of their own, ye ken.'

'You mean that your husband hoped to captain one?' asked Dame Beatrice.

'Just that. It sours on a man, not to get his own ship. But Ian was always hopeful – too hopeful, I thought, times – of getting a command, but he always said that, once he had his wee bit of paper, he trusted the Company to do the right thing by him. I was not so hopeful.'

'Why not, Mrs Baillie?'

'Ian was too old. He was no verra guid at studying. I couldna see him passing an examination. Practical seamanship, ay, certainly; but to write it all down – well, I had ma doubts; I certainly had ma doubts.'

'What did you think of the shipping firm for which he worked?'

'I kenned little about it, but I thought the money was too guid. Not that I scorned the pay – oh, no, not that! – but it was way aboon what the Union were asking.'

'So you suspected that something was wrong?'

'Maybe not just at first. You ken the way it would be. Nobody looks twice at guid siller when it's to your hand. It was only afterwards that I began to wonder.'

'Since the *Saracen* went down, you mean?'

'Ay. Mind ye, there was naething wrong wi' the ship and there was naething wrong wi' the owners – only——'

'Yes?'

'No, no,' said Mrs Baillie, almost with violence. 'It was the money. The money was too guid. Danger money, it was. I can see that fine the now.'

'Did you ever meet the captain of the *Saracen*?'

'I did that. Many's the crack he and Ian had together in this very house. Ou, ay, many and many's the crack. I've left them laughing over their rum mair than twenty or thairty times, I would say. Ay, mair than twenty or thairty times.'

'What about the first officer?'

'That one? There went a bubblyjock of a man for ye. Ay, a right down bubblyjock of a man.'

'A foreigner?'

'Ay, and as black as the minister's hat.'

'Really?'

'Well, he would hae been a fine visitor at the first footing o' Hogmanay.'

'Did he speak English?'

'Ou, ay, in a fashion, but for swearing he relied on his native tongue, whatever that might hae been. My man always had it that he was no sailor. Of navigation he knew nothing.'

'I thought that the mate of a cargo ship was responsible chiefly for the cargo.'

'Ay,' said Mrs Baillie, narrowing her eyes, 'and since I've been capable of thinking about it at all, I've been speiring – in my own mind, ye'll agree – what kind of cargo it would be to blow up like that.'

'A cargo of coal, so we heard.'

'And what way does a cargo of coal blow up and not leave a big enough piece of the ship for them that kens about such things to study? No, no. Coal there may have been, but something mair was underneath it.'

'Did your husband ever mention a man named Grant as being one of the ship's company?'

'Grant? I dinna think so.'

'What did you make of her?' asked Laura, when she and Dame Beatrice were in the car again.

'She has done nothing more than confirm our suspicions, child. There were certainly explosives aboard the *Saracen*. That we know. There was nobody named Grant aboard when she blew up. That is what interests me most.'

'Well, where do we go from here?'

'Back to Slanliebh, child.'

'We're not washing our hands of the case?'

'Time will show.'

'You're not going to visit any more of the relatives of those men?'

'Not at present, if at all. We must wait upon events.'

'At Slanliebh?'

'At Slanleibh. It is a pleasant spot.'

Laura snorted with frustration.

'Action! Give me action!' she said. Dame Beatrice greeted this cry from the heart with an eldritch cackle.

'You will have action, and to spare, before very long, if I am any judge,' she said. 'Sit still; let time pass; enjoy your native land.'

'All right, if you say so,' said Laura. 'By the way, don't you think the inspector may be underestimating our friend Macbeth? And there's still that claim by Grant that his brother was killed when the *Saracen* went up in smoke. Either he was lying or else his brother was going under another name. Fishy, in either case, wouldn't you say?'

Dame Beatrice declined to comment.

*   *   *

'Now,' said Dame Beatrice, later in the week, 'I am wondering whether we know enough of the truth to decide which persons who have supplied us with information are lying, to what extent and what their reasons are for doing so.'

'Everybody has something to hide,' said Laura. They were in the lounge of the hotel at Slanliebh. Outside it was pouring with rain. Laura, who had decided to take a pre-breakfast walk, had been caught on the hillside in a deluge and had hurried back to a boiling hot bath. She was now lounging, in slacks and a wind-cheater, on one of the settees, while Dame Beatrice, upright and straight-backed as a nun, sat in a chair beside her. There were other visitors in the large room, but these were gathered in groups or couples about small tables sufficiently far apart to make private conversations possible.

'Yes, everybody has something to hide,' Dame Beatrice agreed, 'so, while this inclement weather keeps us within doors, let us take the opportunity of examining the evidence, such as it is, of the Grants and the Corries.'

'I hate to think ill of the Corries, so let's take them first and get it over.'

'Very well.' Dame Beatrice took out her notebook. 'But let us banish prejudice from our minds.'

'For me, that's difficult, if not impossible, but I'll do my best. Do you think there was any truth in that crack of Macbeth's that they're not married?'

'If there is, it might provide a motive for the murder of Mr Bradan.'

'You mean blackmail. But an employer wouldn't find it worthwhile to blackmail people like the Corries. I mean, even if you put their earnings together, they can't amount to very much.'

'I was not thinking in terms of money, child. Suppose they had wanted to apply for another post and the laird

180

had not wanted to part with two good and faithful servants? After all, it is not every middle-aged couple who would be willing to spend their lives on a small island in a West Highland loch.'

'I see what you mean, but it still doesn't seem an adequate motive for murder.'

'Suppose, then, that Mr Bradan, whose activities, as we are beginning to find out (thanks largely to the nose for crime of our dear Robert), must have been of a nefarious nature, desired the Corries to connive at, or assist in, some project of which their Lowland consciences could not approve? What then?'

'I suppose . . . yes. But, even so, I can't see the Corries dumping the body in an empty rum-barrel, can you?'

'From what I have seen of them, no, child, I cannot. Do not forget, however, that our young friend Grant may not be the only fanciful embroiderer. We have put down the presence of the *skian-dhu* to him, but there may have been another artist at work, you know.'

'Macbeth, for example?'

'He is a possibility, yes.'

'One thing that strikes *me*,' said Laura, 'is that if the *skian-dhu* was inserted after death, we still don't know what was the weapon which actually killed the laird.'

'A point which had not escaped me, but we must accept the medical evidence, don't you think? A Scottish doctor is not easily deceived, but might hold his tongue.'

'It's a great pity you did not have a chance to examine the body.'

'I should have welcomed the opportunity.'

'You know, we shall need to see young Grant again and make him confess to the *skian-dhu*.'

'And to other matters. You are quite right.'

'If we've guessed about the *skian-dhu*, it stands to reason

181

that he must have been on Tannasgan when the laird was brought home if it was, as seems likely.'

'Quite. Oh, yes, our young Mr Grant has a great deal to explain.'

'We ought to warn young Grant.'

'We will do so when we see him, which may be some time this afternoon or tomorrow morning.'

'You've sent for him, then?'

'Well, this hotel is neutral ground, so to speak. But let us get back to Mr and Mrs Corrie and scrutinise the evidence they have given us. First, there is the uncompromising comment made by Corrie about Mr Bradan.'

'Oh, yes! That he does well enough in his grave.'

'Exactly. That remark interests me for two reasons : first, that he did not love Mr Bradan, and, second, that he must have known perfectly well that it was not to Bradan that I was referring, when I mentioned the laird, but to Mr Macbeth. Then there was his equivocal reply when you asked whether Macbeth had killed the laird.'

' "Maybe he did, and maybe he did not," ' quoted Laura. 'Yes, that was a pretty dodgy answer. It might mean that he knew very well who the murderer was.'

'If he did not know for certain, I think he had very shrewd suspicions.'

'Suspicions which the police didn't get him to voice, then !'

'A country with a Covenanting history and one which steadfastly refused to betray Prince Charles Edward Stuart, would be unlikely to produce sons who could be bullied or cajoled into supplying information which they had intended to keep to themselves,' said Dame Beatrice.

'That's true enough. Then, of course, Mrs Corrie was a bit cagey, too. Remember asking her what she knew about the murder?'

'I do, indeed. Mind you, she qualified what you are

pleased to call the cagey reply by giving us a piece of information.'

'That the son had visited the island. Yes, but we didn't find out *when*. He certainly didn't come over in the boat with Macbeth and me.'

'Reading between the lines, child, I deduced that the visit was paid before the father's death and that the disinheriting was done on the occasion of that visit, and that Mr Macbeth was present. I suppose the inspector has seen a copy of Mr Bradan's will? When I meet him again I shall ask him what was in it, but I see no reason to doubt that Macbeth is the heir. The Corries have accepted him as such, and they, most likely, witnessed the will. Even if they were not permitted to read it, I am sure they knew that Macbeth was to be the new laird of Tannasgan.'

'Corrie seemed to have some suspicions of Mr Grant of Coinneamh, I thought,' said Laura. 'He admitted that there was no love lost between him and Cù Dubh. But what did you make of his statement that the fabulous beasts used to travel to Leith?'

'Of itself, I am certain that the statement was moonshine.'

'Lie number one, you think? Well, it's lies we're looking for, isn't it?'

'I am not prepared to call it a lie. I think it was in the nature of a pointer, you know.'

'To direct our attention to Leith or, perhaps, Newhaven?'

'So I suppose.'

'What about Corrie's story that he had been sent across the loch to telephone about an arrangement for a car to meet Bradan at Tigh-Òsda station?'

'I see no reason to disbelieve it. When young Grant arrives he may be able to tell us a little more about that.'

'But *do* you think Corrie telephoned Cù Dubh? Can we accept that he was alive when Corrie telephoned?'

'That I cannot answer at present. The story that Corrie did tell – and I have not yet decided whether it is true – is that Mr Bradan, *as a living man,* came back to Tannasgan.'

'Yes, I couldn't make out about that, either.'

'Mr Bradan, as we know, did come back to Tannasgan that night, but we do not know whether he was dead or alive.'

'So the piper may have been Macbeth, after all!'

'Yes. He played the pipes because he had seen the body, one might suppose. You remember telling me that the piper began with a lament, went on with an almost indecently triumphant skirling, then the lament again?'

'It was a most extraordinary performance.'

'Yes. He could have mourned his cousin and then realised that he had inherited the family property. Did you ever – no, you're probably too young——'

'Did I ever what?'

'See a slender witch of a girl named, I think, Susan Salaman, perform a ballet solo called *Funeral Dance for a Rich Aunt?*' asked Dame Beatrice. 'It called for the same extraordinary mingling of two emotions.'

'It must have been wildly comic!'

'It was, wildly and brilliantly so.'

'Well, we've sorted the Corries, so what about the Grants? Those of Coinneamh, I mean.'

'Today's thought. Well, now, what strikes you most about the Grants?'

'Fishy people. I've changed my mind about them.'

'By that you infer?'

'I no longer think I can believe a word they say.'

'They have not uttered very many words, child, when one comes to think of it.'

'Granted,' Laura agreed. 'But what have we got on

them, after all? There was the matter of my hired car and then the silly business of Grant's being kidnapped, but – well, what else?'

'Let us see.' Dame Beatrice turned over a page of her notebook. 'We begin, as you very rightly point out, with that so-far unexplained borrowing of your car. There was something very odd indeed about that. We have assumed that it made the journey between Coinneamh and Tannasgan, but there is no evidence, except that of the mileage, to show that that was indeed where the car went that night. Then, as we have already noted, if Mrs Grant cannot drive, it cannot have been she who borrowed the car.'

'But there's nobody else it *could* have been,' Laura protested. 'I think she was lying.'

'There is something in that. I see that it is still raining,' said Dame Beatrice, with apparent inconsequence. 'Would you like some coffee?'

'Yes, with rum in it. Oh, well, no, perhaps not rum. I'd forgotten for the moment. Wonder what Cù Dubh looked like? I ought to have asked Mrs Grant when we were there.' She signalled to the waiter, who had just served morning coffee at another table. 'And now, what about the Grants and the possibility that they were lying at that last interview when we managed to get them both together?'

'Let us have our coffee and enjoy it in peace,' said Dame Beatrice, closing her notebook and restoring it to her skirt pocket. 'I see that the bar is open. There is no reason why you should not drink rum. It is a kindly spirit and may assist thought.'

The waiter brought their coffee while Laura was at the bar and, when she returned to her seat, Dame Beatrice talked about the more amusing aspects of the Edinburgh Conference and then said :

'I want to hear again exactly what happened on that afternoon and evening which you spent on Tannasgan.'

'I don't think you'll pick up anything new,' said Laura, 'but here goes.' When she had concluded her account, her employer, warning her that it was a leading question, asked whether, at any point during her walk, she had suspected that she was being dogged, followed or kept under any form of surveillance.

'You're thinking of the disinherited son,' said Laura, 'but I'm positive that my meeting him like that, at the edge of the loch, was sheer chance.'

'I would still like to know why he signalled the island so that you were taken to An Tigh Mór.'

'Can't we put it down to a chivalrous gesture towards a damsel in distress?'

'Well, we *can*,' said Dame Beatrice doubtfully. 'Let us place this tray on that vacant table and get to work again on the Grants.'

'You noticed that Grant the elder said they had been marooned at Tigh-Òsda station only for about a quarter of an hour?' said Laura, when she had moved the tray.

'I did notice it.'

'Well, that was a fishy answer and I don't think it was the truth. I mean, the Grants can't have it both ways, can they?'

'By which you mean . . .?'

'Either she *can* drive, in which case (as I've felt certain all along) she *did* borrow my car that time I stayed there, or else they must have been at the station a lot longer than a quarter of an hour.'

'Excellent. Pray expound your theory.'

'Well, he was dead set on catching his train, wasn't he?'

'It seemed like it.'

'And their estate car didn't break down until they got to the station, or near enough to the station.'

'True.'

'Well, he *couldn't* have hoped, if the estate car had been all right, to drive his wife to Coinneamh Lodge and get back to the station in time to catch the train, if his account of the quarter of an hour's wait was true.'

'Therefore the original arrangement must have been that Mrs Grant was to drop him at the station and drive herself home, you think?'

'I don't see what else one *can* think.'

'Ably argued, child. You must be right. What did you make of Mr Grant's kindly presenting us with a powerful reason for his having hated Mr Bradan?'

'You mean the loss of his brother when that ship blew up? I think it could have been a bold bit of bluff.'

'In what way?'

'Well, it may have been a clever way of throwing dust in our eyes, I think. In other words, he had a strong motive for killing Bradan and he presents us with a completely phony one instead. It would have put quite a lot of people off the scent, I should imagine.'

'Possibly. I wonder whether he really had a brother on that ship?' said Dame Beatrice. 'Of course,' she added, 'you have not forgotten that Mrs Grant, on the first occasion you met her, made no secret of the fact that she, as well as her husband, hated Mr Bradan?'

'No, I haven't forgotten,' said Laura. She was sitting up straight by this time and her settee faced the window. 'Here comes a motor-cyclist. Can it be – yes, it is.'

'Our young friend Grant?'

'And as wet as a fish. Here he comes.'

'And there was nobody named Grant among the lost crew of the *Saracen,* you remember? But, as we said, that may mean nothing. So many people, even respectable ones, go under an *alias* nowadays.'

'I don't know what you're getting at,' said Laura.

'Well, as I said, it might pay to confess to having a motive for a crime which you cannot possibly have committed, in order to confuse the issue of one which you certainly *could* have committed and which, in point of fact, you did help to commit. I speak merely theoretically, of course.'

'Like hell you do,' said Laura.

CHAPTER EIGHTEEN

Young Grant Comes Not Quite Clean

'The Doctor examined carefully the body of the
dead man. The face of the corpse was distorted and
looked horrible in the candle-light.
' "Shot?" said the Inspector laconically.
' "No," replied the Doctor.'

Barry Pain

YOUNG Grant had shed his waterproof motor-cycling outfit
in the outer vestibule of the hotel. He came forward
buoyantly, bowed to the ladies and was asked to sit down.
Laura went to the bar and ordered him a large whisky.

'And now,' she said, 'what about coming clean?'

'I'd like to,' said young Grant. 'It's about time I shed
the load. Somebody took a pop at me as I came here.
Luckily he missed me and missed my tyres, but it just goes
to show.'

'You were fired on?' asked Dame Beatrice, interested.
'Where did this take place?'

'Not long after I left Crioch. I was passing little Loch
Breac, which is screened, you'll likely know, by bushes——'

'Did you see your adversary?'

'No. I had gone past him when he fired, and although
I have a mirror on the handlebars it was no good to me
in all this rain.'

'Have you decided who it was?'

'The likeliest would be the man Macbeth.'

'Oh? What makes you think so?'

'Wait until you hear my tale, and maybe you'll think so,
too. Oh, and I have an item of news which may interest

189

you. The police have arrested Cosmo Bradan, the dead man's son.'

'Have they, indeed? Then the man who fired at you could not have been he and could not have known of the arrest.'

'That will be so. Mind you, the arrest may be a sort of smoke-screen. It may make the murderer careless.'

'By the murderer, you mean the man who killed Mr Bradan, of course?'

'Whom else should I mean?'

'Do you not remember confirming Mrs Gavin's report of the Edinburgh murder?'

'Oh, yes, certainly. But there would be no reason to suspect Cosmo Bradan of being concerned in that. I told you I saw who did it, and I told you that I should certainly recognise him again.'

'Well, let us have your story. Is it to be the *whole* truth this time? I must tell you that we know all about the *skian-dhu*.'

'You do?'

'And, to clear up a point which has baffled us, do tell us how Mr Bradan was killed.

'I will, so. And this time you shall hear the whole truth. I shall begin with the trouble in Edinburgh. As I told you, I was there to report the Conference in which, Dame Beatrice, you (if I may say so) were a leading light. Well, that left me, as I have also said, with time on my hands, and it was in one of those times that I met a man from Newhaven named Dorg. When he knew that I was a journalist and worked in Freagair he said he had a news item for me.

'Well, I have ambitions, like most people, so I bought him some drinks and, with them, his information. I was disappointed, in a way, for there seemed nothing to print of what he said. He was telling me about some tramp steamers that he thought were gey mysterious in their comings and goings. I speired at him in what way they were mysterious, but, although I plied him with enough whisky to loosen the tongue of anybody but a Dutchman, I could get nothing out of him but an invitation to go and see for myself. I went, but there was nobody able to tell me anything, so I telephoned the Edinburgh office of the *Caledonia* and asked them what they knew of ships under the names Dorg had given me. They had nothing to tell me except that they were owned by a man named Bradan of Tannasgan.

'Well, this had some sort of local interest for the people of my district, I thought, so I thanked them for their information and went back to my lodgings to write up my piece about the Conference and another (rather imaginative) piece about the ships.'

'Which was never published?' asked Dame Beatrice.

'Luckily for me, I'm beginning to think. No, I needed something straight from the horse's mouth – that is, from Bradan himself.'

'Ah, yes, now.' Dame Beatrice, who had produced her notebook, turned back to a former entry. 'Let me remind you of a statement you made at Inversnaid.'

'Please do not !'

'I am not teasing. You claimed that Cù Dubh, as Mr Bradan was sometimes called, died just as you were tying up the boat to set Mrs Gavin ashore. That was, or was not, true?'

'It was not true. That is, it may have been, but I just don't know.'

'I suppose it was because of the *skian-dhu* that you were anxious to persuade Mrs Gavin to give you an alibi. We know a considerable amount about that visit of yours to Tannasgan. That, I may tell you, is a warning.'

'Spare me! I've promised to tell the whole truth.'

'And I am prepared to help you to do so,' said Dame Beatrice. 'We must clear away the mist.'

'By which token, it's stopped raining,' said Laura. 'And what about all that phoney stuff you told us about Corrie being your uncle and getting you a job as *saboteur* at the hydro-electric works near Tigh-Òsda?'

Young Grant laughed uncomfortably.

'I didna really think you'd swallow that,' he said. 'Anyhow, it was put right afterwards, when you found out what my real job was.'

'No thanks to *you* that we did,' said Laura sternly. 'You seem to have acted as a liar and a fool all the way through.'

'I was able to back up your story about the man who was murdered in Edinburgh by being pushed under a car, though, was I not?'

'Pity you don't know who he was.'

'But I *do* know. It was Dorg.'

'Really?' said Dame Beatrice. 'I saw the report in the Edinburgh papers. It was not given much prominence and I should not have been particularly interested except for Mrs Gavin's insistence that it was murder. The name of the dead man was given' – she flipped back another two or three pages – 'as Grant. Quite a coincidence, I feel.'

'It was Dorg,' insisted Grant, 'and one of his murderers was employed by Cù Dubh, as I told you.'

'That sounds as though Dorg was one of Bradan's men, then,' said Laura. 'I wonder who named him as Grant?'

'He might have had papers on him in that name.'

'If he was mixed up in something shady, that's quite likely, I suppose. Do you think he was killed because he had been seen talking to you and perhaps giving away secrets?'

'I do not. If that had been the case, they would not have waited until now to shoot at me. Oh, no! I am certain in my own mind that Macbeth was behind that gun.'

'I suppose the shot *was* intended for you? You don't think it may have been some misguided sportsman potting at something on the other side of the road?'

Young Grant shook his head.

'I do not.'

'Well, you have one good friend in the world, at any rate,' said Dame Beatrice briskly. 'Do you remember Mr Curtis, a travelling salesman for a firm of horticulturalists?'

'Curtis? Oh, yes. An English laddie. I ken him very well. Many's the crack we've had together when he was travelling through Crioch to Gàradh. So he spoke up for me, did he?'

'He indicated that you were harmless. Let us come now to the story you told us at Gàradh. First, what about your determination to blackmail Mr Bradan?'

'That bit was true enough, but I badly needed my story.'

'And your assertion that you made the long journey between Edinburgh and Loch na Gréine on various evenings?'

'Well, there, I admit I did telescope the time a little, but otherwise what I said was true enough. The evening after I had seen Dorg murdered in Edinburgh I motor-cycled to Inverness and spent the night there, before going on to Loch na Gréine to tackle Bradan.'

'One moment! On the Friday afternoon when that Edinburgh murder took place, my Conference had not begun. What, then, were you doing in Edinburgh?'

'Well, as I told you, I wanted to interview some of the notables in their hotels before the Conference started.'

'I see. Now, just let me check some other facts against these things that you are telling me. This death in Edinburgh took place on a Friday, as I have said. Mrs Gavin and I left my home in Hampshire on the previous Wednesday and made a leisurely progress northward. On the Saturday we went sightseeing in Edinburgh, then we spent a quiet Sunday, and the Conference opened at ten o'clock on the Monday morning.'

'Yes, I reported the opening. I can show you my piece in the *Advertiser*. I posted it off immediately after lunch.'

'I see. But, before you reported the opening of the Conference, you had been to Tannasgan. Is that right?'

'Oh, well – no. Not *before* I reported the opening.'

'Please take your time, but you *did* say that on the evening following that on which you had seen Dorg murdered you motor-cycled to Inverness, did you not?'

Grant flushed and scowled.

'Very well,' he said, the scowl changing suddenly to a smile. 'Maybe I'm mixing up the days. What day would it be when I first met Mrs Gavin on Tannasgan?'

Laura glanced at Dame Beatrice and received a nod.

'Let's see,' she said. 'Pitlochry on the Monday, Kingussie on the Tuesday, Inverness on the Wednesday, Freagair on the Thursday. Then on the Friday I motored over to Gàradh to visit Mrs Stewart and stayed the night at Coinneamh Lodge. I drove back to Freagair on the Saturday morning and went to Tannasgan the same afternoon, then got back to Freagair late at night after you'd rowed me ashore and we heard the piping.'

'So we need an account of your adventures on that Saturday and the preceding Friday,' said Dame Beatrice to Grant. 'Pray relate to us what happened after you left Inverness. Can you now recollect which day that would have been?'

'Yes, I can work it out, I think. I took two days – well, one evening and part of the next day – to get to Loch na Gréine and I spent the rest of that day and all the next day on Tannasgan, waiting for Cù Dubh to come home. That means I got to Inverness on the Thursday after I'd written up my report on that session of the Conference. So I must have arrived off Tannasgan on the Friday afternoon, camped out – Mrs Corrie gave me my bread, the good woman – here and there, out of sight of old Macbeth, spent Friday night in the boathouse and – and was in hiding there on Saturday night when Mrs Gavin decided to go back to Freagair.'

'And at what point did you see the dead laird?'

'He was brought back on the Saturday.'

'Who brought him?'

'Who but Corrie?'

'Really? Corrie brought his body across to Tannasgan?'

'He did that. You can ask him if you don't believe me.'

'We have heard Corrie's story.'

'You mean he didn't mention the dead man?'

'He told us that Mr Bradan was alive after Mrs Gavin arrived on Tannasgan.'

'Then he was lying. I tell you it was a *dead* man Corrie ferried over the water.'

'Come, come!' protested Dame Beatrice, giving him a rather unkindly leer. 'Corrie waited with the boat and Mr Bradan turned up at the jetty in the station-master's car. That is his story and I am bound to point out that it is a considerably more sensible one than your own.'

'Have it your own way,' said the young man sulkily.

'But I don't want to. His is the more sensible, but yours is by far the more sensational. Why not tell us the rest of it?'

'There is nothing more to tell.'

'When did you produce your *skian-dhu*?'

'I really forget.'

'And what were you doing with one, anyway.'

'I was wearing the philibeg!'

'Not when I saw you in the boathouse,' said Laura austerely. 'You weren't wearing a kilt then.'

'Was I not?'

195

'You know you weren't. Why on earth don't you come clean and stop wasting our time?'

'Because I don't trust you,' said Grant wildly. 'I don't trust either of you. You'll get me tried for murder if you can. But you've the inspector to reckon with. Do not forget that he kens very well when and where Bradan was murdered and I am telling you that it was a dead man who was brought to Tannasgan that night.'

'And Corrie brought him?' asked Dame Beatrice in a pacific tone which warned Laura not to lose her temper.

'Corrie brought him?' Young Grant asked the question in a stupefied tone. 'I do not know. I canna say. Who else would have brought him? I had better go.'

'There is only one answer to that,' said Dame Beatrice, when he had flung himself out of the lounge. 'Well, he has missed his lunch here. I wonder how much of the truth he knows and how much of it he has told?'

'I really believe he thinks it *was* a dead man who was brought across to Tannasgan that night,' said Laura. Dame Beatrice shook her head, but Laura, unperturbed by this, went on, 'What's more, it must have happened before I left. It was sheer instinct that made me flee the place, I suppose. If only you had been there, instead of me, we wouldn't have had this mystery on our hands.'

'But how much more empty our lives would have been without it,' said Dame Beatrice. 'We could not have prevented the murders, but we can appreciate the puzzle they present.'

'We're still no further forward.'

'Are we not? Suppose that young Mr Grant *was* speaking the truth?'

'Oh, you mean . . . ? Well, what do you mean, Dame B? Have we come to a full stop, do you suppose?'

'By no means,' said Dame Beatrice comfortably. 'For one thing, there is a witness whom we've never contacted.'

'Really? You've got me worried. I thought we'd inter-viewed everybody who might be of the slightest use.'

'Cast your mind back to your first visit to Mrs Stewart at Gàradh.'

'Yes, well, while I was at Gàradh, Mrs Stewart happened to mention that her son had had business dealings with Cù Dubh.'

'Those might be of interest, don't you think?'

'Lord!' said Laura remorsefully. 'It's awful of me to have forgotten it all this time, but I've never given it another thought.'

'There can have been no association of ideas in your mind, that is all. Besides, it is never too late to mend! Pray tell me again what Mrs Stewart said.'

'It isn't so much, really. She just said that her son had had some business to conclude and had invited Bradan to join the house-party at Gàradh and that they had been snowed-up there for a fortnight and she didn't like Bradan at all, but that he had given her some pretty decent rock plants, although she thought it was her son's idea.'

'Excellent. We must return to London forthwith, for I have discovered from his mother, over the telephone, that Alexander Stewart is staying in London on business for his Edinburgh firm. I have the address and have sent him a telegram. I hope he will be able to call.'

'I should have thought of him before,' said Laura.

'Not at all, child. The matter has arisen at the crucial time. Besides, I shall be delighted to meet the young man again.'

'I doubt whether he'll be able to tell us any more than, I suppose, he's told the inspector here, you know,' said Laura. 'I mean, the police are sure to know about the business side of it by this time.'

Morning found them heading south, behind the sturdy,

reassuring back of George, through the Moorfoot hills and by way of Carter Bar. As they left the Border country, Laura was moved to declaim:

> 'O wha will shoe my bonny foot?
> And wha will glove my hand?
> And wha will bind my middle jimp
> Wi' a lang, lang linen band?
> O wha will kame my yellow hair
> Wi' a haw barberry kame?
> And wha will be my bairn's father
> Till Gregory come hame?'

Dame Beatrice looked slightly startled by this confession that Laura was beginning to miss her husband, and insisted on stopping at Newcastle for lunch. They spent the night at Harrogate and were back in Dame Beatrice's Kensington house by tea-time on the following day. From here Laura telephoned Alexander Stewart and received his promise that he would be round to see Dame Beatrice at soon after nine that evening.

He was as good as his word and presented himself, a fair-haired, tall man of about thirty, at nine-ten. Célestine, Dame Beatrice's French servant, showed him in with an inappropriate but obviously excited:

'Monsieur Stewart baisse les mains à madame!'

'Does he, indeed? Very Spanish of him,' said Dame Beatrice, holding out her somewhat monstrously bejewelled hands and embracing the young man warmly instead of allowing him to kiss her fingers. 'And what are you doing in these borrowed French and Spanish plumes, my gay Lothario?'

Célestine, long a trusted and uninhibited member of Dame Beatrice's household, stifled a giggle and withdrew to the kitchen where her husband, a superb and not particularly temperamental chef, was preparing a meal. As usual, as he cooked, he was alternately praising Laura's appetite and lamenting that of Dame Beatrice.

'This one,' his wife stated, describing Stewart, 'is, like all the Scots, demented but adorable.'

'But yes,' said Henri, busy with his own thoughts.

Meanwhile, the demented but adorable Scot under review was being introduced to Laura. His mother, he told her, had written eulogistically about the visits to Gàradh and had expressed the hope that these would occur often. The courtesies having been exchanged, he was provided with a drink and called to order.

'What do you know of a man named Bradan of Tannasgan?' demanded Dame Beatrice.

'Murdered, and then put into an empty hogshead, or whatever you call it, of rum? I knew him, in a sort of business way, very well.'

'Expound.'

'I met him first when I was working up a connection to export dried fish to the Canaries in exchange for bananas. It went all right for a bit, but then the ships – all owned or partly owned by him – seemed an unreasonable time in getting back, and I felt that my firm was losing money and – just as important – goodwill. In the end I stood him off and went to Liverpool for a tender. Their ideas tied in with mine, so I blew Bradan's lot a nice fat raspberry and our relationship ended, just like that.'

'You mean that you realised . . .'

'No, not really. I just thought they were plucking me for a pigeon, and I didn't want to be stood up, that was all.'

'You have never received threatening letters from them?'

Stewart looked surprised.

'Gracious, no!' he replied. 'There was a wee bit of a fuss when I turned them down, but I received the impression that they were just as pleased to see the back of me as I was to see the back of them.'

199

'And when did the break take place?' Dame Beatrice enquired. Stewart wrinkled his brow.

'Oh, a couple of years ago. Yes, about that.'

'Do you remember asking Bradan to stay a day or two at your mother's house at Gàradh?'

'Yes, yes. There was snow. I got away in time, but I believe Bradan was snowed up there for a week or a fortnight. My mother was not very pleased. She did not take to Bradan overmuch.'

'You are right. Is there any reason to think that this forcible exile at Gàradh upset any particular plans made by Mr Bradan?'

'I think not. He told me once that his real business was carried on only in the summer. Something to do with tourists, I understood.'

'Do you carry on your own export business during the winter?'

'Not really. In the winter we mostly do coastal trips, picking up cargo where we can. We carry coal, pit-props and light machinery and make out in a hand-to-mouth sort of way until the Atlantic gets reasonable enough for our rather small ships. Oh, and sometimes we carry potatoes.'

'I see. I hesitate to use the word because I think it is used (in the sense I am about to use it) out of context, but did you ever form the opinion that some, if not all, of Mr Bradan's activities were – *crooked*?'

Stewart frowned thoughtfully.

'Crooked?' he repeated. 'I don't know. Now that you say it, I can see that they might have been, but, as we were not affected in any way except for the excessively slow turn-round (as it seemed to us) of his ships, I can't say that I thought one way or the other about his general business dealings. There isn't time to, you know. So long as the other party isn't doing you down, I'm afraid you don't worry.'

'Yes, I see. Well, thank you very much for your help, my dear Alexander.'

'I'm afraid it hasn't really been of much help, Dame Beatrice, but if there is ever anything else I can do . . .'

'Yes, there is,' said Laura, surprising both herself and her employer. 'What do you know about a red-haired, red-bearded man, obviously cuckoo, who calls himself Malcolm Donalbain Macbeth?'

'Obviously cuckoo?' Stewart considered this description with a truly Scottish mixture of humour and concern. 'Oh, dear, oh, dear!'

'You know him, then?' asked Laura, pressing her point.

'I met him once, and I agree with you.'

'Well, what do you know of him?'

'That he's a great reader of strange tales.'

'Would these strange tales include stories of fabulous beasts?' asked Dame Beatrice. Stewart looked doubtful.

'What kind of fabulous beasts?' he asked. Dame Beatrice looked at Laura.

'Oh, the basilisk, and those sort of things,' she said. Stewart looked astonished.

'You wouldn't be referring to the lion and the unicorn?' he asked. Laura looked to Dame Beatrice for guidance and her employer nodded to her to answer.

'Not so far as I know,' said Laura. 'One of Bradan's ships went up in smoke – the *Salamander*. Did you hear about that?'

Stewart shook his head.

'I have never heard of such a ship,' he said. 'The *Salamander*? No, that is new to me. What more do you require me to tell you?'

'I have no idea. Can you say anything more about the enforced holiday that Mr Bradan spent at Gàradh?'

'I don't know of anything more, beyond what I've already said. I asked him there because, as you will know, there is a relaxed atmosphere at Gàradh and I hoped to be able to get him to make some concessions.'

'In what way?'

'Well, to be a bit easier on the freight charges and all that sort of thing. We used his ships, of course, because our own could not carry all we wanted.'

'Were you hopeful of success?'

'Oh, well, I felt it was worth trying, you know. I was in a position to offer him a fairly substantial increase of business if he could agree to our terms.'

'And how did the negotiations go?'

'Not particularly well. The snow finished matters, I'm afraid. He was a man of few resources and I don't think, during that fortnight, he knew what on earth to do with himself between meals. He didn't care for billiards or snooker and there was nobody at Gàradh anything like as clever at cards as he was.'

'Surely that was a source of satisfaction to him?'

'Well, no. You see, my mother will not allow gambling in her house, not even for the most trifling stakes and, as it *is* her own house, her word is law. When we discovered what a brilliant player he was, I don't think anyone was sorry. I thought you would have known of her little foible in that respect.'

'I do not play cards,' said Dame Beatrice. 'I have always thought card games a waste of time and intelligence.'

'Well, well, so they are, maybe. Then, Bradan was no reader, except of newspapers, and those, of course, could not be got at in that weather. The telephone was off, too, and the man became more and more morose. I am afraid he sorely taxed my mother's patience.'

'You said, I think, that you were not snowed up with him.'

'As it happened, I was not. I had to go to Edinburgh on business and was expected back, but then came the blizzards and I could not make it. When I did manage to get through, I found a very disgruntled Bradan, with his bags packed, just ready to go. It was hopeless to reopen our business conversations. I could see that. I felt it would be wiser to give him time to cool off before I mentioned the matter again. His last words to me were that my invitation to him to visit Gàradh had lost him a business deal worth ten thousand pounds. Oh, he wasn't pleased with me. He wasn't pleased at all.'

'Yet he sent your mother some plants for her rock garden.'

Stewart's eyes twinkled.

'Oh, that!' he said. 'No, no. I let my mother think so, because if she'd known that I bought them myself as a wee bit of compensation to her for having had to put up with the curmudgeonly old fellow, she would have been vexed at my extravagance.' He laughed. 'It amazed me to discover what you can pay for rare little plants for a rockery.'

'And did you ever get the chance to reopen negotiations with Mr Bradan?'

'I tried again, three months later. I visited him on Tannasgan. He was curt to the point of rudeness and told me, in the most uncouth manner, to take my business elsewhere. He was not prepared to carry our extra freight any longer.'

'Really? And what did you deduce from that?'

'As I think I said, there was not much doubt but that he wanted to get rid of us, having found some more lucrative use for his ships. I guessed it might be something questionable, but that was none of my business and I'd found another connection, anyway, in case he should refuse to play ball.'

'You were well out of it,' said Laura. 'I'd like you to meet my husband at some time.'

'It will be a pleasure,' said Stewart courteously.

'You say you visited Tannasgan,' said Dame Beatrice. 'Can you tell me whether anyone besides the laird was living at An Tigh Mór?'

'There were two servants, a man and his wife, named Corrie, Bradan's son (with whom, it struck me, he was at loggerheads) and a rather curious character with red hair and a red beard – a tall, thin man wearing a kilt in a tartan which he said was of his own designing (and I can well believe it!), who told me that, although he had been introduced to me as Bradan's cousin, he was, in fact, the poet Ossian. He was, of course, M. D. Macbeth.'

'Mad, would you say?' enquired Laura. 'He introduced himself to us by the same fancy name.'

'An eccentric; not, I thought, mad. Maybe he had a quirky sense of humour.'

'Not a pawky one?'

'No, no. Mind you, Mrs Gavin, he appeared to take himself very seriously, but it is characteristic of the Scots to be able to keep the solemn face of an elder of the kirk when they're telling a funny story.'

Laura herself had not this gift. She had lived in England too long for that, but she agreed with the observation and, to show this, she gave a vigorous nod of approval.

'On what terms were the poet Ossian and Mr Bradan?' Dame Beatrice enquired.

'On very good terms, I would say. I cannot recall any particular happening or conversation which may have caused me to think so, but the general impression was of two men in harmony. Their relationship was in contrast to the relationship of father and son.'

'How did you yourself get on with Ossian?'

'He seemed an agreeable although an eccentric fellow, but I was so much incensed by Bradan's attitude that I did not stay very long.'

'Who took you across the loch to the island?' asked Laura.

'Who but Bradan himself? He said he liked to scrutinise his guests before he allowed them to land.'

'Oh, yes, so we heard. Who rowed you back across the loch?'

'Oh, Corrie.'

'Did you find him taciturn?' asked Dame Beatrice.

'Yes, to some extent. He broke silence to ask me whether I'd got what I had come for, and I told him that I had not, to which he replied that nobody ever did who had dealings with Cù Dubh.'

'Did he actually call him that?' asked Laura, interested in this unfeudal appellation.

'He did, indeed. I thought it an apt description.'

'Black Dog?' said Laura. 'Oh, yes! But Black Dog was in *Treasure Island*.'

'Ah, but not *on* it,' said Dame Beatrice, 'and that, you know, may prove to be a very significant fact – or, of course, of no importance to us whatsoever.'

'*Treasure Island?*' said Stewart. 'One never knows.'

CHAPTER NINETEEN

The Prodigal Son

'From here the cold white mist can be discerned.'
Matthew Arnold

'WELL!' said Laura, when she and Dame Beatrice were again alone together. 'What did you make of that?'

'I do not think that Mrs Stewart's son can help us any more than he has done. He told us what he could and it has not got us very much farther.'

'What business do you think he had with Bradan?'

'Just what he said. In other words, Mr Bradan's firm was acting as a kind of carrier's service. Beyond that, it was not for Stewart's firm to enquire. I can see that Bradan's business was perfectly respectable at first, but became illegal later.'

'I wonder what Stewart's did when they knew they'd lost the service?'

'I imagine that the other directors were just as much relieved as Stewart was. Firms with a good reputation do not care to be mixed up with even the mildest of shady transactions, and there must have come a point when Stewart's became suspicious.'

'What do we do now?'

'Well, of course, we might endeavour to contact Mr Bradan's son.'

'But he's in prison.'

'It might be interesting to hear his story. But, if I mistake not, I hear our dear Robert at the door.'

'Well, I'm dashed!' said Laura. Her husband was shown in by Célestine. 'What are *you* doing here?'

'Come to eat you, my dear,' stated Detective Chief-Inspector Robert Gavin, fondly embracing his wife. 'How *is* the girl, after all this time?'

'None the better for seeing *you*,' responded his loving spouse. 'Well, what's the news?'

'Very interesting,' said Gavin. 'Meanwhile, what's to eat?' Célestine, summoned from the kitchen, reported that Monsieur Robert's wishes had been complied with, and that a steak and kidney pudding would be at Monsieur Robert's disposal, together with potatoes and greens, in a matter of minutes.

'Oh, many cheers,' said Gavin. 'Just what the doctor ordered.'

'It is as *monsieur* ordered,' retorted Célestine, tossing herself out. 'Over the telephone today.'

'I envy you, Dame Beatrice,' said Gavin. 'Your household never seems to change, except for my wife, who's getting fat.' Laura hit him over the head with a folded newspaper.

'And now, precious idiot, expound. We've been told of your exploits. Be precise,' she said.

'Well, I can't be terribly precise,' said Gavin, relapsing into gravity. 'I don't think that what we've found out will do your case much good, Dame Beatrice. I don't really believe that the rum-running, or even the arms racket, has anything to do with Bradan's death.'

'As I supposed,' said Dame Beatrice. 'But I think I hear your meal going in. Away and sup. We will hear more when you are refreshed.'

'Looks well, doesn't he?' said Laura, when her handsome husband had taken himself off to the dining-room. 'Very bronzed and sunburnt.'

Dame Beatrice agreed.

'I wonder how much money Mr Bradan left?' she added. Laura looked surprised.

'I thought we'd decided it was a revenge job. I certainly

had that impression,' she said. 'Hadn't we discarded the idea of a murder for gain?'

'Well, it would not have been the first of those, child.'

'I suppose,' said Laura thoughtfully, 'that rum-running and gun-running could be pretty lucrative. Yes, it's quite an idea you have there. The only thing about all this which puzzles me – apart from the identity of the murderer, of course – is why you think the police are wrong about Bradan's son. You *do* think they're wrong, don't you?'

'What causes you to ask such a question?'

'Oh, come, now, Mrs Croc. dear! If you thought they were right, you wouldn't still be spending time on the case. Besides, as the police have pinched young Bradan and stuck him in the nick, they must believe that the murder was done for revenge on his part because he'd been disinherited. Now you think it was done to get Bradan's money, and *that* looks like Macbeth.'

'We shall know more when we find out how much Mr Bradan had to leave and exactly how he left it.'

'I'd still like to know more about how the body got on to the island, or, in fact, whether it did. Do you suppose the inspector knows? If he does, he may not tell us. I suppose you're going to use Gavin as a sort of stool-pigeon when we get to Edinburgh.'

'I am not certain that I understand you.'

'Go on with you! Of course you understand me. Gavin is to be our surety. The inspector will be tickled to death to meet him, and will spill all sorts of beans.'

'Possibly in private to our Robert, but with a suggestion that the disclosures are for no ears but Robert's own.'

'Oh, no, that would be too bad. Anyway, he would naturally suppose that Gavin would pass the gen to the wife of his bosom.'

'I am not at all sure about that, and, even if it were so,

it might not be possible for the said wife to pass on the information to a third party – myself.'

'Oh, well, let's not cross any bridges until we come to them. I'll go into the dining-room and tell him what we expect, shall I?'

At this transparent excuse for Laura to have her husband to herself for a bit, Dame Beatrice cackled, but not until Laura had gone out of the room. At the end of about three-quarters of an hour the two returned and seated themselves. Gavin gently patted his stomach.

'Best meal I've had since I dined here last time,' he said. 'And now, Dame B., I am at your service.'

'Well, what can you tell us?'

'As I said before, very little that can help you. We found out – thanks to Laura and my own rather talented young son – that there were some interesting goings-on in the West Indies and so on with regard to liquor and guns, but what on earth can be the connection between them and the death of Bradan is, at present, beyond conjecture. In fact, nothing ties up.'

'I'd better tell you about the Edinburgh murder,' said Laura.

'But, my dear girl, one doesn't murder people in Edinburgh nowadays,' said Gavin, looking incredulous. 'It's no longer done, particularly since the introduction of the Festival.'

'Oh, no?' said Laura. 'Well, big boy, listen to this.' She gave him a vivid but not an exaggerated account of the street death she had witnessed. 'Mrs Croc. was not impressed at first,' she concluded, 'but now I think she believes that what I said was true. It's been confirmed, you see, by an impartial and independent witness.' She went on to tell of their various encounters with the young reporter Grant. Gavin listened without interrupting her until she concluded with the words : 'So you see.'

'Um – yes,' he said. 'I do see. Pity he doesn't know, or won't give, the name of this chap he says he recognised. The fact that he says the chap was in Bradan's employment doesn't help much, as you point out. Got any theories, Dame B.?'

'Well, I have formed some during the investigation (which, now, properly, I should give up), but there is no proof.'

'Why should you give up?'

'Because I began it only to make certain that Laura was not arrested,' replied Dame Beatrice, accompanying, or, rather, concluding, this statement with her unnerving cackle.

'Laura?'

'Well, yes,' his wife admitted. 'I was on the island more or less at the time of Bradan's murder and my story of *why* I was there would have sounded pretty thin in court.'

'And now?'

'Since we have met the inspector, I am no longer concerned for Laura's safety,' said Dame Beatrice.

'What were you doing on the island, anyway, chump?' demanded Gavin. Laura grinned.

'Getting wet. That is to say, I got wet and Bradan's son – I didn't know that's who it was at the time, but we found out afterwards – signalled the island and a huge old man with a terrific red beard brought a boat over and dried, warmed and fed me. But when he wanted to keep me on the island for a week I thought it was time to make my get-away. It was then that I first ran into this reporter. The rest of that story you know.'

'Nice goings-on for a respectable wife and mother! When are you going to grow up?'

'Anyway, now you know it all, what are you going to do?' demanded Laura, ignoring the criticism.

'With Dame B.'s permission, I am going to use her telephone and ring up Edinburgh.'

Dame Beatrice nodded, and he went out of the room.

'Wonder what his idea is?' said Laura.

'He is going to find out whether young Bradan has been arrested for murdering his father, or for some other reason,' said Dame Beatrice. This inspired guess turned out to be correct. Gavin came back looking pleased with himself.

'Well, dog with two tails?' said his wife. Gavin slumped into a chair and spread his long legs over the hearth-rug.

'What do you think?' he asked. Laura, from the opposite side of the fireplace, kicked his ankle. 'Oh, well,' he said resignedly, 'if you're in militant mood, you'd better know all. There's no secret about it. Young Bradan is held in custody for assaulting the police.'

'Really? I shouldn't have thought he had it in him,' said Laura. 'Exactly what did he do?'

'He appears to have gone berserk when your friend Macbeth of the flaming beard sent for the police to order him off Tannasgan, where he was not only trespassing——'

'Who cares about trespass?' demanded Laura, a keen supporter of Access to Mountains.

'Wait for it – but was destroying valuable property – viz. to wit, sculpture owned by the new laird of Tannasgan, Malcolm Donalbain Macbeth.'

'Sculpture? Not the fabulous beasts? And surely he didn't give that pseudonym to the police? I thought it was just his little joke.'

'Sculpture, yes. The fabulous beasts, yes. And his name really *is* Malcolm Donalbain Macbeth. He's got a birth certificate to prove it. So the police from Dingwall stepped in and young Bradan went all hysterical, I gather, and ran at them, brandishing a piece of one of the beasties. It appears that he got in a whack at the law which necessitated the insertion of eight stitches. So he got pinched and is up for trial charged with inflicting grievous bodily harm on a police constable while the latter was in the execution of his duty. He may also be wanted on an even more serious charge.'

'More serious than hitting a policeman? Why, he might have killed him with that chunk of stone,' said Laura. 'I've seen those fabulous beasts. They're tough babies.'

'As it happens – probably luckily for the bobby – it wasn't a lump of stone; it was a lump of metal.'

'Oh, dash it, not the basilisk! That was my favourite!'

'I've no idea what it was called. It's immaterial, anyway. The serious charge against Bradan was that, in his screaming hysterics, he accused Macbeth of assisting him, in Edinburgh, to push a man named Grant under a car so that the said Grant was killed.'

'Is Macbeth arrested too, then?'

'No. It seems that he was able to furnish the police with a complete alibi for that particular time. He was on Tannasgan, and Mrs Corrie swore to him. What is the man Corrie like, by the way?'

'Taciturn and unhelpful,' said Laura, 'but, I should say, honest and loyal and all those things which old-fashioned retainers used to be, and which present-day servants on the whole are not.'

'So you don't think that *Corrie* would have had anything to do with shoving that man under the car?'

'It doesn't seem very likely to me, but I've nothing to go on except instinct.'

'Instinct is not often at fault,' said Gavin thoughtfully, 'and I'd usually trust yours. Anyway, that's all I know and I have work to do. I've been away too long and I have a consultation tomorrow with the Assistant Commissioner about some robberies in – er – well, about some robberies.' He grinned into his wife's furious face. 'No, really, Laura,' he added, 'there's nothing more I can do for you. With the end of Bradan, I think his schemes will just die a natural death. As for his murder, well, that isn't my pigeon.' He glanced at his watch. 'I'm afraid I must go. Apart from seeing the Assistant Commissioner, I seem to have a date with a citizen named Good Egg Symes, who guarantees – for what it is worth – to tip us off about a job that was done in the West End two nights ago. It was a smash and grab. Friend Symes was unlucky enough to receive the smash – in the form of an empty milk-bottle which a scared nightwatchman slung at him – but failed to obtain the grab.'

'His pals welshed on him?' enquired Laura, deeply fascinated by this unadorned and artless history.

'Apparently his reactions to having been struck by the bottle were so positive that they had to make their getaway before the job was done. Their attitude after that was such that he came to us for protection. We shall protect the little lost sheep, of course, but I don't give much for his chances when his pals have served their time.'

'I am sorry that you cannot stay with us here,' said Dame Beatrice. 'Your help would have been invaluable, especially now that there is no reason, apart from what the Americans, I believe, call ornery curiosity, for me to interest myself any further in Mr Bradan's death.'

'You had better carry on,' said Gavin, 'both of you. I can't tell you any more, but if I can get up to Scotland when we've hard-boiled Good Egg Symes I will most certainly do so.'

Laura and Dame Beatrice headed for the north again next day. Laura thought that they were making for Edinburgh until lunch-time, when Dame Beatrice suggested to George that the car turn off at Stamford for Ilkley and Kirkby Lonsdale instead of travelling through Harrogate to Durham.

It soon became clear to Laura that her employer was in

a hurry. Instead of the leisurely journeys, both north and south, which had been indulged in so far, it was not until they arrived in Carlisle by way of Grantham and Appleby that Dame Beatrice had the car pulled up for the night stop, and it was barely five minutes past nine when they were off again on the following morning. They lunched in Glasgow and the second night was spent at Blair Atholl. On the third day they drove through the quiet town of Freagair to the shores of Loch na Gréine.

Here, to Laura's astonishment, Dame Beatrice did nothing at first except gaze across at Tannasgan and An Tigh Mór through the field-glasses which she had brought with her. 'Do you see anything, Sister Ann?' she enquired, handing the glasses to Laura.

'What am I expected to see?' enquired Laura, obediently training the glasses on to the island.

'No, no. You must keep an open mind.'

'Well, I don't see anything at all that I haven't seen before, i.e. the boathouse and An Tigh Mór. Shall I signal the island in the usual manner?'

'It might be a little difficult,' Dame Beatrice pointed out. Laura lowered the glasses and became aware that the tarpaulin and its stones, the handbell it had protected and the red and green lantern had all disappeared.

'So old Macbeth *has* been arrested,' said Laura.

'At any rate, someone is still at An Tigh Mór, for there is smoke arising from the house.'

'Well, anyway, how do we get across now that the bell and the lantern have gone? Do you want me to yodel or something?'

Dame Beatrice gazed at her in admiration.

'What an excellent idea,' she said. 'Yodel, by all means. I had no idea that you could, and that is no reflection upon your not inconsiderable gifts.'

'Do you mean it? Then here goes,' said Laura. The ensuing sounds cleft the air and, it was soon obvious, reached the other side of the loch. A man came hurrying down to the boathouse. It was Corrie. 'It's not Macbeth anyway,' said Laura, 'so it looks as though he isn't here.'

'We must wait and see,' said Dame Beatrice.

Corrie pushed off from the island and rowed across to them.

'What would ye?' he enquired, when he had tied up the boat and approached them.

'Speech with the laird,' said Dame Beatrice, eyeing him in a way he did not like.

'The laird? Ye'll be fortunate. I dinna ken the whereabouts of the laird.'

'What about *Treasure Island*?'

'I dinna ken what ye're speiring about.'

'No?' said Dame Beatrice. 'But I think you do, you know. Tell me, once and for all, what is the meaning of those fabulous animals on the wooded islands?'

'Fabulous animals? What kind of fabulous animals?'

'I suppose you were not the other man concerned in the Edinburgh murder?'

This question seemed to shake Corrie.

'What would that have been?' he asked feebly. Dame Beatrice pressed home what seemed to be an advantage.

'There are two independent witnesses of what you did, you and Grant of Coinneamh,' she said. 'The two of you pushed a man under a fast car. The man stood no chance of surviving. What have you to say about that?'

Corrie looked dumbfounded.

'But I have naething to say about it. I didna do it. I had nae part in it,' he said.

'All the same, you knew about it,' said Dame Beatrice, implacably. 'You overheard something.'

'I did, yes,' Corrie looked even more unhappy. 'But the old laird said that I should keep quiet.'

'The old laird is dead. What have you to tell us?'

'That there are things you'd never guess.'

'Really? There you are wrong, you know. I think that by this time we have guessed nearly everything. Why was the bronze or brass delineation of the basilisk the most important piece of sculpture on the wooded island over there? Moreover, what is the significance of the maze?'

Corrie shook his head.

'I dinna ken.'

'About the metal serpent, or the maze?'

'I hae nae knowledge of either. Will it please you to step into the boat?'

'It will.'

He handed them in with aloof, punctilious courtesy and sat at the oars. His choppy, almost vicious, strokes soon carried them across the water.

'Ye'll be for the house?' he asked doubtfully.

'We are for speaking with Mr Macbeth,' Dame Beatrice replied. Corrie shook his head again.

'He's no here.'

'You mean he is on the other island?'

Corrie stuck out an obstinate underlip.

'Gin ye'll wait in the house, maybe he'll come to you,' he said.

'You go and fetch him,' said Laura. 'I think we'd better wait here.'

'No, no,' said Dame Beatrice. 'Let it be the house. Never mind, Mr Corrie. We have been here before. We can find our own way.'

'Eh, well,' said Corrie. 'The door's open.' He repeated the words and added to them. 'The door's open and syne the spider will be walking in on ye.' For the first time since Laura had known him, he chuckled, a gnome-like, ghoulish sound.

'A bit of a sinister character, our friend, wouldn't you

say?' suggested Laura when, having left Corrie at the boat-house, they were walking up to the house. 'You don't *really* think he was one of the men who pushed that man under the car in Edinburgh, do you?'

'Reporter Grant's insistence that the other man was *employed* by Mr Bradan makes me feel that we cannot dismiss him from our minds.'

'And you believe that the other man was Grant of Coinneamh?'

'I think it is likely. I cannot put it more strongly than that. It may have been Bradan himself.'

'But Grant told us . . .'

'I know. We are not bound necessarily to believe him. Well, Corrie has spoken sooth. The door *is* open.'

They stood in the passage while Laura shouted to find out whether anybody was at home. From the door which led to the kitchen Mrs Corrie appeared. She was wiping her hands on her apron and, clean though it was, it appeared to be no whiter than her face.

'Save and presairve us!' she cried. 'Are ye in the flesh?'

'If you're asking whether we're ghosts, I can tell you that we most certainly are not,' retorted Laura. 'May we come in?'

Mrs Corrie's colour began to come back, but she still wiped nervous hands down her apron.

'Ay, certainly. Come ben,' she said. 'But, gin ye're for calling on the laird, ye've chosen a gey ill time, for he's abroad the day.'

'Yes, but he's expected back,' said Laura. 'We know well enough where he is.'

'Then ye ken mair aboot him than I,' said Mrs Corrie, with something of her old spirit. Laura laughed, but Dame Beatrice said seriously:

'Mrs Corrie, the Edinburgh police have been making enquiries into the death (supposed, at the time, to be accidental) of a man who was killed by a car. I believe they have questioned you about it.'

'They speired at me was the laird ben the house that day.'

'Exactly. You told them that he was.'

'It was the truth. All day, from sun-up to sun-down. He was here, and he had an Inverness gentleman with him and Corrie and I were called in to put our names to a paper.'

'Corrie and you? Both of you?'

'I dinna ken, Mrs Gavin, what way you would be surprised at that. Mind you, I'm no very sure, but I thought – ay, and Corrie thought – that the paper was maybe the laird's will.'

'At what time did you sign it?' asked Dame Beatrice.

'What time? Well, now, the tea – I infused the tea at four o'clock instead of five, because the gentleman wanted to get the Inverness train at Freagair – the tea was cleared at a quarter to five and before I could turn round and wash up the things I was brought back into the room and Corrie was called from splitting kindling wood beyond the hen-house, and we both signed the paper.'

'At soon after a quarter to five?'

'At very soon after a quarter to five. It wouldna have been five minutes after I carried out the trays.'

'I see. Thank you, Mrs Corrie,' said Dame Beatrice. 'Oh, one more question : do you happen to remember what day of the week it was?'

'The police asked me the date, and I remembered that it was the twenty-third.'

'Which *day* of the week was it?' asked Laura, reinforcing Dame Beatrice's question. 'Don't you remember that?'

'It wasna the Sabbath, anyway. Folk up here dinna do business on the Sabbath.'

'So you remember that it was the twenty-third, but not which day it was.'

'For the best of reasons. I mind it was the twenty-third because that was the date on the bottom of the paper.'

Laura laughed. Then she said, 'It might interest you to know——' she began.

'Or, rather, to tell us,' broke in Dame Beatrice, 'whether the present laird, Mr Macbeth, was on Tannasgan at the time.'

'Him? Oh, ay, he was here.'

'All the time?'

'Ay, all the time. I never listen ahint doors, mind ye, but the old laird and the present laird hae muckle big voices, and for twa days they had been talking about Tannasgan and the loch and An Tigh Mór.'

'And the young man? Young Mr Bradan?'

'That one had left Tannasgan lang syne. His father turned him out. Oh, it was an ill business, that, to disinherit and send awa' his only son.'

'Turned him out, you say. How had he offended his father?' asked Dame Beatrice.

'I dinna altogether ken. I think there were debts.'

'Oh, he was that kind of young man.'

'Then there was a lassie. I dinna ken the rights and wrongs of that, either, but when I was about to take in the dishes I heard the old laird say something about making a bed and lying on it, and the young man pleading that without siller he couldna marry on the lassie and make an honest woman of her.'

'But the old man didn't fall for that,' said Laura.

'He did not, indeed. When I went in to clear the table they were still at it and, when I got outside the door again, the old laird told him to get out and tramp the Edinburgh gutters with his fancy woman. It was all they were fit for, to sing in the street for bawbees.'

'Very Victorian. And has the young one ever been back?' asked Laura, interested in this hoary, classical, vintage tale.

219

'Ay, he's been back, but since his father's time, you ken. *And* he's been sent off again with a flea in his ear. The police was sent for and took him awa' with them. Ay, and such a carrying-on as he made! You never heard the like. Accusing here, accusing there! He even spoke against my man. Ay, but for the police my man would have dinged him in the neb.'

'Very proper,' said Laura. Taking this as a sign of dismissal, Mrs Corrie went back to her domain and Laura took Dame Beatrice into the dining-room. 'Why wouldn't you let me tell her that I'd seen the Edinburgh murder and that it did *not* take place on the twenty-third?' she asked, in a low voice, when she had shut the door and had moved away from it to the window.

'Witnesses to a murder are not invulnerable, and neither are people with inconveniently accurate memories. Mrs Corrie herself would not hurt you, but we cannot be certain that she would not talk. Apart from anyone else, she would mention the matter to her husband, you may be sure.'

'Oh, well – Hullo! here comes Macbeth, and from the Island of Strange Beasts, by the look of it. Corrie is just tying up the boat, so now the fun begins.'

CHAPTER TWENTY

Tannasgan Changes Hands

'What a haste looks through his eyes! So should he look
That seems to speak things strange.'

Shakespeare

MACBETH stalked up to the house. He was wearing a faded kilt in what Laura, as he approached, managed to identify as the Wemyss tartan. She was interested.

'The Wemyss family, according to Thomas Innes of Learney,' she explained to Dame Beatrice, 'is descended from a third son of Macduff, twelfth-century Earl of Fife. For a Macbeth to identify himself with a Macduff is interesting, don't you think? – although probably accidental, in this case.'

'I call it fascinating,' replied Dame Beatrice, her eyes not on Macbeth's kilt, however, but upon his sweating bare chest and, alternatively, on his extremely muddy brogues. 'I wonder what is the symbolic value of this latest excursion into history and literature, then?'

'Maybe none. He may have bought it second-hand. He never gives the impression of having any money.'

Macbeth clumped into the hall, followed by Corrie. There came a thunderous knock on the dining-room door and both men marched in.

'Well,' said Dame Beatrice, before anyone else could speak, 'you will catch cold in here, Mr Macbeth. Will you not go and get a good rub down with a rough towel and put a shirt on? You are perspiring very freely.'

'Ay, you shouldna be in the company of ladies. I tellt ye so,' said Corrie. 'Awa' and freshen.'

Crestfallen, Macbeth bowed to the said ladies and departed, followed by his henchman.

'What was the point?' asked Laura, amused by the proceedings.

'The poor man was too hot, both physically and mentally, for his company to be desirable or even tolerable, child. Now he will have time to cool off, in both senses, and we shall be able to converse reasonably with him.'

She was right. In about ten minutes' time a clean, dry, completely clad Macbeth returned to them. His demeanour, so far as could be said of that of such a bristling, red-bearded giant, was still chastened. He apologised, adding :

'I've done hard, dirty work without the reward I expected.'

'I am sorry to hear that,' said Dame Beatrice. 'I do hope our visit has not inconvenienced you.'

'No, no. I was for knocking off, anyway, when Corrie came over. Well, I have done what I could for the place. Tomorrow I must away.'

'You are thinking of leaving Tannasgan?'

'Well is it called Tannasgan! There's nothing here but ghosts. Ay, and they leave their promises behind them, and the promises are as ghostly as their makers. Besides, I'm in danger. The police have been here again. A great fool I was to call them in ! It's true that they've taken off Bradan's wee grilse. I hear he's for trial on a major charge. But the inspector stayed behind and speired at me again about Bradan's death. He means to pin that on me. I ken that very well.'

'I wouldn't run away. It looks bad,' said Dame Beatrice.

'What does the deer do if it gets wind of the stalker? I tell you, yon man needs a scapegoat.'

'Has he anything to build on in thinking that you might be the guilty person?'

'Ay.'

'Oh, really?'

'I found Bradan's body and I piped him a lament. Then it came to me that I was the heir to this' – he waved an arm like the trunk of a young oak – 'and I changed my tune.'

'You certainly did,' agreed Laura. 'It sounded like hell gone mad.'

Macbeth, forgetting his grievances, looked gratified.

'Ay,' he said, 'I'm a guid man on the pipes when I let masel go.' His face changed again. 'But it was an ill night for me when that reporter laddie heard me.'

'We both heard you,' said Laura. 'Nobody could help it. I should think they heard you in Freagair.'

'The newspaper laddie brought back the boat and seeped back into the house. He opened the door and then closed it behind him. I was marching up and down to my piping, you'll understand, and as I turned I saw him. His hair was on end and his face was white, but he stood his ground.

' "You're still here, then?" I speired at him, and at that he nods his head.

' "And I'm no leaving without my story," he tells me.

' "And what story may that be?"

' "I spied Bradan being brought hame?"

' "You did? And what about it?"

' "He was in a verra bad way. There were twa men in the boat. They almost had to carry him ashore."

' "Look, now," I said, "if a gentleman and a landowner canna be fou with his ain friends in his ain boat, where can he be fou?"

' "He was no fou," the laddie said. "The belief is on me that he's dead."

'Well, I had to make up my mind. I wasna so very sure how much the laddie had seen, so I told him that, if he'd a mind to, he could take a keek at anything he liked, and then he was to print what he thought fit. I warned him to be careful what he printed, because a newspaper is fair game to extortionists, and then I left him to it. I kenned he would find the laird, for he was in the cellar.' He turned to Laura. 'And gin I hadna been engaged with you and your fashes, mistress, I'd have heard them bring him in.'

'Sorry,' said Laura. 'Pity neither of us knew. Do tell us more.'

'I dinna ken ony mair. The neist thing I knew was Corrie banging on my door the morn and speiring did I know that the laird was in a barrel over at the quay. I thought the man was haverin', but he was right, so I sent him off for a doctor and the doctor – from Freagair he was – found that Bradan had been killed.'

'Yes,' put in Dame Beatrice, 'but how? By what means?'

'He had a muckle great lump on the back of his head and a *skian-dhu* intil his ribs.'

'The lump on the head would account for his having to be helped up to the house, I suppose, but what about the *skian-dhu*?'

'I dinna ken. It was not mine.'

'Did they test it for fingerprints?' asked Laura.

'I dinna ken that, either. The police move in a mysterious way their wonders to perform, but what they do is no business of mine so long as I keep out of their hands, and that I'm determined to do. So, mistress' – he met Dame Beatrice's eye – 'gin ye ken ony gowk wha will put up good siller for a house and an island, Tannasgan and An Tigh Mór are in feu.'

'I would rent them myself for a fortnight,' said Dame Beatrice.

'A sennight would do. Verra guid.'

'Very well. How much are you asking?'

'I wouldna want to take a cheque. Will ya give me ten

pounds? I'm a man of my word. I want naething signed, ye ken, and I'll no give ye a receipt. Gin ye'll hand me twa five-pound notes, Tannasgan and An Tigh Mór will be yours for seven days. Doubtless ye're thinking of taking a wee holiday.'

'Yes, and a childish one,' said Dame Beatrice. She pulled out a notecase and handed over the money. Laura looked on, amazed, but she realised that there was a tacit understanding that she should say nothing until Macbeth had gone. He wrung Dame Beatrice's yellow fingers, nodded to Laura and went out of the room. In no time he was back, a kit-bag slung over his shoulder.

'Well, *gu'n robh maith agad,*' he said.

'*Is e do bheatha,*' responded Laura, not to be outdone in the civilities. Macbeth bowed and departed.

'Translate, child,' commanded Dame Beatrice. 'I had no idea that you had the Gaelic.'

'I haven't. All he said was, "Thank you," and all I said was, "You're welcome." '

'Poor Sherlock Holmes!'

'You mean the explanations always seem so obvious when they come? Never mind. *You* shall play Sherlock now and, as always, I'll be Watson. Why have we rented this island for a week?'

'First let us sort Corrie as soon as he brings the boat back from taking Mr Macbeth ashore. To do this at leisure, I ought to see that Mrs Corrie is engaged, or embroiled, or in some way prevented from coming to his rescue.'

'Can do,' said Laura, decidedly. 'I'll have a crack with her in the kitchen while you go ahead. It's such a lonely life here for one woman on her own that, once I can get her talking, she'll probably go on until Domesday.'

So they parted, Laura waylaying Corrie on her way to the kitchen on his return from the boathouse to tell him that he was wanted in the dining-room, Dame Beatrice to sharpen her hatchet.

'Well, Corrie,' she said, as soon as he came in, 'you'll have heard from Mr Macbeth that Tannasgan has changed hands for a week.'

'Ay, the laird was telling me.'

'Did he mention his plans?'

'Ay, he's awa' to Skye.'

'To Skye?' (She remembered that Laura had seen young Bradan, as well as young Grant, on Skye, and she wondered where was the connection, if a connection existed.)

'Maybe he'll be climbing Sgurr Dearg,' said Corrie, with a crafty little smile. Dame Beatrice dismissed the unscaleable peak with a wave of her yellow claw.

'Well, never mind that,' she said. 'The point is that he thinks he's running away from the police.'

'The laird has done naething wrang.'

'So he himself seems to think. Why, then, should he be afraid?'

'Maybe it would be the *skian-dhu*?'

'I am asking *you*. What about the *skian-dhu*?'

'Maybe it belonged to the laird.'

'Macbeth?'

'Ay.'

'So that his fingerprints might be on it?'

'They were not.'

'Oh, I see. The police tested it, I suppose?'

'I dinna ken.'

Dame Beatrice was becoming a little tired of this Scottish circumlocution, but she spoke patiently.

'Did the police ask to take your own fingerprints?'

'Ay. I made no objection. I kenned fine it was no masel that put the knife in the old laird's ribs.'

'Man Corrie,' said Dame Beatrice impressively, 'I know so much about the whole affair that it would be better for

226

nearly everybody if I knew all. Tell me about the night you and another brought Mr Bradan back to An Tigh Mór and put him in the cellar.'

'So the laird has split on us!'

'He has indeed, if you choose to put it that way. But as he had not been taken into your confidence and (as I see it) had gone into the cellar simply and solely to get himself something to drink and discovered Bradan there, I scarcely follow your argument. Surely one can only betray one's fellow-conspirators?'

'Ye're in the right of it,' Corrie gloomily agreed. 'Here's for it, then – and this time it's the whole truth I'll be telling ye.'

'And quite time, too. Fire away.'

Corrie's story did not differ, in a sense, from the one he had told before, but there were some significant additions and one or two important contradictions. He maintained that, when Macbeth had taken the boat over to pick up Laura, he had been expecting a visit from young Bradan on the score that the young man who had been disinherited would want to argue with Macbeth about the rights and wrongs of the matter while his father (of whom, Corrie claimed, he had always been in awe) was out of the way.

'You told us that the fabulous beasts travelled to Leith for purposes of advertisement. I don't think that was true,' said Dame Beatrice.

'Well, well!' said Corrie. 'The truth is that they did and they didna.'

'Indeed?'

'The old laird had wee images of them made.'

'Oh, yes, I saw some of them,' said Laura.

'And it was the wee images that were taken across to Grant of Coinneamh and his motor-van. I understand now. Pray go on.'

Corrie again referred to the activities of young Grant and reasserted that he himself had had orders to go to the public telephone on the Freagair road and ring up Bradan.

'And you are certain that his was the voice you heard?' Dame Beatrice deliberately spoke in a tone of doubt, but Corrie was adamant. He could have sworn to it anywhere, he declared.

'I press the point,' said Dame Beatrice, 'because I cannot see how, if Mr Bradan was answering the telephone from Edinburgh at the time you say, he could have reached Loch na Gréine at soon after ten.'

'But wha spoke of Edinburgh?' demanded Corrie. 'It was an Inverness number I was to call.' He went on to speak of meeting the station-master's newly-repaired car and of the sorry state of Cù Dubh. He had smelled strongly of spirits and was in a comotose condition.

'Ye'll appreciate,' said Corrie, 'that I had no suspicion then that he had been hit on the head and was to die.'

'You helped him up to the house and into it, believing that he was drunk.'

'I did that.'

'And you saw nothing of young Grant.'

'I did not.'

'Now, Corrie, Mr Macbeth has told us that you and another man had almost to carry Mr Bradan up to the house, and that young Grant was suspicious about this and, seeing the chance of a scoop for his paper, he bearded Mr Macbeth, who, by that time, must have been aware of what had happened to his cousin, and then Grant was told he might search where he pleased. He found the body in the cellar. What have you to say about that?'

'Only that the puir gentleman must hae crept down there to get himself anither drink, as you said about Mr Macbeth. In my experience, when a man is fou, all he thinks about is how to get his hands on anither bottle. Doubtless that would be the finish of him, gin he'd been clouted over the head – *skian-dhu* or no *skian-dhu*.'

Dame Beatrice agreed that this was very likely.

'There is one other point,' she said. 'Do you know whether young Mr Grant told Mr Macbeth *at the time* that he'd found the body in the cellar?'

'Why else would the laird be piping first a lament and then a reel?'

So you knew what was in the will, thought Dame Beatrice. Aloud she said, 'One more question, Corrie. The man who helped you with Mr Bradan that night was the porter from Tigh Òsda, I take it? He was driving the car.'

'He was.'

'I see. Well, I have met him and I cannot believe that he had guilty knowledge of Mr Bradan's death. Are you and your wife prepared to stay on and look after Mrs Gavin and myself for a week?'

'It will be a pleasure – forbye we have naewhere else to gae.'

'Right. Then I want you to take the boat across and bring back my chauffeur.'

'At once, ma'am?'

'Yes, please – and you had better tell your wife about the new arrangements.'

When he had gone, Laura said :

'What do you make of this business of the body in the cellar?'

'I think that Corrie's explanation is probable, although I have another, even more likely one.'

'You do believe, then, that Bradan was not only alive but blind tight when they brought him home?'

'It is possible. It would explain a good many things. It might even explain why, after a knock on the head which

229

was obviously meant to kill him, he was able to crawl into the cellar. I do not profess to explain it, but it seems to be a fact that when a man is very drunk he can sustain injuries which, in a sober person, might be fatal.'

'Do you speak from experience?' asked Laura, cheekily.

'Professional experience,' said Dame Beatrice, whose only tribute to the grape was an occasional glass of sherry. 'I wonder how Mrs Corrie will react to the news that she has two women and an extra man to cater, cook and clean for, in place of the one man to whom she has been accustomed.'

'Two men, surely?' said Laura. 'At one time, before he was turfed out, young Bradan must have lived here, and, for a bit, I suppose Bradan and Macbeth must both have occupied the house. Besides, one assumes that a Mrs Bradan would have been included, if young Bradan is really Bradan's son.'

'How right you are,' said Dame Beatrice. 'Of course, if he isn't . . .'

'I didn't mean to infer that he wasn't!'

'It might help to explain the disinheriting.'

'I thought the reasons given already were enough to explain that.'

'Anyway, it is no concern of ours. What *is* interesting, though, is that Mr Bradan was not in Edinburgh, but in Inverness.'

'Yes, it explains how he was able to get back here that night.'

'Of course, the medical evidence must always leave a margin in determining the time of death, and the waters of the loch must be extremely cold at this time of year.'

'I'll say they are!' Laura had swum in them. 'I see what you mean. The body being in the tub, *rigor mortis* might have set in earlier than if it had been left in the cellar.'

'Corrie is not an entirely reliable witness, but there is one suspect who certainly could have been in Inverness that night, and that is Mr Bradan's son.'

'I suppose he could. He was on the loch-side ringing bells and turning lanterns, quite well on in the afternoon, but you think he went to Inverness after that and hit Bradan over the head, do you?'

'It is a possibility.'

'But, if so, he must have known he hadn't killed him. There's no doubt that Bradan got on the train and was met at Tigh-Òsda. Of course, Grant of Coinneamh was also in Inverness that night, and told a very fishy story of kidnapping, which he's since denied. If the *other* story is right – that there was bad blood between him and Bradan – there's every reason to think that Grant may have done the job, isn't there?'

'We must keep open minds. Open your keen ears, too, and tell me whether I am imagining I hear the chink of teacups and the footsteps of the excellent Mrs Corrie.'

Dame Beatrice was imagining nothing, for Mrs Corrie entered bearing a tray. She was followed by her husband, who pushed a tea-trolley loaded with scones, cakes and jam.

'What a spread!' said Laura. Mrs Corrie dismissed her husband with a curt nod of the head and, as he closed the door behind himself, she exclaimed :

'My man is no murderer, I'll tell ye.'

'But we did not suppose he was,' Dame Beatrice remarked in her beautiful voice. 'Tell us more, Mrs Corrie. Get another cup and saucer and let us go into conference.'

Mrs Corrie appeared to hesitate. Then, with a grim chuckle, she went off and reappeared with cup, saucer and plate.

'The scones took,' she announced. 'Ye'll do nae better than the scones.'

Dame Beatrice poured tea and for a few minutes there was silence. Judging that this was foreign to Mrs Corrie's nature, Dame Beatrice broke it.

'What do you think of Mr Macbeth's defection – or is there another explanation of his absence?' she asked. Mrs Corrie put down her cup.

'That one is up to his tricks,' she said. 'What caused ye to hold Tannasgan at feu?'

'For fun,' replied Dame Beatrice.

'And games,' added Laura, inexcusably. Mrs Corrie nodded, accepting Laura's interpolation as a genuine contribution to the conversation.

'It was always supposed there was something to be found on Haugr,' she said, 'but maybe folks were just havering.'

'Haugr? A burial mound?' said Laura. Mrs Corrie took up her teacup, looked wise, and sipped thoughtfully. Lowering the cup, she said :

'I haena the Gaelic. All I ken is that the laird was awfu' careful whom he let land on Haugr.'

'That *is* the small island with the trees on it?'

'It is that same.'

'Mrs Corrie,' pursued Laura, breaking in on another silence with some suddenness, 'who was the piper the night I left here?'

'The piper, Mrs Gavin? I dinna recollect ony piper.' She turned a suspiciously mild gaze on the questioner.

'Oh, well,' said Laura, 'I don't suppose it matters.' Privately she decided that it mattered a very great deal that Mrs Corrie should lie. She added, 'Just tell me one thing, though. Who helped your husband put Bradan in the cellar?'

'Naebody put the laird in the cellar. If the laird crawled down intil the cellar, he went of his own free will. It wouldna be the first time.'

'So, according to you, Mr Bradan must have been alive

232

when your husband and Ian, from the station at Tigh-Òsda, landed him here?'

Mrs Corrie looked aggressively and fearlessly at her, and then addressed Dame Beatrice.

'My man is no murderer,' she reasserted. Dame Beatrice spread much-bejewelled yellow claws and nodded.

'Should I really be employing him, although only for a week, if I thought he were?' she demanded. This casuistry did not shake Mrs Corrie. She laughed. At the same moment there came a vigorous thump on the door. It was opened by Corrie, who had knocked, and behind him the stolid, reliable George filled the rest of the aperture.

'Ah,' said Dame Beatrice. 'George will be staying the night. I suppose you can fix him up?'

'His wee bag is in the hall and the bed is aired,' replied Corrie.

'Splendid.'

'And there's a pot of tea ready to infuse in the kitchen, and scones and bannocks for ye,' said Mrs Corrie, addressing her husband.

'Ay,' said Corrie, in dispirited tones, leading the way towards the domestic quarters.

'He's thinking my tongue may rin awa' with me,' said Mrs Corrie. She went over to the door and closed it. 'But *that* it willna do, for I hae nae mair to tell.'

'How long have you been on Tannasgan, Mrs Corrie?' asked Dame Beatrice.

'How long? Oh, a matter of less than two years. We came here last September twelvemonth.'

'So you've spent two winters on Tannasgan.'

'We have that.'

'And you were on your own here for about three weeks last winter?'

'We were. The laird was awa' to Gàradh, where they

keep the gardens open to the public some days during the summer.'

'Did you like it better while he was away?'

'Wha wouldna like it better? We were our own masters.'

'Yes, of course. What were your dealings with Mr Bradan's son?'

'That one? His father had turned him frae the door lang syne.'

'Before you came to work here, you mean?'

'No, no, but not so verra much later. He couldna thole him. He was a natural son, so we heard.'

'Indeed?' said Dame Beatrice. 'Who, then, is said to be his mother?'

But Mrs Corrie was not prepared to answer this question. She muttered that she did not know. Laura made a guess which was destined never to be confirmed or denied.

'I suppose it was the Mrs Grant who lives at Coinneamh,' she said. Mrs Corrie handed her the dish of scones. It might have been an ironic or it might have been a pacific gesture. Conscious that no response to her remark was to be forthcoming, Laura took a scone.

'So,' said Dame Beatrice, taking the conversation along her own line again after this brief digression, 'you cannot have been surprised that this natural son was disinherited.'

'There would hae been no surprise, for we heard he played fause with his father,' said Mrs Corrie.

'Oh? In what way?'

'He took up what he hadna laid down.'

'So, after that, the laird hid it, whatever it was.'

'Naebody kens.'

'Why have you yourself never been on the wooded island of Haugr? Did you never wish to see the models of the fabulous beasts? Did you never wish to see the maze?'

Mrs Corrie shook her head.

'Gin ever I cross the water,' she said, 'I'll be awa' to

Glasgow where there's shops and parks. Sauchiehall Street! Trongate! Argyle Street! Kelvingrove!'

'I thought you came from Kirkintilloch,' said Laura.

'I do, so, but Glasgow is where I would choose to be. As for the wee inch of Haugr, I wouldna set foot on it for ony siller ye could offer.' Asked why, she shook her head and passed her cup for more tea.

CHAPTER TWENTY-ONE

Treasure Island

'Fifteen men on the dead man's chest—
Yo-ho-ho, and a bottle of rum!
Drink and the devil had done for the rest—
Yo-ho-ho, and a bottle of rum!'

Robert Louis Stevenson

LAURA had elected to sleep in the room which had been apportioned to her the first time she had visited An Tigh Mór. She woke at dawn, stared around her for a minute or two, then got up and decided to swim in the loch.

The water was cold, but not unbearably so. She enjoyed her bathe and was on the point of swimming back to the boathouse from which, having no idea of the depth of the water for diving, she had elected to push off, when it occurred to her that she had a priceless opportunity to land on the islet of Haugr and explore it on her own.

It was easy enough to get ashore. The water lapping the island was shallow and the mud was not treacherous. She waded on to the bank and was aware, immediately, that shoes would have been an asset. However, Laura was not deterred by disadvantages. She took the path which she and Dame Beatrice had followed on the only occasion when they had visited Haugr, and soon found herself among the fabulous animals.

Here there was no doubt about the destruction which had been done. The bronze basilisk had been uprooted and all that was left of him was a collection of sections of metal, one of them surmounted by his crowned serpentine head.

The werewolf had been thrown on to his side, but the

enormous gryphon had been left alone. It seemed as though the excavator had boggled at the idea of attempting to uproot him. The salamander, however, had suffered. His large head, spangled with yellow paint in the form of diamonds, lay at an angle to his lizard's body where the stonework had cracked.

Laura, chilly in her wet swim-suit, studied the ruins with concern. Macbeth and young Bradan, between them, had left a sorry mess. Conscious of hunger and cold, Laura left the island and swam back to the boathouse. When she re-entered An Tigh Mór it was to find a warm smoulder of peats in the dining-room and Mrs Corrie polishing the fine old sideboard.

'Well!' exclaimed Mrs Corrie, as Laura approached the fire, wrapped in the towel she had taken down to the boathouse. 'A water-kelpie he called you, and a water-kelpie ye are! Get you into your claes before you catch your death!'

Laura laughed, warmed herself by the fire and then went upstairs to dress. She met Dame Beatrice on the landing.

'Been for a swim,' said Laura. 'Either Macbeth or young Bradan has committed mayhem on the fabulous beasts. You ought to see the carnage!'

'I intend to do so immediately after breakfast, child. I wonder whether the menu includes kippers?'

'It's haddocks' eyes you search for among the heather bright, isn't it?'

'That may well be. Incidentally, I believe I have worked them into waistcoat buttons in the silent night.'

'You have? Whoopee, Mrs Croc., dear. Tell me all.'

'You shall know what there is to be known when we have digested our breakfasts.'

Laura was still young enough in heart to respond to this promise. As it happened, there *were* kippers for breakfast, brought in, said Mrs Corrie, from Aberdeen via Inverness and Tigh-Òsda. As soon as breakfast was over, Laura and

Dame Beatrice went down to the boathouse with George and Corrie and were rowed over to Haugr.

'Now,' said Laura, when they had landed on the wooded island, 'I've almost forgotten my breakfast, so you'd better redeem your promise.'

'We are going treasure-hunting, child. There may have been other reasons for the destruction of the statuary, but young Bradan did not come here merely to destroy. He knew – or believed, at any rate – that most of his father's ill-gotten gains were hereabouts.'

'Ay,' said Corrie, 'there was no a muckle heap of siller at the bank. I ken that verra well, for when the old laird wanted for money, I was despatched tae Inverness wi' a cheque to cash, and mair than aince we were overdrawn there and the laird would go himself to set matters right. Ay, there maun be a hidey-hole hereabouts, as ye say, mistress, but the laird keepit verra close and helpit himself when naebody but the guidwife was on Tannasgan wi' him, and well he kenned that *she* would never set foot on Haugr.'

Laura took the lead, Dame Beatrice was immediately behind her and George brought up the rear so that he could keep an eye on Corrie (his own idea, much appreciated by Dame Beatrice.) She made no reference to it, but thought it both touching and amusing. In this order the party traversed the little path until they came to the maze and, in the centre of it, the smashed and broken statuary.

The two men carried respectively a spade and a garden fork, and, when they reached their objective, a parcel borne by Laura, who had insisted upon relieving Dame Beatrice of it, was found to contain a large hammer.

'Bags I,' said Laura, swinging it up and down. 'What do we do first – slam out or dig?'

'Both, I hope,' her employer replied. 'The stonework has been so badly damaged already that I feel we may be forgiven for adding to the destruction. The basilisk may be left until the last, for it seems clear that the money is not in his possession. George and Corrie must work in partnership with one another and carefully dig up the centre of the maze, by which I mean all the earth except that on which the statues have been standing, for they would appear to be too heavy for one man to have moved when he wanted to uncover his cache. You, my dear Laura, may do what you will with your hammer. When you are tired, you may hand it over to me.'

The Amazonian Laura grunted. She did not tire easily. The three then went to work. The ground in the centre of the maze had been well trampled and digging was not easy. Soon each man removed his coat and was perspiring freely. Laura swung her hammer with zeal tempered by discretion, for it was her firm, although unspoken, opinion that some, at any rate, of Bradan's treasure might be in the form of precious stones, a kind of wealth which had world-wide currency.

A couple of hours passed. The men had dug up most of the centre of the maze to a depth of a couple of spits. First Corrie had broken up the soil with his fork, to be followed by George prospecting with the spade. Every half-hour they had exchanged tools, as the work with the fork was considerably more exhausting than that performed with the spade. Laura had broken up the werewolf and was attacking the gryphon when an overcast sky, which had been threatening rain for the past hour, discharged a true West Highland deluge. Hastily the men retrieved their coats and Dame Beatrice, rising from the remains of the salamander (which had suffered destruction, she supposed, when the ship he represented had blown up) announced firmly that work was over until the rain ceased. So the party hastened back to the boat and made across the lake for Tannasgan and An Tigh Mór.

'Well,' said Laura, damp-haired and wearing a change

of clothing, 'that's put paid to that for the rest of the day, I suppose. Wonder what's for lunch? The usual mutton, I expect.' She was at the window watching the rain sweeping over the loch. 'I love my native land, but I do think it could do with a little less rain.'

'It may clear up this afternoon,' said Dame Beatrice. She mended the fire with more peats. 'In any case, I am beginning to wonder . . .'

'Whether your hunch has gone wrong? Oh, I don't know. There's still quite a bit of digging to be done, and I've hardly touched the gryphon yet. I had a feeling that the stuff would be in the werewolf's tummy. That's why I tackled him first. Do you think the police have got hold of the right man? You know, I still don't believe Corrie has told us the whole truth about that night.'

'I think he has told it as far as he knows it. What he has said now checks pretty well with what we already know. If the rain eases off a little this afternoon, I propose to drive in to Tigh-Òsda and have another talk with the lad Ian.'

'If it eases off, I'm going to have another go with my hammer, then. I don't mind confessing, childish though it may seem, that treasure-hunt fever is on me.'

'Tak' tent!' said Mrs Corrie, coming in to lay the table. 'Ye're blethering, lassie!'

Laura grinned and Dame Beatrice said:

'The treasure can wait. It won't run away. Besides, I should like you to be with me when I talk to Ian. I may need a translator if he becomes excited and decides to address me in Gaelic.'

Laura began to look mulish. She saw through this flimsy reason for not leaving her behind on Tannasgan with nobody but the Corries in the house.

'You won't need me. The station-master can translate for you,' she said.

'Ah, but I don't choose that he should,' said Dame Beatrice implacably. Laura laughed.

'All right,' she said. 'You win. But' – she lowered her voice, for the door into the hall was ajar to facilitate Mrs Corrie's re-entry with the soup – 'don't you think the C's may get up to something while we're away?'

'I don't think it matters if they do, child. As the discovery of the hoard cannot possibly benefit either you or me in any way, it does not really matter who discovers it.'

'It does to me. I'm simply longing to find it. All my life I've wanted to find treasure or some cave paintings or something, and now you don't care if the cup is dashed from my lips.'

Mrs Corrie carried in a steaming tureen, said, 'Saumon tae follow,' and marched out again.

'Terrible as an army with banners,' said Dame Beatrice absently, going to the head of the table.

'I say!' said Laura, dismayed. 'You don't really think that, do you?'

'Think what, child?'

'That Mrs Corrie is mixed up in any funny business.'

'I think she knows one thing that Corrie does *not* know. Sit down.' Dame Beatrice removed the lid from the tureen. 'I always look upon Scotch broth as a meal in itself,' she added.

'Well,' said Laura, abandoning an abortive argument, 'I suppose, in poor homes, it had to be. It's what they call, in England, filling, nourishing and cheap. Anyway, in my opinion, it has Irish stew licked to a frazzle. Serve me a good deep plateful, please. My demolition job has made me hungry.'

When lunch was over, the rain was still coming down and a grey mist had settled on the loch. Laura stood at the window and stared moodily out at the weather. By three o'clock, however, there was a primrose-coloured promise in the sky, and by half-past three it had stopped raining and Dame Beatrice announced her intention of repairing forthwith to Tigh-Òsda. Corrie was summoned to row the boat back and forth, George warned that the car was required and at four o'clock precisely the car moved off from the loch-side and headed for the west.

From every hillside narrow waterfalls cascaded on to the road and were received by deep drains. Heavy cloud hung over the mountains, obliterating all the peaks and giving the impression of an improbable stage-set seen from the back of the gallery. Except for the sound of the waterfalls and the almost undetectable sound of the car, an eerie silence brooded everywhere. Laura, gazing out of the window and sometimes through the windscreen behind George's solid, broad-shouldered back, wondered whether, or to what extent, the mystery of two violent deaths was about to be cleared up. Dame Beatrice was thinking about the lion and the unicorn, who were fighting for the crown. She had remembered that the royal arms had been introduced into England by that oddity King James I on the strength of his believing the rhyme to be a Scottish story, a strangely patriotic gesture for the son of the half-English Lord Darnley and the half-French Mary, Queen of Scots.

As they passed the private trackway which led to Coinneamh Lodge, Laura remarked :

'I suppose we shall never know why she borrowed my car that night I stayed there.'

'I do not despair of finding that out, child,' responded Dame Beatrice. George drew in at a passing-place to give an estate wagon a clear road.

'The Grants,' said Laura, on whose right-hand side the estate wagon had passed them. 'Wonder where *they're* going?'

'It is Friday,' said Dame Beatrice.

'Yes, but we understood that he always goes to Inverness by train and that she never goes with him.'

'*Aliud alia dicunt, puella.*'

'They jolly well *do* say different things! One trouble about this case is that no two people concerned in it seem to speak the same language.'

No other traffic was encountered on the road, and the car drew up sedately outside Tigh-Òsda station. Ian was available, since no train was expected for some time, and he greeted the visitors shyly.

'The same old story,' said Dame Beatrice. 'We are still concerned with the death of Mr Bradan of Tannasgan. Now you will remember that he had ordered your station-master's car and that you drove him to the shores of Loch na Gréine.'

'*Marbhphaisg air a' bhrùid mhi-thaingeil!*' muttered Ian. Laura was delighted.

'Curse the ungrateful brute!' she translated. 'Lesson number eight in *Gaelic Without Groans.*'

'Indeed?' said Dame Beatrice, uncertain whether Laura was jesting.

'By John MacKechnie, M.A.,' added Laura, supplying the necessary footnote. 'Didn't Cù Dubh pay you, then, Ian?'

'He paid for the car, but nothing for me.'

'Mingy hound!'

'Not hound, please you! Hound is a good word in the Gaelic,' said Ian, with a nervous giggle.

'Oh, Lord, so it is! Come to me, sons of hounds, and I will give you flesh! How does it go?'

'It is the slogan of Cameron of Lochiel, Mrs Gavin, and it goes : *Chlanna nan con thigibh a's gheibh sibh feòil!*'

'Jolly good. But we're holding up Dame Beatrice.'

'You believed, with Corrie, Mr Bradan's man, that Mr Bradan was very drunk that night, did you not?' she asked.

243

'I did. He had a great smell of spirits on him and he could not stand on his feet.'

'Did you see anybody help him out of the train?'

'I did. It was a young Englishman, works at the hydro-electric plant further up the *dalr*. He helped him on to the platform and I went to help and so did Mr Corrie. The Englishman said, "I'm afraid this bloke's pickled." That will be an English idiom, no doubt.'

'That's right. The English will say a man is *a* drunk, but not, if they can help it, that he *is* drunk.'

'Fancy that, now. The study of language, and the circumlocutions of the same, make very interesting thinking.'

'So when you first saw Mr Bradan being helped out of the train, you thought he was ill,' said Dame Beatrice. 'However, you accepted the theory that he was drunk because of what the young Englishman said and because of the strong smell of spirits.'

'Spilt over him, I expect,' said Laura. 'It's been done before to lend verisimilitude, etc. Quite a well-established gag.'

'I believe you crossed over in the boat with Corrie,' said Dame Beatrice to Ian.

'It was a case of necessity. Mr Corrie would never have managed him alone, small, wee man though he was.'

'The laird?'

'Yes, yes, the laird.'

'That is the first I have heard about his size. Was he thin as well as short?'

'He was as thin as a *caolbhain*.'

'Lead pencil,' murmured Laura. 'Lesson number fifteen.'

'So, in your opinion, the person who murdered him could quite easily have placed his body in the barrel where it was found?'

'Very easily, och, yes. But when he was alive and, as we thought, having taken spirits, it was a different matter.'

'Did Mr Bradan say anything during the journey home?'

'He would moan, "My head! My head!" But much to drink will always go to a man's head, as they say.'

'Very true. Did you actually go into the house?'

'No. I would not like to go into a big, fine house such as that. There was, also, Mr Corrie's wife to help, and Mr Macbeth, the new laird, so I parted from them at the door.'

'Did you see a young man sitting in the boathouse?'

'No, indeed. There was nobody there.'

'Well, what next?' asked Laura, when Ian had received a gratuity and they were about to return to the car. 'Evidence from the young Englishman?'

'You have hit it.'

'We don't know his name.'

'There cannot be many young Englishmen there, I take it except for Curtis, of course.'

'I shouldn't think there are, and, by the look of things, I should say that work is about finished for the day.' She referred to the fact that cars and pedestrians had begun to appear on the narrow road. 'We'd better wait here and get Ian to identify our bird for us.'

'Let us hope he always travels by train, then. Otherwise we shall miss him.'

They were fortunate. In the booking-hall doorway which led on to the platform, Ian readily identified a young fellow whose dark suit and carefully-rolled umbrella seemed to speak of London and a white-collar job.

'Good heavens!' said the young man, when Ian had introduced Dame Beatrice. 'Do you mean that he was the fellow who was croaked and put in a barrel? We merely thought he was tight. The chap who bundled him into my compartment said he was.'

A description of the 'chap' followed, at the urgent request of Dame Beatrice.

'Well?' she said to Laura, as they walked back to the car.

'An eye-witness's description of young Bradan.'

'I thought it might be. Now I really *am* in a quandary.'

'As how?'

'Well, it's obvious that young Bradan may have hit his father on the head with intent to kill him, but it doesn't seem possible that it actually did kill him.'

'Oh, Lord!' exclaimed Laura. 'No wonder young Grant chased me for that alibi after he'd read the papers! You mean . . .'

'That the *coup de grace* was not delivered by young Bradan. The medical evidence was perfectly clear. It *was* the *skian-dhu* which killed Cù Dubh.'

'But young Grant had no motive!'

'He thought that Cù Dubh was already dead, and that the *skian-dhu* and the barrel would provide a nation-wide sensation. And I have no doubt whatever of his absolute horror when he found out what he had done. I have very little doubt, either, mind you, that Mr Bradan eventually would have died of the injury to his head, but that we must check.'

'And tonight? If it were bright moonlight we could go back and tackle the fabulous beasts again.'

'No, child, not even by moonlight. We have to find the lion and the unicorn, and I believe I know where to look for them. *Where a man's heart is,* you know.'

'The cellar!' exclaimed Laura. 'He was badly hurt, but he did manage to crawl into the cellar! He'd shifted the treasure from Haugr when he knew his son was stealing it! I can't wait to get back to An Tigh Mór.'

It did not take them long to do this. The cars and the pedestrians from the hydro-electric plant were gone by the time they took the road for Tannasgan. Laura wondered whether they would pass the Grants' station-wagon again, and she looked out for it, but there was nothing on the road except a solitary small ambulance which seemed in no hurry and from which a cheery greeting was waved as they passed it.

Tannasgan looked deserted. It seemed so, too, for Laura jangled the handbell and turned the lantern in vain.

'Goodness! What's happened to Corrie?' she demanded. The answer came from just behind her.

'I am saying that Corrie was away to Freagair.'

Laura swung round, but it was not young Bradan (as, from the Gaelic construction of the sentence, she had half-expected) but young Grant. He smiled at her. Laura, who now knew him to have been, however unintentionally, the actual killer of Cù Dubh, looked as astounded as she felt.

'What on earth are *you* doing here?' she demanded. 'And if Corrie is in Freagair, why isn't the boat tied up on this side?'

'Mrs Corrie rowed it back to the boathouse,' said Grant, in his ordinary tones. He put two fingers to his mouth and split the air with a screeching, piercing, almost ferocious whistle. This had an effect, for, a minute later, Mrs Corrie was at the boathouse and was untying the heavy, clumsy boat. As Grant helped her to hold it against the side of the small quay, while she tied up, she said to him :

'I am not having ye set foot again on Tannasgan.'

'Why not, then?'

'Because ye did enough mischief the last time ye were here.'

'Oh, come, now, Maggie, you must make some allowance for the Press. It was only a story I was after.'

'Ay, and ye got one, too! How dared ye stab the old laird and gie him his death-blaw?'

'*What?*' said Grant, in a kind of strangled yelp. 'What are you saying, you old . . . ?'

'I'm no an old what you said the now, and my name's not Maggie. I say I ken verra well how Mr Bradan came by his death. I haena told any other body, but gin ye dinna

247

tak' yoursel' awa' from here and let me never set een on ye mair, I will go to the police and swear to them on my aith that ye murdered the old laird.'

Grant was unable to speak, but Laura said :

'You've bought it, chum. So my word wouldn't have helped you, even if I had been able to give it, you see.'

Grant turned and ran. The three women gazed after him until they lost him at the bend in the road. George joined them on the quayside.

'Well,' said Dame Beatrice, 'you have saved me from a most unwelcome duty, Mrs Corrie. I thought I should have been obliged to present the same home truth to young Mr Grant as you have done.'

'Are ye for the boatie?' Mrs Corrie demanded.

Her passengers stepped in and George relieved her of the oars.

'Had Corrie any particular reason for visiting Freagair?' Dame Beatrice enquired. 'He said nothing about it before we left this afternoon.'

'He was needing a pick-axe and he kens a man in Freagair will no be sweer to gie him the loan of one. My man was fair fashed tae be howking over at Haugr wi' a fork and shovel the morn.'

'Oh, I see. He thought that a pick-axe would do the work more quickly and easily, and, if we were going on with that same work, there is no doubt that he would be right.'

'Ye'll no be howking over there the morn's morn, then?'

'No, the digging I intended is all done.' No more was said until they had tied up the boat and were at the front door of An Tigh Mór. Then Dame Beatrice added, as though there had been no break in the conversation, 'I suppose there is a key to the cellar?'

'And what would ye be wanting wi' the cellar?' asked Mrs Corrie, preparing to make her way to her own regions at the back of the house. 'There's naething of interest in the cellar but a dozen bottles, maybe, of whisky.'

'I should like the key of the cellar, all the same.'

'It will be in the door, then. That is where my man left it when he took all the old laird's siller and hid it where nane o' ye will find it.'

'When was this?'

'Just after ye left for Tigh–Òsda. Oh, ye need not think we were stealing it. It's a' there for them it's meant for.'

'And who might they be?'

'The Grants of Coinneamh Lodge, maist like. It's common talk that Mistress Grant was closer to the old laird than some others.'

CHAPTER TWENTY-TWO

The Last Word

' "I tell 'e," he said to the vicar, bringing his fist
with a smack into the palm of his hand, "I tell 'e the
burials be goin' to the daags . . . But four holes to fill
in a twalmonth, setting aside the Lunnon man kilt by
the Ramps, and the corpse pickt out o' Spook Pool,
neither o' them the rightful property o' the parish." '

Angus Evan Abbott

'WELL,' said Detective Chief-Inspector Gavin, when he rejoined his wife and Dame Beatrice at the latter's Kensington house, 'you both seem to have had quite a holiday.'

'I think it's absolutely stinking,' said Laura, 'that we
didn't discover the treasure.'

'Dame B. didn't intend that you should. What do you
say, Counsel for the Defence?'

'It might have been embarrassing,' Dame Beatrice admitted. 'It seemed better to give Corrie the hint and allow
him to get rid of it in our absence.'

'Good heavens!' said Laura, disgusted. 'Is that why we
went to interview Ian at Tigh-Òsda? But Mrs Corrie said—!
Wasn't her story true?'

'Partly,' said Dame Beatrice soothingly, 'but only partly.
The treasure was still in the cellar when we left for Tigh-
Òsda and I have no doubt whatever that, as soon as we
were safely away from Tannasgan, Mrs Corrie told her
husband where it was and advised him to move it while
we were out of the house. Unless I am greatly mistaken, we
shall see no more of your sometime host, though. There
is nothing now for him on Tannasgan.'

She was not mistaken. Later they heard, through Gavin's contact with the Edinburgh police, that Macbeth had been flown to South America, with the treasure, having made only a pretence of leaving the neighbourhood of Tannasgan in order to keep watch on the Corries. Young Grant had given himself up to the authorities and had made a full confession of how, unwittingly and without malice, he had delivered the *coup de grace* to the already dying laird. Young Bradan contrived to commit suicide before he could be brought to trial.

'Marmaduke,' quoted Gavin solemnly, after having given these melancholy details, 'was a bad lad, I'm afraid. There's no doubt he hit his father over the head in Inverness with, as we say, intent.'

'Well, I don't wonder,' said Laura, 'with a father like Cù Dubh. And was Mrs Grant of Coinneamh Lodge really young Bradan's mother?'

'I didn't find that out, but there is no other story, and there *was* the Salmon which went astray.'

'You mean that Cù Dubh wasn't a Scot?'

'Devil a bit of it. May partly account for his unpopularity, of course. Ours are a prejudiced, sentimental, insular, irrational people.'

'Irrational?' said Laura, seizing on the one adjective with which she totally disagreed. 'Why? What makes you say that?'

'The kilt. The sporran. The Gaelic language. The Highland weather. Robert Burns. Tossing the caber. Deerstalking. Bannockburn. That is to name a few items which leap immediately to the mind. There are probably dozens more.'

'Explain yourself, you renegade!'

'Now, now! No rude epithets. Who on earth else but us Scots would sport a kilt except in a warm country? It's simply shrieking for rheumatism. Who else would carry his purse on his lower abdomen – to put it politely – when he could use pockets? Who else would spell the word *lamhan* (hands) when it's pronounced *lávin*? Who else would live in a country where it's always raining? Who else would revere a poet who wrote in a dialect that scarcely any civilised person can understand? Who else would have invented a sport which is both terribly strenuous and completely unspectacular? Who else would crawl on his belly up mountain burns and over supersaturated heather, peat hags and other assorted bogs, to bag an animal whose flesh has to be practically putrified before it's chewable? Who else would have won Bannockburn?'

'Ah, now you're talking!' said Laura. 'Did you ever find out, by the way, why Mrs Grant borrowed my car that morning?'

'Oh, yes. I was going to tell you that. She did go to Tannasgan, as you thought at the time.'

'What for?'

'To throw stones at An Tigh Mór.'

'*What?*'

'Apparently that which had made you drunk had made her bold, and she hated Bradan. Of course, we don't really know why.'

'I *wasn't* drunk!'

'No, but, as the Irish policeman (was it?) said, you had drink taken. I only hope (from the same source) that you had not the appearance of a woman who had knocked at a back door.'

'I'm ashamed of you,' said Laura. 'To think that I should listen to all of this rot, not only from my husband and the father of my child, but from a Scotsman born and bred!'

'Talking of your child,' said Gavin, 'I sent for him. Doubtless that is the winsome boy even now at the door.'

'Oh, *no*!' cried Laura. The door opened and Hamish went straight to his father.

252

'I have been in Scotland,' he said. 'I wore my kilt and grandfather bought me a new sporran. I can speak seven sentences in Gaelic. It rained most of the time. I can recite *Cowrin' Beastie*. Grandfather once won a prize for tossing the caber. I have an inkpot made from a deer's horn. Grandmother took me to the field of Bannockburn, but there were not any pits or any dead soldiers.'

'You've had quite a time,' said Laura, glowering at her husband who was laughing in a loud, rude way.

'Well, you yourself can't grumble,' said Gavin. 'A loch, an island, a treasure, two corpses and a couple of mad-men . . .'

'Oh, yes! Did you find out who the man was who was pushed under the car in Edinburgh before the rest of the fun started?' asked Laura, abandoning her threatening attitude.

'His name was Grant, not Dorg.'

'Not *another* Grant?'

'Yes, indeed. Father of the reporter.'

'Who pushed him?'

'Nobody knows, and never will now, I suppose, but in Edinburgh they think it was Bradan and a ship's captain we contacted when I was on the other side. A barracuda overturned a small boat he was in while I was there and, as you probably know, the barracuda is a killer, so *that* captain's day was done. He was a bit of a scoundrel, any-way.'

'How did you find out?'

'As I say, we didn't, but they mix the drinks pretty strong in some of those ports and men are apt to talk in their cups. You were luckier. You only seem to have slept in yours.'

Laura put out her tongue at him, but only half-heartedly. She was thinking of a beautiful sub-tropical garden over-looking a shallow and idle bay with a formidable mountain on the other side of the water and a softly-spoken owner repeating the Latin names of both common and most exotic plants.

'You don't think,' she said suddenly, 'that young Grant *knew* that Bradan wasn't dead when he stuck the *skian-dhu* into him?'

'You mean because of his father?'

'Yes. You see, he was there and saw it happen, just as I did.'

'You've told me that. Would *you* have risked killing a man to avenge your father? I know *I* would.'

'Yes, and if it was Uncle Hamish, I would, too,' said Laura, decidedly. Her husband grinned .

'Uncle Hamish!' he said. 'Remember his telling us that Crioch means The End?'

'Well, so it does,' said Laura.

MORE VINTAGE MURDER MYSTERIES